The Red Widow
Or
The Death-Dealers Of London

by

William Le Queux

Double9
BOOKS

The Red Widow
Or
The Death-Dealers Of London
by William Le Queux

ISBN: 978-93-59951-46-1

Published by

DOUBLE 9 BOOKS

2/13-B, Ansari Road
Daryaganj, New Delhi – 110002
info@double9books.com
www.double9books.com
Tel. 011-40042856

This book is under public domain

ABOUT THE AUTHOR

Anglo-French journalist and author William Tufnell Le Queux was born on July 2, 1864, and died on October 13, 1927. He was also a diplomat (honorary consul for San Marino), a traveler (in Europe, the Balkans, and North Africa), a fan of flying (he presided over the first British air meeting at Doncaster in 1909), and a wireless pioneer who played music on his own station long before radio was widely available. However, he often exaggerated his own skills and accomplishments. The Great War in England in 1897 (1894), a fantasy about an invasion by France and Russia, and The Invasion of 1910 (1906), a fantasy about an invasion by Germany, are his best-known works. Le Queux was born in the city. The man who raised him was English, and his father was French. He went to school in Europe and learned art in Paris from Ignazio (or Ignace) Spiridon. As a young man, he walked across Europe and then made a living by writing for French newspapers. He moved back to London in the late 1880s and managed the magazines Gossip and Piccadilly. In 1891, he became a parliamentary reporter for The Globe. He stopped working as a reporter in 1893 to focus on writing and traveling.

CONTENTS

CHAPTER I
CONCERNS A MAN IN WHITE

"I can't understand what it all means. The whole thing is a mystery—*a great mystery*! I have my suspicions—grave suspicions!" declared the pretty blue-eyed girl emphatically.

"Of what?" asked the young man strolling at her side along the sunny towing-path beside the Thames between Kew and Richmond.

"Well—I hardly know," was her hesitating response. "But I don't like auntie to remain in that house any longer, Gerald. Some evil lurks there; I'm sure of it!"

Her companion smiled.

"Are you quite sure you are not mistaken, Marigold?" he asked in a dubious tone. "Are you absolutely certain that you really saw Mr. Boyne on Thursday night?"

"Why, haven't I already told you exactly what I saw?" asserted the girl excitedly. "I've related in detail all I know. And I repeat that I don't like auntie being there any longer."

"Well," said the young man, as they strolled leisurely along near the water's edge on that Sunday afternoon in summer, their intention being to take tea at Richmond, "if what you have described is an actual fact, then I certainly do think we ought to watch the man very closely."

"You don't doubt me—do you?" exclaimed the girl, with quick resentment.

"Not in the least, Marigold," he replied, halting and looking straight into her clear, almost child-like eyes. "Please do not misunderstand me. But what you have said is so extraordinary that—well, it seems all so weird and amazing!"

"That's just it. The affair is extraordinary, and, as I've said, I hope auntie will leave the place. She has a very good post as housekeeper to Mr. Boyne. Her affliction is against her, I know, but there is something in progress at Bridge Place that is too mysterious for my liking."

"Then let us watch and try to discover what it really is," said Gerald Durrant determinedly.

"Will you really help me?" she asked eagerly.

"Of course. Rely upon me. If I can be of any assistance to you where your aunt is concerned, Marigold, I shall only be too delighted. Surely you know that!" he added, looking again into her eyes with an expression of unspoken admiration and affection.

She murmured her thanks, and the pair—a handsome pair, indeed, they were—went on along the gravelled path in a silence that remained unbroken for some minutes.

Marigold Ramsay was just twenty-one, and an uncommonly pretty girl, though unconsciously so. Men turned to glance a second time at her as she passed. Though a typical London business girl who carried her leather dispatch-case on weekdays, she bore an air of distinction which was unusual in one of her class. Her clear, deep blue eyes, her open countenance, her grace of carriage, her slim suppleness, and the smallness of her hands and feet, all combined to create about her an air of well-bred elegance which was enhanced by a natural grace and charm. There was nothing loud about her, either in her speech or in her dress. She spoke softly, and she wore a plain coat and skirt of navy gaberdine, and a neat little velvet toque which suited her admirably. She was, indeed, as beautiful as she was elegant, and as intelligent as she was charming.

Many a young man about Lombard Street—where Marigold was employed in the head office of a great joint-stock bank—gazed upon her with admiration as she went to and fro from business, but with only one of them, the man at her side, had she ever become on terms of friendship.

Though Gerald Durrant had spoken no word of love, the pair had almost unconsciously become fast friends. He was a tall, good-looking young fellow, with well-brushed hair and a small moustache carefully trimmed, in whose rather deep-set eyes was an expression of kindly good-fellowship. Erect and athletic, his clear-cut features were typical of the honest, clean-minded young Englishman who, though well-born, was compelled, like Marigold, to earn his living in the City.

He had served in Flanders through the first year of war, but, being invalided out, had been since employed as confidential secretary to the head of a great firm of importers in Mincing Lane.

As, in his well-cut grey tweeds and straw hat, he strode beside her in silence in the sunshine, he reflected. What she had told him was utterly amazing. The whole affair was, indeed, a mystery.

Marigold had first met Gerald at a little corner table of a certain small teashop in Fenchurch Street, where she daily took her frugal luncheon.

One morning as he sat opposite to her he politely passed the salt. From that chance meeting they had each day chatted at the Cedar Tea-Rooms, gradually becoming friends, until one Saturday, he had invited her to Hampton Court, and they had spent the afternoon in the old-world gardens of the Palace so reminiscent of Henry the Eighth and Cardinal Wolsey.

That day's excursion had frequently been repeated, for Marigold's great blue eyes attracted the young man, until one day he cleverly arranged that she should meet his sister—with whom he lived out at Ealing—and the outcome was an invitation to tea on the following Sunday. Thus the chance-made acquaintance ripened until they found themselves looking eagerly forward to lunch time on five days each week, when they would rush to their meeting-place to chatter and enjoy the hour's relaxation from work. Hence it was not surprising that Gerald had fallen violently in love with Marigold, though he had never summoned up sufficient courage to declare his affection.

"What you've told me is a problem which certainly requires investigation," he remarked reflectively after a long silence. "If your aunt is in any real danger, then she should, I quite agree, leave the house. At present, however, I cannot see that she is, or why she should know anything. It is our duty to watch and to form our own conclusions."

"Ah!" cried the girl gratefully, "it's really awfully kind of you, Gerald, to promise to help me. As you know, I have very few men friends, and not one, save yourself, in whom I would place this confidence."

"You know me, Marigold," he said, with a smile of satisfaction. "You know that I will do all I can to help you to solve this extraordinary problem."

The problem which the girl had placed before her admirer was certainly a most puzzling one—sufficiently puzzling, indeed, to excite the curiosity of anybody to whom it was presented.

Had Marigold Ramsay but foreseen the terrible vortex of uncertainty and peril into which their inquiries would lead them, it is probable that she would have hesitated ere she embarked upon an investigation so full of personal risk to both.

In her ignorance of the cunningly-devised counter-plot, which shielded from exposure and justice one of the most diabolical and remarkable conspiracies of modern times, she and her admirer entered cheerfully upon a policy which led to many exciting and perilous adventures, some of which I intend to chronicle in these pages.

That you, my reader, shall clearly understand the cause of Marigold Ramsay's suspicions, it will be as well to here unfold certain queer circumstances which had happened on the previous Thursday night.

Mr. Bernard Boyne, whom Marigold viewed with such distinct suspicion, was a work-a-day man who tramped daily the bustling pavements of Hammersmith, Chiswick, and Bedford Park as an insurance agent, and was well known and very highly respected. He lived in a cheaply-furnished, nine-roomed house in Bridge Place, Hammersmith, a dingy third-class neighbourhood. The exterior of the place was, in summer, rendered somewhat more artistic than its neighbours in the same row by the dusty Virginia creeper which covered its walls and hung untrimmed about its windows. Upon the railings was fastened a brass plate, always well polished, which bore the name "Bernard Boyne—Insurance Agent."

Mr. Boyne had resided in that house for some six years. He was well known to all the tradespeople in the neighbourhood—for he paid his bills weekly—as well as by the working classes whose policies he was so frequently effecting, and whose small premiums he so assiduously collected.

He was agent for several insurance companies of second-class standing. He was also in touch with two well known underwriters at Lloyd's who would insure his commercial clients against practically anything—except bankruptcy.

Year in, year out, he was to be seen, always respectably, and even nattily dressed, passing actively in and about the neighbourhood, keenly on the alert for any new clients and any fresh "proposals."

Probably Mr. Boyne was one of the best known of local personalities. He was a regular attendant at the parish church of St. George the Martyr, Hammersmith, where he acted as sidesman. Further, he was honorary secretary to quite a number of charitable organisations and committees in Hammersmith, and in consequence had become acquainted with most of the wealthiest residents.

"Busy" Boyne—for that was what the people of Hammersmith called him—was a widower, and lived in that small unpretentious house, a very deaf old woman named Mrs. Felmore—the aunt of Marigold Ramsay—looking after him. For several years she had performed the domestic duties, and she did them well, notwithstanding her infirmity.

Now this is what happened.

On Thursday night, on his return after a strenuous day at about ten o'clock, Boyne had entered his small sitting-room and taken his bulky notebook and papers from his pocket. Then he had thrown off his coat and sat down to the cold meal which Mrs. Felmore had prepared for him prior to retiring. Though the house was so dingy, yet everything appertaining to its master's comfort was well ordered, as shown by the fact that the evening paper was lying neatly folded, ready for his hand.

Beneath the hissing incandescent gas-jet Bernard Boyne looked very pale, his eyes deeply set, his brow furrowed and careworn. He seemed weary and out-of-sorts.

"Fool!" he grunted aloud to himself. "I'm growing nervous! I suppose it is that big cheque that I had to-day—seven thousand, eight hundred—the biggest I've ever had. I wonder if I ought to tell Lilla?"

The room was the typical home of a man earning an income on commission just sufficient to enable him to "rub along" in comfort. It was certainly not the room of a man who was receiving cheques for such sums as seven thousand, eight hundred pounds.

At first glance Bernard Boyne, as he stood there in his shirt-sleeves, was an excellent type of the steady, reliable insurance agent, with no soul above "proposals" and "premiums." They constituted his sole aim in life, now that his "dear wife" was dead.

Nobody suspected the man who so piously passed round the bag in St. George the Martyr on Sundays to be a man of mystery. Nobody, indeed, would ever have dreamed that the active man in question would be placing cheques to his account of such value as seven thousand odd pounds.

"I wonder how long I shall remain here?" he whispered to himself. "I wonder what all these good people would say if they but knew—eh? *If they knew*! But, happily, they don't know!" He chuckled to himself.

He was silent for a moment as he crossed to rearrange the dusty old Venetian blinds.

Then he turned to a half-open cupboard beside the fireplace, and from it took a small wire cage from which he released a tame white rat, which instantly ran up his arm and settled upon his shoulder.

"Poor little Nibby!" he exclaimed, tenderly stroking its sharp pink snout with his forefinger. "Have I neglected you? Poor little fellow!—a prisoner all day! But if I let you out when I'm away some nasty terrier might get you—eh? Come let me atone for my neglect."

And he placed his pet upon the table, over which the rodent ran to investigate the remains of the meal.

Boyne stood watching his pet nibbling at a scrap of sausage.

"Ah!" he gasped in a whisper. "If they knew—but they will never know. They *can't!*"

A few minutes later his actions were, to say the least, strange.

He flung himself into the old armchair from which the flock stuffing protruded from the worn-out American cloth, and unbuttoning his dusty boots, took them off. Then, in his socks, he crept upstairs, and on the landing listened at the deaf old woman's door. Sounds of heavy snoring apparently satisfied him.

Back again he returned to the parlour, and with a key opened the opposite cupboard beside the fireplace, from which he took a very long, loose coat which seemed to be made of white alpaca. This he shook out and submitted to close scrutiny. It was shaped like a monk's habit, with a leather strap around the waist—a curious garment, for it had a hood attached, with two slits in it for the eyes.

After careful examination of the strange garment, he put it on over his head, drawing down the hood over his eyes, which gave him a hideous appearance—like the ghost of an ancient Inquisitor of Spain, or a member of the mediæval Misericordia Society of Italy, dressed in white instead of black.

Thus attired, he fumbled beneath in his pocket, and then noiselessly ascended the two flights of stairs to an attic door upon which was the circular brass plate of a Yale lock. This he opened, and passing within, closed the door softly behind him.

Bernard Boyne naturally believed himself alone in the house with old Mrs. Felmore sound asleep—but, truth to tell, *he was not!*

As he ascended the stairs, Marigold's pale face peered around the corner. The shock of seeing such a hideous ghostly form moving silently upstairs proved almost too much for her. But clinging on to the banisters, she managed to repress the cry of alarm which rose to her lips, and she stood there rooted to the spot—full of wonder and bewilderment. She listened breathlessly, still standing in the dark passage which led to the kitchen stairs. Then she detected the sound of the key going into the lock of the upstairs room where she knew Mr. Boyne kept his private papers.

But was it Mr. Boyne? Or was it an intruder who had adopted that garb in order to frighten any person he might encounter? Besides, why should Mr. Boyne assume such a strange disguise before entering the room where his business papers were stored?

Now upon that summer night Marigold had called about nine o'clock to visit her aunt, who had in years past been as a mother to her, to have a snack of supper, as she often did. Afterwards she had helped her aunt to prepare Mr. Boyne's frugal meal. Then old Mrs. Felmore, feeling rather unwell, had gone to bed, leaving her niece in the kitchen to write an urgent letter to Gerald, which she wanted to post before midnight.

As she finished the letter, she had heard someone enter, and not desiring that Mr. Boyne should know of her presence there at that hour, she had moved about quietly, and was just about to escape from the house when she had seen that strangely-garbed figure ascending the stairs.

The girl's first impulse had been to waken her aunt and raise an alarm that an intruder had entered the place. But on seeing that the supper had been eaten, and that Mr. Boyne's hat and coat lay upon the sofa, she at once decided that the figure that had ascended the stairs to the locked room was actually that of the master of the house.

"Why is he dressed like that?" she asked herself in a whisper, as she stood in the front parlour. "What can it mean?"

She glanced around the room. The cupboard beside the fireplace, which stood open, and from which Boyne had taken his strange disguise, caught her eye. She had never before seen that cupboard open, for her aunt had always told her that Mr. Boyne kept some of his important insurance papers there. Therefore, with curiosity, the girl approached it, finding it practically empty, save for a woman's big racoon muff, and with it a photograph— that of a handsome, well-preserved woman of about forty, across the front of which had been scrawled in a thin, feminine hand the signature, "Lilla, January, 1919."

Who was Lilla? She wondered.

Mr. Boyne she knew as a pleasant, easy-going man, full of generosity so far as his limited means allowed. He was a widower, who frequently referred to his "poor dear wife," and would descant upon her good qualities and how affectionately they had lived together for ten years.

The photograph, which she examined beneath the light, was quite a new one, and dated—hence it could not be that of the late Mrs. Boyne.

"I'll come back and tell auntie to-morrow," she said to herself. "She ought to know—or one night she'll see him and get a shock like I've had.

And her heart is not too strong. Yes—I must warn her—then no doubt she'll watch."

With those words she dabbed her hair in front of the cheap mirror over the mantelshelf, and then treading on tiptoe, went to the front door and let herself out.

This was the strange story Marigold had related to Gerald Durrant on that sunny afternoon beside the Thames—a story which had aroused his curiosity and held him fascinated.

CHAPTER II
WHO IS MRS. BRAYBOURNE?

Bernard Boyne was certainly a mystery man in Hammersmith, yet nobody suspected it. In all the years he had lived in the neighbourhood his actions had never aroused a single breath of suspicion.

In pious black he passed the collection bag around to the congregation of St. George the Martyr each Sunday morning, and afterwards, with a deep bow, handed the bag to the rubicund vicar of his parish.

Often he had been approached to serve upon the municipality of the borough, but he had always declined because of stress of work and for "family" reasons. Mr. Boyne could have achieved the highest local honours, aldermanic and otherwise, had he cared for them, but notwithstanding his great popularity, he was ever retiring, and even anxious to efface himself.

When that night he descended the stairs of his house in Bridge Place, all unconscious that he had been observed ascending them, he entered his little parlour, where he divested himself of the ugly white overall and locked it away, together with the woman's muff and the photograph. Then he paced the room in indecision, ignorant that Marigold had only vacated it a few minutes before.

He caught his pet, Nibby, after several attempts, and having replaced him in his cage, again stood with knit brows, still apparently uncertain how to act. He was in a bad humour, for now and then he uttered imprecations beneath his breath. Whatever had occurred upstairs had no doubt upset him. A further imprecation fell from his lips as he cursed his luck, and then, with sudden resolve, he resumed his boots, took his felt hat and stick, turned out the gas, and, going out into the narrow hall, extinguished the light and left the house.

He was in a bad temper on that warm summer's night as he strode hurriedly to the Hammersmith Broadway station, whence he took ticket to Sloane Square.

"Rotten luck! Lionel is a fool!" he declared to himself viciously, as he approached the pigeon-hole to take his ticket. "But one can't have all the good things of life. One must fail sometimes. And yet," he added, "I can't think why I've failed. But so long as it isn't a bad omen, I don't care! Why should I?"

And he took his ticket and descended the stairs to the train.

On arrival at Sloane Square he walked along to Pont Street to a large, red-brick house, into which he admitted himself with the latchkey upon his chain, a key very similar to that of the locked room in Bridge Place.

In the well-furnished hall he encountered a smart, good-looking French lady's maid.

"Ah! Good-evening, Annette. Is Madame at home?" he asked.

"Oui, monsieur," the girl promptly replied. "Madame is upstairs in the boudoir."

Boyne, who was evidently no stranger there, hung up his hat and passed upstairs to a room on the second floor, a cosy, tastefully-furnished apartment, where, at a table upon which stood a reading-lamp with a green silk shade, a handsome, dark-haired woman in a pearl-grey evening frock sat writing a letter.

"Hallo, Lilla! I'm glad you haven't gone to bed!" he exclaimed. "I want to have a chat with you. I met Annette downstairs. A pity that infernal girl hasn't gone to her room. I don't want her to overhear anything. Recollect Céline!"

"I'll send the girl to bed," said the woman, pressing an electric button. "Anything wrong?"

"Nothing very seriously wrong," was his reply.

And at his words the woman, who had betrayed alarm at sight of him, gave a sigh of relief.

Bernard Boyne flung himself into a silk-covered easy-chair, and, clasping his hands behind his head, gazed around the luxurious little room. It was, indeed, very different to his own surroundings in drab, work-a-day Hammersmith. Here taste and luxury were displayed on every hand; a soft, old-rose carpet, with hangings and upholstery to match—a woman's den which had been furnished regardless of expense by one of the best firms in the West End. Truth to tell, that elegant West End house was his own, and the handsome woman, Lilla, though she passed as Mrs. Braybourne, and was very popular in quite a good set, was his own wife.

Husband and wife lived apart. They did so for a purpose. Bernard was a hard-working insurance agent, a strict Churchman, perfectly upright and honest, though he lived his struggling life in Hammersmith. Truly, the *ménage* in Pont Street was both unusual and curious. Boyne, known to the servants as Mr. Braybourne, was very often away for weeks at a time. Then suddenly he would return and spend a week with his wife, being absent, however, all day. Neither dear old Mrs. Felmore nor all his wide circle of Hammersmith friends ever dreamed that he kept up another establishment in one of the best streets in London, a thoroughfare where a few doors away on either side were the legations of certain important European States.

"My dear Lilla, we can't be too careful," he said, with a kindly smile. "Our business is a very ticklish one. Ena agrees with me that Annette, your maid, has picked up too much English, and in consequence is a danger."

"Rubbish, my clear old Bernard!" laughed the handsome woman, upon whose fingers sparkled several valuable rings. "All that we need is to exercise due discretion."

"I know. When the game is crooked one has to be all the more careful."

"You don't seem to be in the sweetest of tempers to-night," remarked his wife, rather piqued. His visit was unexpected, and to her it portended unpleasantness. Not because discord ever existed between them. On the contrary, they were bound together by certain secrets which neither one nor the other dared to disclose. Lilla Boyne feared her husband to exactly the same extent that he feared her.

In that house in Pont Street, Mr. Boyne kept his well-cut suits, his evening clothes, his opera hat, and his expensive suit-case marked "B.B.," for on entry there he at once effaced his identity as the humble insurance agent, and became Bernard Braybourne, a man of means, and husband of the good-looking woman who in the course of five or six years had been taken up by quite a number of well-known people.

"I didn't expect you to-night," she remarked rather wearily. "I thought you'd have been here yesterday."

"I couldn't come. Sorry!" he replied.

"To-night I went to dine at Lady Betty's. You accepted, you know. So I apologised and said you had been called suddenly to Leeds last night," she said. "That idea of your candidature at Leeds at the next election works famously. You have to go and meet your committee, I tell them, and it always satisfies the curious. All of them hope you'll get in at the by-election when old Sammie dies, as he must very soon. They say the doctors have only given him three months more."

"Then before that date I'll have to retire from the contest," remarked her husband, with a grin.

"Oh! I'll watch that for you all right. Have you got that cheque?"

"Yes—to-day. It came from my new solicitor—seven thousand, eight hundred!"

"Good! I'm glad they've paid up. I began to fear that there might be some little hitch. They were so long-winded."

"So did I, to tell you the truth. But it's all right, and the new lawyer, a smart young fellow in the City, suspects nothing. I've already sent him his fee—so that's settled him."

"Will you employ him again?"

"I never employ a solicitor a second time, my dear Lilla. That would be a fatal mistake," was his reply. "But what I came to tell you mainly is that I've had a failure—a mysterious failure! Things haven't turned out exactly as I expected they would."

"Failure!" gasped the woman, with disappointment upon her dark, handsome face. "Then we must postpone it? How annoying!"

"Yes. But perhaps it's all for the best, Lilla. There was an element of danger. I told you that from the first."

"Danger! Rubbish!" declared his wife, with boldness, the diamonds flashing upon her fingers. "There's no danger! Of that I'm quite convinced. There was much more in that other little affair last winter. I was full of apprehension then—though I never told you of it."

"Well, at any rate, I haven't succeeded in the little business I've been attempting this last fortnight, so we'll have to postpone it."

"Perhaps your failure is due to the presence of your deaf old lady in the house," laughed his wife. "I passed the place in the car about a fortnight ago. Ugh! What a house!" and she shuddered.

"Yes, you might say so if you lived there and ate Mrs. Felmore's cold sausage for your supper, as I have to-night. Yet it must be done. If one makes money one has to make some sacrifice, especially if the money is made—well, not exactly on the square, shall we say?" And he grinned.

*　　*　　*　　*　　*

Away in North Wales three days later.

A beautiful moonlit evening by the Irish Sea. Over the Great Orme the moon shone brilliantly across the calm waters lazily lapping the bay of Llandudno, which was filled at the moment with an overflowing crowd of holiday folk, mostly from Yorkshire and Lancashire.

All the hotels and boarding houses were crowded out, and there were stories of belated trippers, many of whom were on their first seaside holiday after the stress of war, being compelled to sleep in bathing machines.

The lamps along the promenade were all aglow, the pier blazed with light, and across the bay came the strains of the orchestra playing selections from the latest revue.

In the big lounge of the Beach Hotel, which faces the sea in the centre of the bay, sat a well-preserved, middle-aged woman in a striking black dinner gown, trimmed with jade-coloured ninon, and wearing a beautiful jade bangle and ear-rings to match. The visitor, whose hair was remarkable because of its bright chestnut hue—almost red, indeed—had been there for three weeks. She was a widow, a Mrs. Augusta Morrison, hailing from Carsphairn, in Kirkcudbrightshire, Scotland, whose late husband had great interests in a big shipbuilding works at Govan.

Of rather loud type, as befitted the widow of a Scotch shipbuilder who had commenced life in the shipyard, she dressed extravagantly, greatly to the envy of the bejewelled wives of a few Lancashire war millionaires, who, unable to gain admittance to that little piece of paradise, the Oakwood Park Hotel, beyond Conway, were compelled to mix with the holiday crowd on the seashore of Llandudno.

The hotel lounge was at the moment almost empty, for most of the visitors were either on the pier or had gone out for a stroll in the moonlight. But Mrs. Morrison sat near the door chatting with Charles Emery, a young Manchester solicitor who had only been married since he had been demobilised six months before, and who had come to Llandudno with his wife, as is the custom of young married folk of Lancashire.

Once or twice the rich widow—who had hired a car for her stay in North Wales—had invited Emery and his wife to go for runs with her to Bangor, and across the Menai Bridge to Holyhead, or to Carnarvon, Bettws-y-coed, St. Asaph, and other places. From time to time she had told them of her loneliness in her big country house in one of the wildest districts in Scotland, and her intention to go abroad that winter—probably to Italy.

"My wife has gone to the theatre with Mr. and Mrs. Challoner," Emery was saying, as he lazily smoked his cigarette. "I had some letters to write—business letters that came from the office this morning—so I stayed in."

"Have you finished them?" asked the handsome widow, whose hair was always so remarked, and her eyes large and luminous.

"Yes," he replied. "I suppose I shall soon have to be back in harness again in Deansgate. But we shall both cherish the fondest memories of your great kindness to us, Mrs. Morrison."

• "It's really nothing, I assure you," laughed the widow merrily. "You have taken compassion upon me in my horribly lonely life, and I much appreciate it. Ah!" she sighed. "You can never imagine how lonely a woman can be who goes about the world aimlessly, as I go about. I travel here and there, sometimes on trips abroad, by sea, or by rail, often to the south of Europe, but I make no friends. Possibly it is my own fault. I may be too exclusive. And yet I never wish to be."

"I really don't think that!" he said gallantly. "At any rate, you've given us both a real ripping time!"

"I'm so glad you've enjoyed the little runs. But not more, I'm sure, than I have myself. I cannot live without movement. I love crowds. That's why I love cities—Manchester, London, Paris, and Rome. Where I live, up in Kirkcudbrightshire, it is one of the wildest and least explored districts of Great Britain. Between Loch Ken and Loch Doon, over the Cairnsmuir, the people are the most rural in all our island, quiet, honest folk, with no soul above their sheep and their cows. You and your wife must come north one day to Carsphairn and stay with me."

"I'm sure we should both be only too delighted to accept your hospitality, Mrs. Morrison," he said. "I'm afraid we can never repay you for your kindness to us. We are leaving next Monday."

"Oh, you have four more days! I'm motoring to Bettws-y-coed again to-morrow. You must both come with me, and we'll lunch at the Waterloo, as we did before. There has been rain these last few days, and the Swallow Falls will no doubt be grand."

And so it was arranged.

Next day all three went in the car up the beautiful valley of the Conway, with the wild hills on either side, through Eglwys Bach and Llanrwst, past Gwydyr Castle, and on by the Falcon Rock to that gem of North Wales, Bettws-y-coed.

To Mrs. Emery the widow was exceedingly amiable, and the day passed most pleasantly.

As they were motoring back through the mountains, purple in the sunset, between Capel Curig and Bangor, the widow, turning to Emery, suddenly said:

"I wonder, Mr. Emery, if you would advise me upon a little point of business? I'm rather perturbed, and I would so much like your professional advice. Can I see you after dinner to-night?"

"Most certainly," was his reply. "Any advice I can give you I will do so to the best of my ability," said the sharp young lawyer, well pleased at the prospect of a wealthy client.

That night at dinner Mrs. Morrison, radiant and handsome, wore a striking gown of black-and-gold, with a gold band in her red hair, and her string of fine pearls. In the big white-and-gold dining-room she was the most remarked of all the women there, but she pretended to take no notice of the sensation caused by her entrance into the room. Yet that gown had cost her sixty guineas in Dover Street, and, in secret, she was amused at the excitement its appearance had caused among the moneyed folk of Lancashire-by-the-Sea, who, after all, be it said, are honest people and who are more thorough than the shallow "Society" of post-war London.

After dinner, while Mrs. Emery went into the lounge and joined a woman and her daughter whom she knew, her husband went to Mrs. Morrison's sitting-room, where he found coffee awaiting him.

She produced a big silver box of cigarettes, and when she had served him with coffee and liqueur she lit a cigarette and settled herself to talk.

"The fact, Mr. Emery, is this," the woman with the wonderful hair commenced, when he had seated himself. "My late husband was a shipbuilder at Govan. Only recently I discovered that some twenty years ago he was guilty of some sharp practice in a financial deal which, while he and his friends enriched themselves, a man named Braybourne and his wife were both ruined. Braybourne died recently, but his widow is living in London. Now knowledge of this affair has greatly upset me, for I had the greatest faith in my dear husband's honesty."

"Naturally," remarked the young lawyer. "The knowledge of such a stigma attaching to his name must grieve you."

"Exactly. And I want somehow to make reparation. Not while I am alive—but after my death," she said. "I have been wondering what course would be best to pursue. I don't know Mrs. Braybourne, and probably she is in ignorance of my existence. Yet I should much like to do something in order to relieve my conscience. What would you advise?"

The young solicitor was silent for a few moments. At last he replied:

"Well, there are several courses open. You could make her an anonymous gift. But that would be difficult, for with a little inquiry she could discover the source of the payment."

"Ah! I don't want her to know anything!"

"I quite agree with that. You could, of course, make a will in her favour—leave her a legacy."

Mrs. Morrison remained silent for a while.

"Yes," she said at last, "that would be a way of easing my conscience regarding my husband's offence."

"Or, another way, you could insure your life in her favour. Then, at your death, she would receive the money unexpectedly," he suggested.

"That's rather a brilliant suggestion, Mr. Emery!" she replied eagerly. "But I know nothing about insurance matters. How can I do it? What have I to do and where shall I go to insure?"

"Well, Mrs. Morrison, I happen to be agent for a first-class life assurance company, the Universal, whose head offices are in Cornhill, London. If you so desire, I would be very happy to place a proposal before them," he said enthusiastically, for it meant a very substantial commission.

"I shall be very glad indeed, Mr. Emery, if you can carry the business through for me."

"With the utmost pleasure," was the young man's reply. "Er—what amount do you propose?"

"Oh! I hardly know. Some really substantial sum, I think. My husband, I have learned, got some twenty thousand pounds out of Mr. Braybourne. At least I would like to give her back half that sum."

"Ten thousand! How extremely generous of you, Mrs. Morrison. Of course, it's a large sum, and will mean a special premium, but no doubt the company will, providing you pass the medical test, issue the policy."

She thanked him for his promise to take up the matter for her. Then he went down to the writing-room to pen a letter to the Universal Assurance Company, while the handsome red-haired widow passed along the lounge and, with her merry chatter, rejoined his wife.

CHAPTER III
THE "GAME"—AND ITS PLAYERS

On the following morning Mr. Emery, the young solicitor, entered Mrs. Morrison's sitting-room at Llandudno with a telegram in his hand.

"I've just had this from the manager of the Universal. They are prepared to do the business and are writing me full particulars. I shall get them by to-morrow morning's post. I've wired to my clerk, Wilson, to post me a proposal form and some other papers."

Emery, his one thought being the big commission upon the business, entered Mrs. Morrison's room twenty-four hours later with a number of papers in his hand.

He sat down with the rich widow, and put before her the proposal form—a paper which had printed upon it a long list of questions, mostly inquisitorial. The bed-rock question of that document was "Who are you, and are you subject to any of the ills that human flesh is heir to?"

Question after question she read, and her answers he wrote down in the space reserved for them. Once or twice she hesitated before replying, but he put down her hesitation to a natural reserve.

The filling up of the form took some time, after which she appended her signature in a bold hand, and this completed the proposal.

"I fear it will be necessary for you to go to London to pass the doctor," he said. "When would that be convenient?"

"Any time after next Wednesday," she replied. "As a matter of fact, I have some shopping to do in town before I return to Scotland, so I can kill two birds with one stone."

"Excellent! They will, of course, make it as easy for you as possible. You will hear from Mr. Gray at the head office. Where shall you stay in town?

"With a friend of mine—a Mrs. Pollen." And she gave him an address in Upper Brook Street which he wrote down.

Before eleven o'clock Mrs. Morrison had dispatched a telegram addressed to "Braybourne, 9b, Pont Street, London," which read:

"All preliminaries settled. Shall be in London end of week.—AUGUSTA MORRISON."

Meanwhile, the solicitor, greatly elated at securing such a remunerative piece of work, sent the completed proposal to the head office of the company in London, and on the following day, accompanied by his wife, returned to his home in Manchester, after what had turned out to be a very profitable as well is beneficial holiday.

Before leaving, Mrs. Morrison arranged that he should carry the whole matter through, her parting injunction being:

"Remember—tell the Company to write to me at Upper Brook Street, and not to Scotland. And always write to me yourself to London."

Now that same evening, after Emery's departure, there arrived at the Beach Hotel, wearing rimless pince-nez, a dark, strongly-built man, well dressed, and with a heavy crocodile suit-case which spoke mutely of wealth. He signed the visitor's form as Pomeroy Graydon, and gave his address as "Carleon Road, Roath, Cardiff, Shipbroker."

He was late, and ate his dinner alone. Afterwards he went out for a stroll on the esplanade in the direction of the Little Orme, when, after walking nearly half a mile, he suddenly encountered the red-haired widow, who was attired plainly in navy blue with a small hat, having evidently changed her dress after dinner.

"Well, Ena!" he exclaimed, lifting his soft felt hat politely. "I'm here, you see! I thought it best to come up and see you. I'm at your hotel as Mr. Graydon of Cardiff."

"I'm awfully glad you've come, Bernie," she said. "I rather expected you."

"As soon as Lilla got your wire I started, and was fortunate to get to Euston just in time for the Irish mail—changed at Chester, and here I am!"

The pair strolled to a convenient seat close to where the waves lazily lapped upon the wall of the esplanade—for the tide was up—and the night a perfect one with a full white moon.

"Everything going well?" asked the smartly dressed man, whose pose in Hammersmith was so entirely different. He spoke in an eager tone.

"Yes, as far as I can see it's all plain sailing. I'm doing my part, and leave you and Lilla to do the rest. I've met here a very nice young fellow—as I intended—a useful solicitor named Emery, of Manchester. He is carrying the matter through for me. He's agent of the Universal."

"A first-class office."

"Well, I'm insuring with them in Lilla's favour."

"Have you carried out the plan we discussed?"

"To the very letter! Trust me, my dear Bernie."

"I always do, Ena," he declared, gazing across the moonlit sea. They were alone on the seat, and there was none to overhear:

"Ten thousand is a decent sum. Let's hope it will be all over soon. I sometimes have bad quarters of an hour—when I think!" he remarked.

"The sums assured have been higher and higher," she said. "We started with five hundred—you recollect the woman Bayliss?—and now we are always in thousands. Only you, Bernard, know how the game should be played. I do my part, but it is your brain which evolves all this business for which the companies are so eager, and which is so wonderful."

"True, our plan works well," Boyne admitted, still gazing over the sea. "We've all of us made thousands out of it—haven't we?"

"Yes. I can see no loophole by which the truth might leak out—save one," she said very seriously.

"And what's that?"'

"Your visits to your wife," was her reply. "Suppose somebody watched you, and saw you leave your frowsy little house in Hammersmith, go to Lilla in Pont Street, and blossom forth into a gentleman of means; it would certainly arouse a nasty suspicion. Therefore you should always be most careful."

"I am. Never fear," he said. "Recollect, nobody in Hammersmith knows that Lilla Braybourne is my wife."

"They don't know. But they might suspect things, which may lead eventually to an awkward inquiry, and then——?"

"Oh! my dear Ena, don't contemplate unpleasant things!" he urged, with a shrug of the shoulders. "I know you are a clever woman—more clever by far than Lilla herself—therefore I always rely upon your discretion and foresight. Now, tell me—what has happened up to date?"

In reply she told him briefly of her meeting with the young solicitor Emery—which she had prearranged, by the way—and how she had entertained the newly-married pair.

"They, of course, believe you to be Mrs. Augusta Morrison, of Carsphairn, widow of old Joe Morrison, the great shipbuilder of Govan?" he remarked, smiling.

"Exactly. As you know, I paid a visit in secret to Carsphairn six weeks ago, and found out quite a lot. This I retailed to the Emerys, and they took it all in. I described Carsphairn to them, and showed them the snapshots of the place which I took surreptitiously when I was up there. Indeed, I gave a couple of them to Mrs. Emery—to make evidence."

"Excellent!" he exclaimed. "You never leave anything undone, Ena."

"One must be thorough in everything if one desires success."

"And what is your address?"

"I gave it to my own flat in Upper Brook Street—care of Ena Pollen—widow."

"So you will come to London?"

"Yes—I have to go there shopping before I return to Scotland," she replied grimly. "I am staying with Mrs. Pollen."

"Good! It will be far the best for their London doctors to examine you. If you were examined up here they might resist the claim. If they did that—well, it would open up the whole business, and we certainly can't afford to arouse the very least little bit of doubt."

"Hardly," she laughed. "Well, I've played the game properly, my dear Bernie. My name is Morrison, and I am the widow of old Joe Morrison, the woman with the red hair, and I live at Carsphairn, Kirkcudbrightshire, the fine sporting estate left me by my late husband. All that is upon the records of the Universal Life Assurance Corporation."

"Excellent! You've established an undeniable identity—red hair and everything!" he said, again gazing reflectively out across the rippling waters. "You have taken the first step."

"The second move is that Mrs. Morrison goes to London on a shopping visit, prior to going abroad," the widow said.

"Really, you are marvellous, Ena!" declared the humble insurance agent of Hammersmith. "Your foresight always carries you to success."

"In a number of cases it has done so, I admit," the woman laughed. "When one's identity is not exactly as one represents, one has to have one's eyes skinned day and night. Men—even the shrewdest lawyers—are always easily gulled. Why? Because of the rapacious maws the legal profession have for fees. Women are always dangerous, for they are too frequently jealous of either good looks or pretty frocks. A man I can usually manage—a woman, seldom, unless she is in love. Then I side with her in her love affair and so gain her confidence."

"Ena, I repeat I hold you in admiration as one of the cleverest women I have ever known. Nothing deters you—nothing perturbs you! You fix a plan, and you carry it through in your own way—always with profit to our little combination."

"And very substantial profit, I venture to think, eh?" "I agree," he said, with a grim laugh.

"All thanks to you, my dear Bernie," the red-haired woman said. "But really I am growing just a little apprehensive. Why—I don't know, I cannot tell. But somehow I fear we may play the game once too often. And what then—eh?"

"Funnily enough, I've experienced the same curiously apprehensive feeling of late," he said. "I always try, of course, to crush it out, just as I crush out any other little pricks of conscience which occur to me when I awake in the mornings."

"Very strange that we should both of us entertain apprehensive feelings!" she remarked very thoughtfully. "I hope it's no ill omen! Do you think it is?"

"No," he laughed. "Don't let us seek trouble—for Heaven's sake. At present there is not the slightest danger. Of that I feel confident. Let us go forward. When shall you go up to London?"

"To-morrow. I go to visit my dear friend, Mrs. Pollen—as I have told you."

He laughed.

"So really you are going on a visit to yourself—eh? Excellent! Really you are unique, Ena!"

"Well—it is the only way, and it will work well."

Then the strange pair, who were upon such intimate terms, rose and strolled leisurely side by side back towards the opposite end of the promenade, chatting merrily the while.

When approaching the Beach Hotel they halted, and the woman bade the man good-bye. Afterwards he sank upon a seat in one of the shelters, while she walked on and entered the hotel.

Not until half an hour later, after he had taken a stroll along to the end of the pier, where the band was still playing, did he return to the hotel. Mrs. Morrison was at the moment sitting in the lounge chatting with two men visitors. The eyes of the pair met as he passed, but neither gave any sign of recognition.

To those in the lounge the two were absolutely strangers to each other.

Little did the other visitors dream of the dastardly, even demoniacal, plot that was being so skilfully woven in their midst.

Next afternoon Bernard Boyne stepped from out of the Holyhead express upon Euston platform and drove in a taxi to Pont Street, where he was greeted warmly by his wife, who had been informed of his advent by telegram from Chester.

"Well?" she asked, when the door of the luxurious drawing-room was closed and they were alone. "And how did you find Ena?"

"She's splendid! All goes well," was his enthusiastic reply. "She's got hold of a young Manchester solicitor who is carrying the policy through all right. He happens to be an agent of the Universal. She's on her way back to London now. I wasn't seen with her in the hotel, of course."

"When is she coming here?"

"To-night at nine. She wants to see you."

"I think the less she sees of me just now the better, don't you, Bernie?"

"I quife agree. We don't want anyone to recognise you as friends when the time comes," replied Boyne. "As soon as she gets passed by the doctors—both of them unknown to any of us—which is a blessing—she'll have to go up to Scotland."

"To New Galloway again?"

"No. To Ardlui, that pretty little village at the head of Loch Lomond. The inquiries I have been making of the servants at Carsphairn show that it is the lady's intention to go with her maid to Ardlui for a fortnight, and thence to Edinburgh for another fortnight."

"Really, Bernie, you are wonderful in the way you pry into people's intentions."

"Only by knowing the habits and intentions of our friends can we hope to be successful," was his reply, as he flung himself back among the silken cushions of the couch and lazily lit a cigarette.

"So Ena will have to go to Scotland again?"

"Yes. She ought to pass the doctors in a week, for this young fellow is pushing it through because of the handsome fee she will give him, and then, in the following week, she must put on her best frocks and best behaviour and take a 'sleeper' on the nine twenty-five from Euston to Glasgow."

"What an adventure!" remarked the handsome woman before him.

"Of course. But we are out for big money this time, remember."

"You have examined the whole affair, I suppose, and considered it from every standpoint—eh?"

"Of course I have. As far as I can discover, there is no flaw in our armour. This young solicitor is newly married, and is much gratified that the wealthy Mrs. Morrison should take such notice of his young wife. But you know Ena well enough to be sure that she plays the game all right. She's the rich widow to the very letter, and talks about her 'dear husband' in a manner that is really pathetic. She declares that they were such a devoted couple."

"Yes. Ena can play the game better than any woman in England," agreed his wife. "Have some tea?"

"No; it's too hot," he replied. "Get me some lemonade."

And she rose, and presently brought him a glass of lemonade. She preferred to wait upon him, for she was always suspicious of the maids trying to listen to their conversation, which, however, was discreet and well guarded.

That night at about half-past nine, husband and wife having dined together *tête-à-tête*—being waited on by the smart young Italian footman—Ena Pollen was ushered into the drawing-room.

"Oh! Welcome back, dear!" cried Mrs. Braybourne, jumping up and embracing her friend, making pretence, of course, before the servant. "Sit down. I had no idea you were in London! I thought you were somewhere in the wilds of Wales."

Then, when the door had closed, her attitude altered to one of deep seriousness.

"Well," she said, "according to Bernie, everything goes well, doesn't it?"

"Excellently," replied the other. "You see in me Mrs. Augusta Morrison, widow, of Carsphairn, New Galloway, who is in London on a visit to her friend, Ena Pollen, and who is about to be passed as a first-class life!" And she laughed, the other two smiling grimly.

"I congratulate you upon finding that young solicitor. What's his name?"

"Emery—just getting together a practice and looking out for the big commission on the first of my premiums," she said. "We've met those before. Do you recollect that fellow Johnson-Hughes? Phew! what an ass!"

"But he was over head and ears in love with you, my dear Ena," said Boyne, "and you know it."

"Don't be sarcastic, Bernie!" she exclaimed, with a pout. "Whether he was in love with me or not, it doesn't matter. We brought off the little affair successfully, and we all had a share of the pickings. In these post-war profiteering days it is only by callous dishonour and double-dealing one can make both ends meet. It begins in the Cabinet and ends with the marine store dealer. Honesty spells ruin. That's my opinion."

"I quite agree," Lilla declared. "If we had all three played a straight game, where should we be now?"

"Living in Bridge Place," remarked Boyne, whereat the two women laughed merrily.

That night Marigold met Gerald at Mark Lane Station, and they travelled westward together on the way home. In the Underground train they chatted about the mystery of Bridge Place, but amid the crush and turmoil of home-going City workers they could say but little.

Marigold had been again to see her deaf aunt, who was still unsuspicious of the strange state of affairs in her master's humble home.

Gerald was next day compelled to accompany his principal up north to a conference upon food prices, and for ten days he remained away. Therefore Marigold could only watch and wait.

She went to Bridge Place several times, and saw Mr. Boyne there. He was always cheerful and chatty. About him there seemed nothing really suspicious. Indeed, when she considered it all, she began to wonder whether she had not made a fool of herself.

CHAPTER IV
PROGRESS OF THE PLOT

In the dull, sombre consulting-room of Sir Humphrey Sinclair in Queen Anne Street, Cavendish Square—a room with heavy mahogany furniture, well-worn carpet, a big writing-table set in the window, and an adjustable couch against the wall—sat the pseudo Mrs. Augusta Morrison, who desired to insure her life.

At the table sat the great physician, a clean-shaven, white-haired man, in large, round, gold-rimmed spectacles. He was dressed in a grey cashmere suit—for the weather was unbearably hot that morning—and, truth to tell, he was longing for his annual vacation at his pretty house by the sea at Frinton.

In the medical world Humphrey Sinclair had made a great name for himself, and had had among his patients various European royalties, besides large numbers of the British aristocracy and well-known people of both sexes. Quiet mannered, soft spoken, and exquisitely polite, he was always a favourite with his lady patients, while Lady Sinclair herself moved in a very good set.

Having arranged a number of papers which the Universal had sent to him, he took one upon which a large number of questions were printed with blank spaces for the proposer's replies. Then, turning to her, he said, with a smile:

"I fear, Mrs. Morrison, that I shall be compelled to ask you a number of questions. Please understand that they are not merely out of curiosity, but the company claim a right to know the family and medical history of any person whose life they insure.

"I perfectly understand, Sir Humphrey," replied the handsome woman. "Ask me any questions you wish, and I will try to reply to them to the best of my ability."

"Very well," he said. "Let's begin." And he commenced to put to her questions regarding the date of her birth, the cause of the deaths of her father and her mother, whether she had ever suffered from this disease or that, dozens of which were enumerated. And so on.

For nearly half an hour the great doctor plied her with questions which he read aloud from the paper, and then wrote down her replies in the spaces reserved for them.

Never once did she hesitate—she knew those questions off by heart, indeed, and had her replies ready, replies culled from a budget of information which during the past three months had been cleverly collected. Truth to tell, she was replying quite accurately to the questions, but only so far as Mrs. Morrison of Carsphairn was concerned. The medical history she gave was correct in every detail concerning Mrs. Morrison.

But, after all, was not the proposal upon the life of Mrs. Morrison, and did not the famous physician believe her to be the widow of Carsphairn?

Sir Humphrey asked her to step upon the weighing machine in the corner of the room, and afterwards he measured her height and wrote it down with a grunt of satisfaction.

Then, after further examination, and putting many questions, he reseated himself, and turned to the page upon which his own private opinion was to be recorded.

"I hope you don't find much wrong with me?" asked the lady, with a little hesitation.

"No, my dear madam—nothing that I can detect," was the physician's reply as he gazed at her through his big glasses. "Of course, my colleague, Doctor Hepburn, may discover something. I shall have to ask you to call upon him."

"When?"

"Any time you care to arrange. To-day—if you like. He may be at home. Shall I see?"

"I do so wish you would, Sir Humphrey," Ena said. "I want to get back to Scotland, as I have to go to Ardlui next week."

The great doctor took the telephone at his elbow, and was soon talking to Doctor Hepburn, with whom he arranged for the lady to call in an hour.

Then Sir Humphrey scribbled the address in Harley Street on a slip of paper, and with a few polite words of reassurance, rang his bell, and the man-servant conducted her out.

"An exceptionally pretty woman," grunted old Sir Humphrey to himself when she had gone. "Highly intelligent, and a first-class life."

And he sat down to record his own private views as to the physical condition of the person proposed for insurance.

Ena idled before the shop windows in Oxford Street for three-quarters of an hour, and then took a taxi to Harley Street, where she found Doctor Stanley Hepburn, a short, stout, brown-bearded man of rather abrupt manner.

In his smart, up-to-date consulting-room he put the same questions to her, wearying as they were, and parrot-like she answered them.

"Truly, I'm having a busy morning, doctor," she remarked, with a sigh, laughing at the same time.

"Apparently," he said, smiling. "I must apologise for bothering you with all these questions. Sir Humphrey has, no doubt, gone through them all."

"He has."

"Well, never mind. Forgive me, and let's get along," he said briskly.

And he proceeded with question after question. At last, after an examination exactly like that conducted by Sir Humphrey, Doctor Hepburn reseated himself at his table, and said:

"Well, Mrs. Morrison, I don't think I need keep you any longer."

"Are you quite satisfied with me?" she asked boldly.

He was silent for a few seconds.

"As far as I myself am concerned I see no reason whatever why the company should not accept the risk," was his reply. "Of course, I don't know the nature of Sir Humphrey's report; but I expect it coincides with my own. I can detect nothing to cause apprehension, and, in normal circumstances, you should live to quite old age."

"Thanks! That is a very agreeable piece of information," she said.

Then, his waiting-room being crowded—for he had given her a special appointment—he rose and, bowing, dismissed her, saying:

"I shall send in my report to the company to-night, therefore the matter should go through without delay."

Afterwards, as she walked along Harley Street, a great weight having been lifted from her mind, she hailed a taxi and drove back to her pretty flat in Upper Brook Street, where a dainty lunch awaited her.

To answer frankly and correctly those questions had been an ordeal. Those queries were so cleverly arranged that if, after death, the replies to any of them are found to be false the company would be able to resist the claim upon it. To give a true and faithful account of your parents' ailments and your own illnesses is difficult enough, but to give an equally true account of those of another person is extremely difficult and presents many pitfalls. And none knew that better than Ena Pollen.

After lunch, she rested for an hour, as was her habit in summer, and then she took a taxi to Pont Street, where she had tea with Lilla Braybourne.

To her she related her adventures among the medicos, adding:

"All is serene! There's nothing the matter with Mrs. Morrison of Carsphairn! She's in excellent health and may live to be ninety. Hers is a first-class life!"

"Bernie predicted it," said the wife of the humble insurance agent of Hammersmith. "You were passed fit in the Fitzgerald affair—you recollect."

"Yes," snapped the handsome woman. "What a pity the sum wasn't five thousand instead of five hundred."

"I agree. But we didn't then realise how easy was the game. Now we know—a few preliminary inquiries, a plausible tongue—which, thanks to Heaven, you've got, Ena—a few smart dresses, and a knowledge of all the devious ways of insurance and assignments—and the thing is easy."

"Well, as far as we've gone in this matter all goes well—thanks to Bernie's previous inquiries regarding the good lady of Carsphairn."

"She's a bit of a skinflint, I believe. Can't keep servants. She has a factor who is a very close Scot, and things at Carsphairn are usually in a perturbed condition," Lilla said. "Bernie has gone back to Bridge Place. What an awful life the poor dear leads! Fancy having to live with that deaf old woman Felmore!"

"Yes. But isn't it part of the game? By living in Hammersmith, and being such a hard-working, respectable man, he acquires a lot of very useful knowledge."

"Quite so; but it must be very miserable there for him."

"He doesn't mind it, he says," was the reply. "It brings money."

"It certainly does that," said Lilla. "When shall you go north? Will you wait till the policy is issued?"

"I think not. The sooner I meet Mrs. Morrison the better. Don't you agree?"

"Certainly. What does Bernie say?"

"That's his view," answered Ena. "So I shall go to Scotland at the end of the week. I shall stay at the Central, in Glasgow, for a night or two, and then on to Loch Lomond."

"Bernie has heard from one of his secret sources of information that the widow is leaving Carsphairn three days earlier than she intended. She goes to visit a niece who lives in Crieff, and then on to Ardlui."

"I've been to Ardlui before—on a day trip from Glasgow up the Loch," Ena said. "A quiet, remote little place, with an excellent hotel right at the extreme end of the Loch, beyond Inversnaid."

"Then you'll go north without waiting for the policy?"

"Yes. Letters will come to me addressed care of myself, and Bernie will send them on. As soon as I have notice that the company will accept me, I'll pay the premium. I've already opened a little account in the name of Augusta Morrison, so that I can send them a cheque. In the meanwhile, we need lose no time."

"And yet I don't think we ought to rush it unduly, do you?" asked Lilla.

"Oh! we shan't do that, my dear Lilla. There's a lot to be done in the matter of inspiring confidence. Perhaps dear Augusta will not take to me. What then?"

"You always know how to make yourself pleasant, Ena. She'll take to you, never fear!"

"According to the reports we've had about her, she's rather discriminating in her friendships," said the handsome woman, smiling grimly.

"Well, I rather wish I were coming with you for a fortnight on Loch Lomond," said Lilla.

"No, my dear, you have no place in the picture at present. Much as I would like your companionship, you are far better here at home."

"Yes, I suppose you are right!" answered her friend, sighing. "But I long for Scotland in these warm summer days."

"Get Bernie to take you to the seaside for a bit. There's nothing urgent doing just now."

"Bernie is far too busy in Hammersmith, my dear," Lilla laughed. "He wouldn't miss his weekly round for worlds. Besides, he's got some important church work on—helping the vicar in a series of mission meetings."

"Bernie is a good Churchman, I've heard," said Ena.

"Of course. That, too, is part of the big bluff. The man who carries round the bag every Sunday is always regarded as pious and upright. And Bernie never loses a chance to increase his halo of respectability."

Ena remained at Pont Street for about half an hour longer, and then, returning to her own flat, she set about sorting out the dresses she would require for Scotland, and assisted her elderly maid to pack them.

Afterwards she returned into her elegant little drawing-room and seated herself at the little writing-table, where she consulted a diary. Then she wrote telegrams to the hotels at Glasgow and at Ardlui, engaging rooms for dates which, after reflection, she decided upon.

Ena Pollen was a woman of determination and method. Her exterior was that of a butterfly of fashion, careless of everything save her dress and her hair, yet beneath the surface she was calm, clever, and unscrupulous, a woman who had never loved, and who, indeed, held the opposite sex in supreme contempt. The adventure in which she was at that moment engaged was the most daring she had ever undertaken. The unholy trio had dabbled in small affairs, each of which had brought them profit, but the present undertaking would, she knew, require all her tact and cunning.

The real Mrs. Augusta Morrison, the widow of Carsphairn, was one of Boyne's discoveries, and by judicious inquiry, combined with other investigations which Ena herself had made, they knew practically everything concerning her, her friends, and her movements. The preliminaries had taken fully three months, for prior to going to Llandudno, there to assume the widow's identity, Ena had been in secret to New Galloway, and while staying at the Lochinvar Arms, at Dairy, she had been able to gather many facts concerning the rich widow of Carsphairn, a copy of whose birth and marriage-certificate she had obtained from Somerset House.

After writing the telegrams, she took a sheet of notepaper and wrote to Mr. Emery in Manchester, telling him that she had passed both doctors, and asking him to hurry forward the policy.

"*My movements during the next fortnight or so are a little uncertain,*" she wrote, "*but please always address me as above, care of my friend, Mrs. Pollen. Please give my best regards to your dear wife, and accept the same yourself .— Yours very sincerely,* AUGUSTA MORRISON."

Three nights later, Ena left Euston in the sleeping-car for Glasgow, arriving early next morning, and for a couple of days idled away the time in the great hotel, the Central, eagerly awaiting a telegram.

At last it came.

The porter handed it to her as she returned from a walk. She tore it open, and when she read its contents, she went instantly pale.

The message was disconcerting, for instead of giving information regarding the movements of the woman she had been impersonating, it read:

"*Remain in Glasgow. Am leaving to-night. Will be with you in morning. Urgent.*—BERNARD."

What could have happened? A hitch had apparently occurred in the arrangements, which had been so thoroughly discussed and every detail considered.

It was then six o'clock in the evening. Boyne could not be there until eight o'clock on the following morning. She glanced bewildered around the busy hall of the hotel, where men and women with piles of luggage were constantly arriving and departing.

"Why is he not more explicit?" she asked herself in apprehension.

What could have happened? she wondered. For yet another fourteen hours she must remain in suspense.

Suddenly, however, she recollected that she could telephone to Lilla, and she put through a call without delay.

Half an hour later she spoke to her friend over the wire, inquiring the reason of Boyne's journey north.

"My dear, I'm sorry," replied Lilla in her high-pitched voice, "but I really cannot tell you over the 'phone. It is some very important business he wants to see you about."

"But am I not to go to Ardlui?" asked Ena.

"I don't know. Bernie wants to see you without delay—that's all."

"But has anything happened?" she demanded eagerly.

"Yes—something—but I can't tell you now. Bernie will explain. He'll be with you in Glasgow early to-morrow morning."

"Is it anything very serious?"

"*I think it may be—very!*" was Lilla's reply; and at that moment the operator cut off communication with London, the six minutes allowed having expired.

CHAPTER V
CONTAINS A NOTE OF ALARM

Ena Pollen was on the platform when the dusty night express from London ran slowly into the Caledonian Station, at Glasgow.

Bernard Boyne, erect and smartly-dressed, stepped out quickly from the sleeping-car, to be greeted by her almost immediately.

"What's happened?" she demanded anxiously beneath her breath.

"I can't tell you here, Ena. Wait till we're in the hotel," he replied. She saw by his countenance that something was amiss.

Together they walked from the platform into the hotel, and having ascended in the lift to her private sitting-room, the man flung himself into a chair, and said:

"A very perilous situation has arisen regarding the Martin affair!"

"The Martin affair!" she gasped, instantly pale to the lips. "I always feared it. That girl, Céline Tènot, had some suspicion, I believe."

"Exactly. She was your maid, and you parted bad friends. It was injudicious."

"Where is she now, I wonder?"

"At her home in Melun, near Paris. You must go at once to Paris, and ask her to meet you," Boyne said.

"To Paris?" she cried in dismay.

"Yes; not a second must be lost. Inquiries are on foot. I discovered the situation yesterday, quite by accident."

"Inquiries!" she cried. "Who can be making inquiries?"

"Some friend of that girl—a Frenchman. He has come over here to find me."

"To find you! But she only knew you under the name of Bennett!"

"Exactly. In that is our salvation," he said, with a grin. "But the affair is distinctly serious unless we can make peace with Céline, and at the same time make it worth her while to withdraw this inquiry. No doubt she's looking forward to a big reward for furnishing information."

"But why can't we give her the reward—eh?" asked the shrewd, red-haired woman quickly.

"That's exactly my argument. That is why you must leave this present little matter, turn back to Céline, and make it right with her."

"How much do you think it will cost?"

Bernard Boyne shrugged his shoulders.

"Whatever it is, we must pay," he replied. "We can't afford for this girl to remain an enemy—and yours especially."

"Of course not," Ena agreed. "What is her address?"

Boyne took a slip of paper from his pocket-book and handed it to the handsome woman.

"But what excuse can I possibly make for approaching her?" she asked bewildered.

"Pretend you've come to Paris to offer to take her into your service again," Boyne suggested. "She will then meet you, and you can express regret that you sent her away so suddenly, and offer to make reparation—and all that."

"There was an object in sending her away so peremptorily. You know what it was, Bernie."

"I know, of course. She might have discovered something then. You adopted the only course—but, unfortunately, it has turned out to have been a most injudicious one, which may, if we are not very careful and don't act at once, lead to the exposure of a very nasty circumstance—the affair of old Martin."

"I quite see," she said. "I'll go to Paris without delay."

"You'll stay at the Bristol, as before, I suppose?"

"Yes. I will ask her to come and see me there."

Boyne hesitated.

"No. I don't know whether it would not be better for you to go out to Melun for the day and find her there," he queried. "Remember, you must handle the affair with the greatest delicacy. You've practically got to pay her for blackmail which she has not sought."

"That's the difficulty. And the sum must be equal, if not more, to that which she and her French friend who has come over here to seek and identify you hope to get out of it by their disclosures. Oh! yes," she said, "I quite see it all."

"I admit that the situation which has arisen is full of peril, Ena," remarked the man seated before her, "but you are a clever woman, and with the exercise of tact and cunning, in addition to the disbursement of funds, we shall undoubtedly be able to wriggle out—as we always do."

"Let's hope so," she said, with a sigh. "But what about Ardlui and Mrs. Morrison?"

"Your visit to Paris is more important at the moment. You must lose no time in getting there. Before I left London, I instructed my bank to send five thousand pounds to you at the head office of the Credit Lyonnais. You will be able to draw at once when you get there, and it will give you time to get more money if you deem it wise to pay any bigger sum."

"Really, you leave nothing undone, Bernie.

"Not when danger arises, my dear Ena," he laughed. "In the meantime, I'll have to remain very low. That infernal Frenchman may be watching Lilla with the idea that I might visit Pont Street. But I shan't go near her again till the danger is past."

"Then I'd better get away as soon as possible," she said. "I can be in London this evening, and cross to Paris by the night mail."

"Yes," he replied. "Don't waste an instant in getting in touch with her. Have a rest in Paris, and then go to Melun. You can be there to-morrow afternoon."

"Shall you go back to London with me?"

"No. Better not be seen together," he said. "Let us be discreet. You can go by the ten o'clock express, which will just give you time to cross London to Victoria and catch the boat train, and I'll leave by the next express, which goes at one. The less we are together at present the better."

"I agree entirely," Ena said, with a sigh. "But this affair will, I see, be very difficult to adjust."

"Not if you keep your wits about you, Ena," he assured her. "It isn't half so difficult as the arrangements you made with that pious old fellow Fleming. Don't you recollect how very near the wind we were all sailing, and yet you took him in hand and convinced him of your innocence."

"I was dealing with a man then," she remarked. "Now I have to deal with a shrewd girl. Besides, we don't know who this inquisitive Frenchman may be."

"You'll soon discover all about him, no doubt. Just put on your thinking-cap on the way over to Paris, and doubtless before you arrive, you'll hit upon some plan which will be just as successful as the attitude you adopted towards old Daniel Fleming." Then he added: "I wish you'd order breakfast to be served up here, for I'm ravenously hungry."

She rose, rang the bell, and ordered breakfast for two.

While it was being prepared, Boyne went along the corridor to wash, while Ena retired to her room, and packed her trunk ready for her departure south at ten o'clock.

Afterwards she saw the head porter and got him to secure her a place on the train, and also in the restaurant-car, which is usually crowded.

They breakfasted *tête-à-tête*, after which she paid her bill, and at ten o'clock left him standing upon the platform to idle away three hours wandering about the crowded Glasgow streets before his departure at one o'clock.

Next morning Ena Pollen took her déjeuner at half-past eleven in the elegant table d'hôte room of the aristocratic Hôtel Bristol, in Paris, a big white salon which overlooks the Place Vendôme. Afterwards she took a taxi to the Gare de Lyon, whence she travelled to Melun, thirty miles distant— that town from which come the Brie cheeses. On arrival, she inquired for the Boulevard Victor Hugo, and an open cab drove her away across the little island in the Seine, past the old church of St. Aspais, to a point where, in the boulevard, stood a monument to the great savant, Pasteur. The cab pulled up opposite the monument, where, alighting, Ena found herself before a large four-storied house, the ground floor of which was occupied by a tobacconist and a shop which sold comestibles.

Of the old bespectacled concierge who was cobbling boots in the entrance she inquired for Madame Ténot, and his gruff reply was:

"Au troisième, à gauche."

So, mounting the stone steps, she found the left-hand door on the third floor, and rang the bell.

The door opened, and the good-looking young French girl, who had been her maid for six months at Brighton, confronted her.

"Well, Céline!" exclaimed Ena merrily in French. "You didn't expect to see me—did you?"

The girl stood aghast and open-mouthed.

"*Dieu*! Madame!" she gasped. "I—I certainly did not!"

"Well, I chanced to be passing through Melun, and I thought I would call upon you."

The girl stood in the doorway, apparently disinclined to invite her late mistress into the small flat which she and her mother, the widow of the local postmaster, occupied.

"I wrote to you, Madame, two months ago—but you never replied!"

"I have never had any letter from you, Céline," Ena declared. "But may I not come in for a moment to have a chat with you? Ah! but perhaps you have visitors?"

"No, Madame," was her reply; "I am alone. My mother went to my aunt's, at Provins, this morning."

"Good! Then I may come in?"

"If Madame wishes," she said, still with some reluctance, and led the way to a small, rather sparsely-furnished salon, which overlooked the cobbled street below.

"I have been staying a few days at Marlotte, and am now on my way back to Paris," said her former mistress, seating herself in a chair. "Besides, I wanted particularly to see you, Céline, for several reasons. I feel somehow that—well, that I have not treated you as I really ought to have done. I dismissed you abruptly after poor Mr. Martin's death. But I was so very upset—I was not actually myself. I know I ought not to have done what I did. Please forgive me."

The dark-haired, good-looking young girl in well-cut black skirt and cotton blouse merely shrugged her well-shaped shoulders. She uttered no word. Indeed, she had not yet recovered from her surprise at the sudden appearance of her former mistress.

"I don't know what you must have thought of me, Céline," Ena added.

"I thought many things of Madame," the girl admitted.

"Naturally. You must have thought me most ungrateful, after all the services you had rendered me, often without reward," remarked the red-haired widow. "But I assure you that I am not ungrateful."

The girl only smiled. She recollected the manner in which she had been suddenly dismissed and sent out from the house at five minutes' notice— and for no fault that she could discover.

She recollected how Madame had two friends, an old man named Martin, and a younger one named Bennett. Mr. Martin, who was a wealthy bachelor, living in Chiswick, had suddenly contracted typhoid and died. Madame, who had been most grief-stricken, received a visit from Bennett next day, and she had overheard the pair in conversation in the drawing-room. That conversation had been of a most curious character, but its true import had never occurred to her at the time. Next day her mistress had summarily dismissed her, giving her a month's wages, and requesting her to leave instantly. This she had done, and returned to her home in France.

It was not until nearly two months later that she realised the grim truth. The strange words of Mr. Bennett, as she recollected them, utterly staggered her.

And now this woman's sudden appearance had filled her with curiosity.

"Your action in sending me away in the manner you did certainly did not betray any sense of gratitude, Madame," the girl said quite coolly.

"No, no, Céline! Do forgive me," she urged. "Poor Mr. Martin was a very old friend, and his death greatly perturbed me."

Céline, however, remembered how to the man Bennett she had in confidence expressed the greatest satisfaction that the old man had died.

Ena was, of course, entirely ignorant of how much of that conversation the girl had overheard or understood. Indeed, she had not been quite certain it the girl had heard anything. She had dismissed her for quite another reason—in order that, if inquiries were made, a friendship between Bernard Boyne and the dead man could not be established. Céline was the only person aware of it, hence she constituted a grave danger.

Ena used all her charm and her powers of persuasion over the girl, and as she sat chatting with her, she recalled many incidents while the girl was in her service.

"Now look here, Céline," she said at last. "I'll be perfectly frank with you. I've come to ask you if you'll let bygones be bygones, and return to me?"

The girl, much surprised at the offer, hesitated for a moment, and then replied:

"I regret, Madame, it is quite impossible. I cannot return to London."

That was exactly the reply for which the clever woman wished.

"Why not, pray?" she asked the girl in a tone of regret.

"Because the man to whom I am betrothed would not allow me," was her reply.

"Oh! Then you are engaged, Céline! Happy girl! I congratulate you most heartily. And who is the happy man?"

"Henri Galtier."

"And what is his profession?"

"He is employed in the Mairie, at Chantilly," was her reply.

"He is at Chantilly now?"

The girl again hesitated. Then she replied:

"No—he is in London."

Ena held her breath. It was evidently the man to whom Céline was engaged who was in London in search of Richard Bennett. Next second she recovered from her excitement at her success in making the discovery.

"In London? Is he employed there?"

"Yes—temporarily," she answered.

"And when are you to marry?"

"In December—we hope."

"Ah! Then, much as I regret it, I quite understand that you cannot return to me, Céline," exclaimed Ena. "Does Monsieur Galtier speak English?"

"Yes; very well, Madame. He was born in London, and lived there until he was eighteen."

"Oh, well, of course he would speak our language excellently. But though you will no doubt both be happy in the near future, I myself am not at all satisfied with my own conduct towards you. I've treated you badly; I feel that in some way or other I ought to put myself right with you. I never like a servant to speak badly of me."

"I do not speak badly of Madame," responded the girl, wondering whether, after all, her late mistress suspected her of overhearing that startling conversation late on the night following Mr. Martin's death.

Ena hesitated a moment, and then determined to act boldly, and said:

"Now Céline, let us be quite frank. I happen know that you have said some very nasty and things about me—wicked things, indeed. I heard that you have made a very serious allegation against me, and——"

"But, Madame! I——!" cried the girl, interrupting.

"Now you cannot deny it, Céline. You have said those things because you have sadly misjudged me. But I know it is my own fault, and the reason I am here in Melun is to put matters right—and to show you that I bear you no ill will."

"I know that, Madame," she said. "Your words are sufficient proof of it."

"But, on the contrary, you are antagonistic—bitterly antagonistic towards myself—and"—she added slowly, looking straight into the girl's face—"and also towards Mr. Bennett."

She started, looking sharply at the red-haired widow.

"Yes, I repeat it, Céline!" Ena went on. "You see I know the truth! Yet your feeling against Mr. Bennett does not matter to him in the least, because he died a month ago—of influenza."

"Mr. Bennett dead!" echoed the girl, standing aghast, for, as a matter of fact, her lover, Henri Galtier, was searching for him in London.

"Yes; the poor fellow went to Birmingham on business, took influenza, and died there a week later. Is it not sad?"

"Very," the girl agreed, staring straight before her. If Bennett were dead, then of what avail would be all her efforts to probe the mystery of Mr. Martin's death?

"Mr. Bennett was always generous to you—was he not?" asked Ena.

"Always," replied the girl. "I am very sorry he is dead!"

"Well, he is, and therefore whatever hatred you may have conceived for him is of no importance," she replied; and then adroitly turned the conversation to another subject.

At length, however, she returned to Céline's approaching marriage, expressing a hope that she would be very comfortably off.

"Has Monsieur Galtier money?"

"Not very much," she replied. "But we shall be quite happy nevertheless."

"Of course. Money does not always mean happiness. I am glad you view matters in that light, Céline," Ena said. "Yet, on the other hand, money contributes to luxury, and luxury, in most cases, means happiness."

"True, Madame, I believe so," replied the ex-maid, whose thoughts were, however, filled by what her late mistress had, apparently in all innocence, told her, namely, that Bennett, the man her lover meant to hunt down, was dead. She had no reason to doubt what Mrs. Pollen had said, for only on the previous day Henri had written her to say that his inquiries had had no result, and that he believed that the man Bennett must be dead, as he could obtain no trace of him. The reward which they hoped to gain from the insurance company when they had established Bennett's identity had therefore vanished into air.

Céline Tènot sat bewildered and disappointed, and the clever woman seated with her read her thoughts as she would have read a book.

"Now let's come to the point," she said, after a pause. "I want to make amends, Céline. I want you to think better of me, and for that purpose, I want to render you some little service, now that you are to marry. My desire is to remove from your mind any antagonism you may entertain towards myself. The best way in which I can do that is to make you a little wedding-present—something useful."

"Oh, Madame!" she cried. "I—I really want nothing!"

"But I insist, Céline!" replied the wealthy widow. "Poor Mr. Bennett remarked that I was very harsh in dismissing you. At the time I did not think so, but I now realise that the fault was on my side, therefore I shall give you thirty thousand francs to put by as a little nest-egg."

"But, Madame, I could not really accept it!" declared the girl, exhibiting her palms.

"I have an account at the Credit Lyonnais, and to-morrow I shall place the thirty thousand francs there in your name," said Mrs. Pollen. "I shall want you to come to Paris—to the Hôtel Bristol—so that we can go to the bank together, and you can there open an account and give them your signature. If I were you, I would say nothing whatever to Monsieur Galtier about it—or even tell him of my visit. Just keep the money for yourself—as a little present from one who, after all, greatly valued your services."

Though the girl pretended to be entirely against receiving any present, yet she realised that possession of such a respectable sum would be able to assist in preparing her new home. After all, it was most generous of Madame. Yes! she had sadly misjudged her, she reflected, after Mrs. Pollen had left. So, adopting her late mistress's suggestion, she refrained from telling her mother of the unexpected visit.

That night she wrote to Galtier, who was staying in a boarding-house in Bloomsbury, telling him that she had heard of the death of Bennett, but not revealing the source of her information. She therefore suggested that he should spend no further time or money on the inquiry, but return at once to his duties at Chantilly.

Next day Céline called at the Hôtel Bristol, when mistress and maid went together to the bank in the Boulevard des Italiens, and there the girl received the handsome present. After this, she returned much gratified to Melun, while her late mistress left Paris that same night for London.

She had cleverly gained the girl's complete confidence, thereby preventing any further inquiry into the curious circumstances attending the death of Mr. Martin, of Chiswick.

CHAPTER VI
THE LOCKED ROOM IN HAMMERSMITH

"I'll go in first, and see if Mr. Boyne is at home," said Marigold Ramsay excitedly to her companion, Gerald Durrant, as they turned into Bridge Place, Hammersmith, about half-past nine one night ten days later.

"Yes. If he's there I won't come in. We'll wait till another evening," the young fellow said.

"If he's out, I shall tell auntie that you are here, and ask whether I can bring you in," said the girl, and leaving him idling at the corner, she hurried to the house, and went down the basement steps.

What Marigold had told Durrant had aroused his curiosity concerning the occupier of that creeper-covered house, and after much deliberation, he had, after his return from Newcastle, decided to make an investigation. Certainly the exterior of the place presented nothing unusual, for the house was exactly the same as its neighbours, save for the dusty creeper which hung untrimmed around the windows. Yet the fact that the man who lived there disguised himself when he went to a locked attic was certainly mysterious.

After a few moments, the girl emerged, and hastening towards him, said eagerly:

"It's all right. Mr. Boyne is not expected home before half-past ten. I'll introduce you to my aunt, and before she goes to bed—as she always does at ten—I'll manage to unbolt the basement door. Then we'll go out, and return without her being any the wiser."

"Excellent!" he replied, as they walked to the front door which Marigold had left ajar.

In the hall Mrs. Felmore met them fussily.

"Very pleased to know you, Mr. Durrant," declared the deaf old lady without, of course, having heard Gerald's greeting as he shook her hand.

"My aunt is very deaf," the girl said. "She can read what I say by my lips, but it will be useless for you to try and converse with her. Mr. Boyne can just manage to do so."

"Then I'll do the same," said Gerald, glancing around the front parlour, into which Mrs. Felmore had then ushered them.

He noted the cheapness of the furniture, combined with scrupulous cleanliness, as Mrs. Felmore, turning to him, said in that loud voice in which the deaf usually converse:

"I hope you'll make yourself at home, Mr. Durrant! Any friend of my niece is welcome here. Would you like a cup of tea? I know Marigold will have one."

He thanked her, and she went below to prepare it, leaving the pair in Mr. Boyne's room.

Quickly Gerald rose, remarking:

"There's nothing very curious about this, is there?" He made a critical tour of the apartment.

He noticed the cupboards on either side of the fireplace, and on trying the handle of one, found it locked.

"He keeps his insurance papers in there," said his companion in a low voice.

"What? More insurance papers! I thought he kept them in the locked room upstairs!" exclaimed Durrant.

"So he does, but there are some others here," she said. "This cupboard is open. He keeps Nibby here."

"Nibby—who's that?"

"Here he is!" replied the girl, opening the door and taking out the cage containing the tame rat.

"Is that his pet?" asked the young man, bending to examine the little animal, whose beady eyes regarded him with considerable apprehension.

"Yes. Nibby always feeds off his master's plate after he has finished. A sweet little thing, isn't he?"

Durrant agreed, but the possession of such a pet showed him that Boyne was a man of some eccentricity.

"Would you like to see the door of the locked room?" Marigold asked. "If so, I'll go downstairs and keep my aunt there while you run up to the top floor."

"Excellent! I've brought my electric torch with me."

So while Marigold descended to the kitchen to talk to her aunt and help to prepare the cup of tea, young Durrant switched on his light and rushed up the stairs, half fearing lest the front door should suddenly open and Boyne appear.

Arrived at the top of the stairs, he was confronted by the door which led into the attic, a stout one of oak, he noted. The doors of all the other rooms were of deal, painted and grained. This, however, was heavy, and of oiled oak.

After careful examination, he came to the conclusion that the particular door was much more modern than the others, and the circular brass keyhole of the Yale latch gave it the appearance of the front door of a house, rather than that of a room.

Some strange secret, no doubt, lay behind that locked door.

If it had an occupant he would, in all probability, have a light, therefore he switched off his torch and tried to discover any ray of light shining through a crack.

Carefully he went around the whole door, until he drew away the mat before it, when, sure enough, *a light showed from within!*

With bated breath he listened. He could, however, distinguish no sound, even though he placed his ear to the floor. Then, raising himself, much gratified at his discovery, but nevertheless increasingly puzzled, he recollected that the occupant, whoever he might be, would no doubt have heard his footsteps and was now remaining quiet, little dreaming that his light had betrayed his presence.

Suddenly, as he stood there straining his ears, he heard the sound of low ticking—the ticking of a clock. Again he bent his ear to the bottom of the door, and then at once established the fact that the clock was inside that locked room.

He heard Marigold coming up from below, and at once slipped down again, meeting her in the hall. When within the sitting-room, he said to her in a low, tense voice:

"There's somebody in that room! There's a light there!"

"Your first surmise is correct then, Gerald!" she exclaimed. "Who can it possibly be?"

"Ah! that we have to discover!" he said. "Let's be patient. I wonder, however, who can be living up there in secret. At any rate, he has both light and the time of day. In this weather he only wants food and water."

"But it's extraordinary that somebody should live here without my aunt's knowledge."

"It is. But there are dozens of people hidden away in London—people believed by their friends to be dead, or abroad," he said. "In a great city like ours it is quite easy to hide, providing that one is concealed by a trusty friend. I wonder," he added, "how many people whose obituary notices have appeared in the papers are living in secret in upstairs rooms or down in cellars, dragging out their lives in self-imprisonment, yet buoyed by the hope that one day they may, when changed in appearance by years, reappear among their fellow-men and laugh up their sleeves because nobody recognises them."

"Really, do you honestly think that Mr. Boyne is concealing somebody here?" asked the girl anxiously.

"Everything points to it—a light in the room, and a clock."

"But why should he pay visits to him in disguise?"

"Ah! That's quite another matter. We have yet to discover the motive. And we can only do so by watching vigilantly."

Then he described to her how he had pulled away the mat from before the door, and how the light had been revealed.

"Well," exclaimed the girl. "I'm greatly puzzled over the whole affair. May I not be frank with auntie, and tell her what we suspect?"

"By no means," he answered. "It would be most injudicious. It would only alarm her, and upset any plans we may make."

"I wonder who can really be up there?"

"Some very close friend of this Mr. Boyne, without a doubt. He must have some strange motive for concealing him."

"But if he's a friend, why does he disguise himself when he visits him?" queried the girl.

"Yes, that's just the point. There's something very curious about the whole affair," declared the young man. "When your aunt is in bed, he goes up, evidently to take his friend food and drink. And yet he puts on a gown which makes him look—as you have described it—like a Spanish Inquisitor."

"Only all in white. Why white?"

"Can it be that the person upstairs is not self-imprisoned?" suggested the young man, as a sudden thought occurred to him. "Can it be that whoever is confined there is without proper mental balance? Solitary confinement produces madness, remember. In Italy, where solitary confinement for life takes the place of capital punishment for murder, the criminal always ends his days as a lunatic—driven mad by that terrible loneliness which even a dog could not suffer."

"That's certainly quite another point of view," she remarked. "I hadn't thought of that!"

"Well, it is one to bear in mind," he said. "Your aunt, a most worthy lady, is devoted to Mr. Boyne and serves him well. For the present let her hold him in high esteem. In the meantime we will watch, and endeavour to solve this mystery, Marigold."

Hardly had the words left his mouth, when the old lady entered the room with two cups of tea upon a brass tray.

"There!" she said, addressing Marigold. "I know you like a cup o' tea at this hour of the evening, and I hope, Mr. Durrant, it will be to your liking. Mr. Boyne often has a cup out of my teapot if he gets home before I go to bed."

"It's awfully good of you, auntie," the girl declared. "I know Mr. Durrant highly appreciates it."

"That's all right," laughed the old lady. "I'll soon be going to bed. It's near ten o'clock now."

Gerald glanced at his wrist-watch and saw that it was just ten.

Then, when Mrs. Felmore had gone, he said to the girl:

"Hadn't we better be going? Boyne will be back soon."

"Right," she said, drinking her tea daintily. "I'll go down and unfasten the basement door. Auntie has no doubt bolted it. Then, when she's gone to bed, we can get in again."

And a few moments later she left him. Five minutes later she reappeared, followed by Mrs. Felmore.

"Auntie is going to bed," she said. "We must be off, Gerald."

The young man rose, smiled pleasantly, and shook the deaf woman's hand in farewell. Then, a few moments later, the young pair descended the front steps and left the house.

About ten minutes later, however, they returned to it, slipping unobserved down the area steps. Marigold turned the handle of the door, and in the darkness they both entered the kitchen, where they waited eagerly, without lighting the gas, and conversing only in whispers. Mrs. Felmore had gone upstairs, and stone-deaf that she was, would hear no noise below.

She had left the gas turned low in the hall in readiness for her master's return, retiring fully satisfied with the appearance and manners of the young man to whom her niece had that night introduced her.

The pair, waiting below in the darkness, remained eagerly on the alert.

It was a quarter past ten, and Bernard Boyne might return at any time. But each minute which passed seemed an hour, so anxious and puzzled were they, and at every noise they held their breath and waited.

At last footsteps sounded outside—somebody ascending the stone steps above—and next second there was a click as a key was put into the latch of the front door.

"Here he is—at last!" the girl whispered. "Now we'll watch!"

They watched together—and by doing so learned some very strange facts.

CHAPTER VII
WHAT HAPPENED IN BRIDGE PLACE

Together Marigold and her lover crept up the kitchen stairs in the darkness, and heard Mr. Boyne moving about in the front parlour.

They heard him yawn as he threw off his coat, for the night was sultry, and there were sounds which showed that he was eating his evening meal. They heard the loud fizzing as he unscrewed a bottle of beer, and the noise of a knife and fork upon the plate, for he had left the door open.

After about ten minutes, for he seemed to eat his supper hurriedly, he flung off his boots, and in his socks crept upstairs to Mrs. Felmore's door, apparently to satisfy himself that she had retired.

"Hadn't we better get down," suggested Durrant, in a low whisper. "He may take it into his head to come down and search here."

"No, he never comes into the kitchen. So long as auntie has gone to bed he does not mind. Let's wait and watch."

This they did. After a few moments Mr. Boyne came down again and walked along the narrow passage back to his room, satisfied that all was quiet.

He had removed his boots, apparently for some other purpose than to be able to move about in silence, for however heavily he trod his old housekeeper would not hear him. Perhaps, however, he feared that her sense of feeling had been so highly developed that she might have detected the vibration caused by his footsteps.

He remained for nearly a quarter of an hour in his room, while the pair stood breathless in the darkness.

"This is just what happened when I last watched," the girl whispered into the ear of the young man who held her arm affectionately in the darkness.

"I wonder when he'll come out," remarked young Durrant, highly excited over the curious adventure. That something remarkable was afoot was proved by the man's action in ascending the stairs to ascertain that his housekeeper had retired and would not disturb his movements.

At last they heard a soft movement, and next moment, peering over the banisters, they saw a tall, ghostly form clad from top to toe in a long, loose white gown advancing to the stairs.

In one hand he carried a glass jug filled with water, and in the other a plate piled with bread and other food.

"See!" whispered Durrant. "There is somebody upstairs in that locked room. He's carrying food and water to his prisoner!"

"Hush!" the girl said softly, and in excitement. "He may hear you! He's very quick!"

But the strange occupant of the house had already ascended out of view, and a few moments later they heard a click as he put his key into the Yale lock of the closed room.

They distinctly heard him open the door, and as distinctly heard him close it again.

"You wait here, Marigold," the young fellow whispered. "I'll creep up and see what I can. Perhaps I shall hear them talking."

"Yes, do," she said. "But take the greatest care. Mind the stairs don't creak. He'll be alarmed in a moment."

"Leave that to me," he replied, and next moment he left her side, and slowly ascending the few remaining steps, gained the hall, and then the foot of the stairs which led to the first floor.

Though he had not removed his shoes he made no noise, for he trod slowly and cautiously, never lifting one foot until the other was down silently. Thus very slowly he followed the mysterious man in white.

Hardly had he ascended four steps when an electric bell sounded, apparently in the locked room. He halted, and in an instant decided to retreat. Scarcely before Marigold had realised that the alarm had sounded, he sprang down, rejoined her, and whispering:

"Quick! Let's get down!" he descended into the dark kitchen. There, clutching her by the arm, he felt his way to the door.

Without pausing to listen to the effect of the alarm upon the man upstairs, the pair passed out into the area, closed the door after them, hurried up the steps, and out into the street.

"Let's get away before he sees us!" Gerald urged, and they both ran light-footed along to the corner into King Street, where they escaped.

"There's a trap in that house!" Durrant declared, as after hurrying breathlessly they walked along in the direction of the Broadway Station.

"Upon one of those stairs is an electrical contact which gives to the locked room the alarm of an intruder. He switched it on from his room below!"

"Yes!" said the girl. "I feel sure there is."

"And that shows that there's something very wrong somewhere. Mr. Boyne has, in secret, a guest who is in hiding upstairs. He takes him food and water every night—as we have seen with our own eyes. And, further, he had taken the precaution of installing an electrical alarm in case anyone followed him upstairs while he was there with his friend."

"True," said the girl. "But why does he disguise himself whenever he goes up there?"

"That we cannot yet tell. At present it is a complete mystery."

"And a most uncanny one!"

"It is, I can't see the motive of that disguise."

"Is it not weird? He was covered from head to foot in that white cloak, and only those two slits for his eyes."

"Yes. And he moved as silently as a shadow."

So the pair conversed until they reached the Broadway Station, and left by the Underground a few moments later.

What they had witnessed that night had increased the mystery a hundredfold.

In the meantime Bernard Boyne had been startled by the ringing of the bell, yet in the full knowledge that Mrs. Felmore could hear nothing. That secret alarm had, as a matter of fact, been installed with his own hands about two months before, with its switch concealed in the upstairs room.

On hearing it, he instantly flung off his white cloak and dashed headlong down the stairs.

In the hall, however, he halted and burst out laughing.

"Fool you are, Bernard!" he exclaimed aloud to himself. "Yes, you are getting more nervous every day!"

The reason of this was because close to the front door sat Mrs. Felmore's black cat, waiting to be let out for the night.

"Ah, pussy!" he exclaimed. "So it is you who ran silently down the stairs and set off the gong, eh?"

And, opening the door, he let out the cat, saying:

"Out you go, Jimmy, and don't do it again."

Then he reascended the stairs to the locked room, perfectly satisfied with the solution of what a few moments before had caused him very considerable alarm.

No intruder would be tolerated in that dingy house—the house of great mystery.

He carried in his hand a small bottle of meat extract which he had taken from the sideboard in the parlour, and was fully satisfied that it was the cat who had set off the alarm.

As Gerald and Marigold sat side by side in the train, they could not converse because of the noise, but at Earl's Court, where they changed, the girl for Wimbledon Park and her lover bound in the opposite direction, Marigold halted on the platform, and said:

"I feel worried about auntie, Gerald. There's something wrong in that house. Don't you think so?"

"Frankly, I do," was the young man's reply. "That he sets an alarm when he visits the mysterious person concealed in that locked room is in itself a most remarkable feature of the affair, which is one we must certainly probe to the bottom."

"But Mr. Boyne is such a nice man. Everyone speaks so well of him. In all Hammersmith I don't think he has a single enemy, save those who are jealous of his local popularity. And there are always such."

"As I've said before, Marigold, the men who are deep schemers always take care to establish a high reputation locally. This Mr. Boyne has, no doubt, done so with some ulterior motive."

"And that motive we mean to find out," said the girl decisively.

"We will," he said, in a hard voice. "I feel confident that we are on the track of some very sensational affair."

"Who can be the person who is hiding?"

"Ah! that remains to be seen. It is evidently someone who dare not show his face—not only in the light of day, but even at night."

"But why does Mr. Boyne wear that hideous robe with slits for the eyes?" asked Marigold, bewildered, as they walked to the stairs.

"At present, I can't imagine. But we shall know the truth very soon, never fear," the young man replied. And then, lifting his hat politely, he shook her hand, and they parted after a very adventurous evening.

As Gerald Durrant travelled back to his home, he reflected deeply upon the whole affair. Though he had not dared to mention the fact to Marigold, he was more deeply in love with her than ever. She was the most dainty and most beautiful girl he had ever met. She was chic to the finger-tips, and among the many girl clerks he met daily she was outstanding on account of her refinement, her modesty, and the sweet expression always upon her countenance.

Yet the problem which she had put forward to him was certainly an inscrutable one. Boyne, the highly respectable, hard-working insurance agent, lived in that dingy and rather stuffy house surrounded by meagre comfort which, in itself, betokened modest means. For every penny Bernard Boyne gained he worked very hard. Insurance agency is not highly-paid, for everything is nowadays cut to a minimum, while since the war the cost of living has soared.

Nevertheless, as he sat in the train taking him westward, he examined the facts. Boyne employed as housekeeper a woman who was stone-deaf. Why? Was it because the person confined behind that stout door upstairs sometimes shouted and made noises which would have attracted the attention of any person who possessed the sense of hearing?

That this was so he was convinced. Had it not been proved by Boyne carrying food to the mysterious person who was his captive, or who remained in voluntary concealment?

If the latter, why did he disguise himself each time he paid him a visit?

No. Somebody was held there captive against his will, and the reason of the wearing of that cloak was in order that the captor should remain unknown and unidentified. Truly, there was an element of sensationalism in the whole affair!

He was, however, determined to get to the bottom of it. Marigold had, in her perplexity, consulted him, and he had given his aid. Now, having witnessed what he had, he meant to carry the affair through, and solve the mystery of Bernard Boyne and his locked room in Hammersmith.

It occurred to him that perhaps by watching Boyne's movements he might learn something of interest. The unfortunate part of it was that in his position he was engaged all day, and could never have any time to devote to the affair till six or seven o'clock. Nevertheless, he had made a firm resolve to discover the reason of that locked room, and the identity of the person concealed within.

Supposing the person to be some relative who was insane, or whose personal appearance was too horrible to be seen in public—and there are all sorts of human monstrosities living in concealment in London—then there could be no reason why Boyne should hide his face when visiting him. No. Somebody was held there, a prisoner in solitary confinement.

He recollected the heavy door, and the light beneath. Did they not tell their own tale?

"London contains many mysteries of crime," he said to himself as he alighted at the station and strolled home. "And here is one, I feel sure. Boyne is playing some clever game. Perhaps he seeks to inherit property belonging to the person whom he holds in captivity, and whose death may indeed have been registered!"

Such a case—and more than one—was on record. Cases of people presumed by the law to be dead, yet they were still alive, held in confinement by those who benefited by their money.

Durrant, who had read deeply of the mysteries of crime, recollected the case of Mrs. Marvin, of Hounslow; of George Charles Pepper, of Richmond; or Doctor Heaton, of Curzon Street; the celebrated case of the sisters Tredgold, and others, all of whom were concerned in the holding in bondage of those whose fortunes they secured.

His inclination led him to go direct to Scotland Yard, and reveal what he had heard and seen, but Marigold had urged him to refrain from doing so until they had investigated further. She held Mr. Boyne in such high esteem, and her aunt held such a comfortable post, that she was most reluctant to put any suspicions before the police. It was in accordance with the girl's wishes that he did not go straight to the Criminal Investigation Department. Yet he knew too well that the police, who discover so many "mare's nests" daily, are slow to move until a tragedy occurs. And then it is often too late, for the perpetrators of the crime have vanished, either abroad, or into one or other of the criminal bolt-holes which are ever open to those who know.

The public never realise that in the great underworld of London there are people who make a living—and a very good one, too—by successfully concealing for weeks, months, nay, years, those for whom the emissaries of Scotland Yard are in search. The clever criminal knows of these burrows where he can live quite cosily, and surrounded by comforts, defying all police inquiries until the hue and cry has died down, and then as a stoker-fireman, or in some menial capacity, he gets abroad a free man—free to enjoy the proceeds of his crimes.

At first Gerald Durrant had suspected Bernard Boyne to be one of those obliging persons who offer safe asylum to criminals, but the wearing of that ghostly cloak by the owner of the house dispelled any such theory.

No. As he entered the house, after that exciting evening, he was firmly convinced that Boyne held somebody—man or woman—in captivity.

And he intended, at all hazards, to learn the truth.

CHAPTER VIII
ON LOCH LOMOND

A bright brilliant day on glorious Loch Lomond, which, with its wooded islands, is one of the most picturesque of all the Scottish lakes.

The grey little steamer, which that morning had left Balloch Pier at the southern end of the loch, was slowly threading its way through the green islets in the afternoon sunshine. Crowded as it always is in fine weather with visitors from the south, all full of admiration as at every turn there came into view fresh aspects of the woods and mountains around Ben Lomond, standing high and majestic, Ben Vane, Ben Vorlick, the twin peaks of Ben Cruachan, and the tent-shaped Ben More.

The silent grandeur of the loch, where in the deep waters, smooth as glass, the heron fishes undisturbed, is always impressive. Even on that unusually clear autumn day—for mists and rains are more often than not drifting up and down that twenty-five miles or so of picturesque water, which is sometimes as wide as five miles—those who had come up from Edinburgh or Glasgow to make the trip, stood open-mouthed at the ever-changing scene as the steamer wended its way up the loch after leaving the remote little village of Luss.

Among those on board, seated in a deck-chair and enjoying the beautiful afternoon, was a well-dressed woman of middle-age, with auburn hair, and rather sad-faced, but very well preserved. Once or twice her maid, a short, stout little Scotchwoman, whose speech was that of a Glaswegian, came to wait upon her, afterwards retiring to another part of the boat.

The lady's eyes were fixed upon the gorgeous panorama. Beside her chair was a well-worn dressing-bag in dark-green cover, which showed that she was not a mere day traveller, but had come to Loch Lomond to stay at one of the unpretentious lakeside hotels, of which there are several at Tarbet and at Inversnaid. Though she was greatly enjoying the scenery, it was not in the least fresh to her. Indeed, Mrs. Morrison, of Carsphairn, was an annual visitor to Loch Lomond, staying a fortnight each year at the little hotel at Ardlui, a spot which her late husband had loved so well.

Though an extremely wealthy man, the summer attractions of Harrogate, Dinard, Aix, or Ostend, had never appealed to him. Bluff and hearty, he loved Loch Lomond in the days of his prosperity just as when, in his youth, he used to save his coppers to enable him to have a one-day trip from Glasgow each summer—red-letter days in his otherwise grey workaday life.

It had, indeed, been in his mind to build a fine summer residence on the shore of the loch at Ardlui, and he had actually bought the site—one that gave a magnificent view of Ben Lomond and a wide-reaching expanse of the lake—when a sudden illness cut him off, and his wife was left to mourn his loss.

Augusta Morrison was thinking of the last occasion when she and her devoted husband had come for the annual fortnight at Ardlui, and of how daily they walked to the site on the mountain-side where their new home was to be.

That was four years ago. Yet each year she never failed to pay her pilgrimage to the spot which they both so loved.

A young couple, evidently Londoners, seated beside her, had been reading aloud from a guide book the legend of the rocky Craig Royston, where there is a cave known locally as "Rob Roy's Prison," and then, full of admiration, had turned to the splendid view afforded of the mountains around Arrochar.

Just then the steamer slackened, and after some shouting from the captain, was moored to the pier at Inversnaid, the little loch-side village with its wooded mountains beyond. There most of the passengers left the boat to cross by coach or motor that ridge which lies between Loch Lomond and Loch Katrine, Inversnaid being one of the points of departure from Loch Lomond to the Trossachs. Therefore, when the boat went on to the head of the loch at Ardlui, there remained but few passengers.

At last the steamer drew up at the quaint little landing-stage, the postal official brought out the last bag of mail for delivery, and, Mrs. Morrison's maid collecting up all their belongings, they both waited until the paddles had ceased to revolve.

Scarcely had the widow risen from her chair, when a big, burly Scot presented himself, and, touching his cap, respectfully bade the lady welcome.

"Ah! so you're here still, McIntyre!" remarked the widow pleasantly.

"Yes, Mistress Morrison, David McIntyre never leaves Ardlui," laughed the man, who acted as porter, boots, and general factotum to the Tillychewan Arms Hotel.

Mistress and maid walked ashore, and were very soon at the little hotel facing the loch, a very cosy, unpretentious place, where one could get excellent food, and go mountaineering and fishing to one's heart's content.

On the threshold Mrs. Morrison was greeted enthusiastically by the proprietor's wife, a stout, homely woman, and very soon the widow from Kirkcudbrightshire and her maid were installed in the rooms she annually occupied, both of which gave magnificent views of water and mountains.

At Ardlui the daily steamer waits for an hour and a half, and then returns to Balloch, where the express for Glasgow is waiting. Therefore, when the siren sounded and the boat left on its return journey, the little place relapsed into its lethargy of rural solitude and remoteness from the stress of the southern world.

The hotel, half covered with creeper, stood in its well-kept garden, which ran down to the lake. It was not quite full of visitors. The guests, however, were all of the better class, mostly Glasgow merchants and their wives, with a couple of families from London, and the usual youthful, well-dressed idler which one finds in every hotel the world over.

At dinner, as Mrs. Morrison sat alone in a corner by the window overlooking the loch, now crimson in the sunset, she glanced around, but none of her fellow-visitors appeared to be very interesting. The only person who attracted her was one woman who, seated alone, was apparently taking no interest in anyone, for she had propped up before her the *Glasgow Herald*, which had just arrived by the steamer, and was absorbed in it.

Augusta Morrison raised her eyes again, and saw that the woman was exceedingly well, though very quietly, dressed, while there was about her a distinct air of refinement. She also noticed that she possessed very remarkable hair.

Suddenly the eyes of the two women met, and the widow, a little confused for she had been staring hard, turned to look out of the window.

An hour later, when the well-dressed woman had gone out for an after-dinner stroll in the direction of the landing-stage, Mrs. Morrison inquired her name of the proprietor's wife.

"Oh!" replied the other. "She's a very nice lady from London. She has never been up here before. She's a Mrs. Pollen."

Then, referring to the visitors' book, she added: "She lives in Upper Brook Street, London. She came here about four days ago."

"Is she making a long stay?"

"She took her rooms for a fortnight," was the woman's reply. "She seems quite nice," she added.

Mrs. Morrison, of Carsphairn, agreed, and then, getting a wrap, went out into the garden where several of the other visitors were sitting on the verandah, as the dull red afterglow deepened into twilight.

With one of the women she got into conversation, and, taking the empty chair next to her, remained there chatting for nearly an hour. Then, just as darkness was falling, Mrs. Pollen, in a short skirt and carrying a little ash walking-stick, re-entered the garden and sank into a seat in the corner to rest.

Next morning after breakfast—the usual Scotch breakfast with cold grouse and scones—Mrs. Morrison again strolled out into the sunlit garden after Mrs. Pollen, and broke the ice.

At first Mrs. Pollen preserved a somewhat dignified attitude. She spoke in her best Mayfair manner, and it was apparent that she considered herself socially superior to the widow, who, by her speech, was so palpably Scotch.

"No," said Ena, "I have never been in Scotland before. I find it most delightful up here, but rather dull when one is alone, as I am."

"I, too, am alone, except for my maid," replied the widow. "But I love this place. It is so quiet and out of the world. Besides, the scenery is as grand as any in Scotland. I'm Scottish, and I've travelled the whole country through with my husband. He was always enchanted with Ardlui. Indeed," she added, "we bought a site for a home out here at the back—where one has a lovely view—but unfortunately he died before he gave the order to build the place."

"How very unfortunate," said Ena Pollen, with quick sympathy, and in pretence that she knew nothing whatever of her fellow-guest's identity, or of her past, whereas she knew every fact of importance concerning her. "I live in London, and though I travel a good deal, mostly on the Continent or in Egypt, I must say that I think Loch Lomond really beautiful. I took a long ramble by the lochside yesterday afternoon, and found it most enjoyable."

"Ah!" said Mrs. Morrison. "You must take the trip over to Stronachlachar and up Katrine. It is quite pretty, but not so grand as this. Besides, there are always too many trippers in the Trossachs. But while you are here you must really go across and see Ellen's Isle."

And so the pair, seated in the garden with the sunlit waters at their feet, gossiped on, and quickly became good friends.

That same evening, indeed, Mrs. Morrison invited the lady from London up to her sitting-room to take coffee after dinner, and there they sat gossiping and smoking cigarettes until it was time to retire.

When Ena Pollen gained her room she locked the door, and, flinging herself into a small easy chair, exclaimed beneath her breath:

"Thank Heaven! That's over! The first few hours when one cultivates a friendship are always full of pitfalls. A word in the wrong place, and the person one seeks to know may instantly conceive a strong dislike. In this case, however, the woman has approached me. It was a good job I got up here first."

Ena Pollen was much fatigued by the recent rapid journeys to and fro to Scotland, over to Paris and back, and then north again to Loch Lomond. She was, however, a cosmopolitan, and had travelled very extensively ever since she had been left a widow ten years earlier. Her husband had been a solicitor, whose practice was in Bedford Row, but after his death she had embarked upon an adventurous career which had culminated in her association with Bernard Boyne and his wife.

That association had brought her considerable wealth—sufficient, indeed, to allow her, through payments from Boyne and his wife, to live in an expensive flat and indulge in jewellery, furs, smart frocks, and all that appealed to her natural vanity.

That evening, however, she felt worn out. The strain of ingratiating herself with Mrs. Morrison of Carsphairn, whom she found to be an exceedingly shrewd woman, had been considerable, and this, combined with the fact that she had taken a long walk that afternoon, had utterly fagged her.

From a tiny silver tube with a cap upon it, which she took from her dressing-case, she extracted a single little white tabloid, and swallowed it.

"I wonder—I wonder if we shall really be successful?" she murmured to herself. "There must be no slip this time—no recurrence of that unfortunate contretemps in the Martin affair. Phew! That was a narrow shave. I was in Melun only just in time. A few days later, and all chance of dispelling suspicion would have gone!"

She reflected how on more than one occasion they had sailed very near the wind—far too near to be pleasant—and how they had narrowly escaped a closer inquiry. Lilla, however, was always fearless, even when her husband expressed doubts. It was she, indeed, who was the moving spirit of the whole affair, for she went about in her circle of society with her eyes and ears ever open until she saw an opportunity to put into motion that deadly machinery which, worked with such subtle cunning, never failed to increase their bank balance.

She stood at her window as the full moon rose over the loch, transforming the scene into a veritable fairyland, and here she remained in deep reflection. She was contemplating the course she should pursue when she met Mrs. Morrison on the morrow. Already they had become friends, the widow from Kirkcudbrightshire being, of course, in entire ignorance that the pleasant woman from London had come to Ardlui for the sole purpose of making her acquaintance. Ena Pollen was possessed of a cunning that few women possess unless they are adventuresses. She saw that she must allow this Mrs. Morrison to seek her society. Already she realised that the Scotch widow had been greatly attracted by her conversation; hence she decided that on the morrow she must not be too eager to meet and chat with her.

She was in no mood for sleep, therefore she pulled down the blind, and seating herself at a little table in the room, penned a letter which she addressed to "B. Braybourne, Esquire, 93, Pont Street, London," and in the course of which she wrote:

"Things are going even better than I expected. Mrs. M., who made the first advance, is extremely affable to me. I hope that within a week or ten days I can be back in London. Mrs. M., on leaving here, is going to Brighton to visit a niece, so I may see something of her. Do not write here, as I may be leaving any day. I have had a letter from Emery. It was sent to Upper Brook Street, and fortunately enclosed to me in an envelope. It would have been unfortunate if it had come here addressed to Mrs. M.! Would it not? But do not be alarmed! I have given instructions that no letters are to be forwarded in future."

Next day after breakfast she went out to the post-box and there dropped in the letter, so that it would leave by the afternoon steamer for the south. And after she took a long walk alone along the loch-side, under Ben Voirlich, as far as the little village of Inveruglas, and thence up the Inveruglas water, a pretty stream which comes rushing down through the woods from Loch Sloy. And there in the cool shade she at last sat down upon a moss-grown boulder and took out a book and read.

She was playing a waiting game, and one that succeeded, for as she rose from her table after lunch, Mrs. Morrison came up to her, saying:

"Why, wherever have you been, Mrs. Pollen? I've been seeking everywhere for you."

"Have you?" she asked quite innocently. "I've been for a walk to the Inveruglas water."

"Oh! Isn't it delightful there in the woods?" said the widow. "I've been there often. We used to go and picnic there sometimes—right on up Loch Sloy. It is very grand and lonely up there, and the view in all directions is superb."

"I've only been in the woods at the bottom of the mountain," the Red Widow replied.

"Well, I was going to ask you whether, if you haven't anything better to do, you would drive with me up Glen Falloch to Crianlarich," said Mrs. Morrison.

"I shall be most delighted," replied Ena. "I'm sure it is awfully good of you."

"Well, as we are both alone, it will be a pleasure for me to have your company," Mrs. Morrison assured her.

Therefore at three o'clock they left in a carriage which took them away into the picturesque glen for six miles or so, past the little village of Inverarnan, until they reached that pleasant little spot Crianlarich, sheltering beneath the high Ben More at the head of the narrow Glen Dochart, with Loch Fay beyond.

They wandered about the heather gossiping on all sorts of subjects, the Red Widow telling her a number of purely fictitious stories about herself and her travels, while Mrs. Morrison told her much about the happiness of her own married life.

"I have never cared to enter society because, while my husband lived, it never attracted me," she said, as they sat together upon a rock among the heather whence they had a magnificent view up Glen Dochart. "My husband hated it. He was a self-made man. A baronetcy was offered him, but he refused it. He did not agree with the system whereby donations to party funds makes an honest man a pinchbeck gentleman."

Ena laughed.

"True!" she declared. "I admire Mr. Morrison for his outspokenness."

"Well, that is why I never entered society," Mrs. Morrison said, with a sigh.

"But why don't you see a little more of life?" Ena suggested. "You appear, from what you say, to be buried alive at Carsphairn!"

"I see but very few people, but I take a great interest in the estate, and I have a few shooting parties—mostly friends of my late husband."

"Why not come to London for a month or so? Go to the theatres and restaurants, and have an enjoyable time? I do, and I find that I'm amused and meet many interesting people. You are going to Brighton. Why not remain in London for a bit after your visit there?" the Red Widow suggested. "I know a good many people, and I think you would have a nice time. Besides, you would do shopping also. Paris and London are the only places where one can buy anything decent to wear nowadays."

"You are really very good, Mrs. Pollen, to offer to entertain me in London," she declared. "Of course, I have other engagements, but— —"

"Oh, but those can be broken. If you are going to Brighton, make a stay in London on your return. I live in Upper Brook Street. Do you know it?"

"Oh yes. I once, long ago, had a friend who lived there. I know it quite well."

"I have only a small flat, otherwise I would offer you hospitality."

"Oh—no," said the widow. "I can easily stay at the Carlton, the Ritz, or somewhere."

"Then think it over," said the pleasant woman from London.

"Yes, I will," replied the other. "We have many things in common, I believe, and I am sure that we shall be good friends."

"I'm delighted to hear that your thoughts coincide with my own. I make very few new acquaintances; I have so many old friends."

"And I make none. Not that I'm at all exclusive, I hope. But the majority of women I meet I find too shallow and frivolous, and they don't attract me."

"Then I consider myself highly honoured!" laughed Ena, as the pair rose to walk back to the Crianlarich Hotel to tea.

And while Mrs. Morrison of Carsphairn, ignorant of what was in progress, believed that she really had found a delightful friend—a woman after her own heart—the Red Widow smiled within herself, highly gratified at her success.

CHAPTER IX
A GENTLEMAN NAMED GREIG

The days passed pleasantly enough at Ardlui. Mrs. Morrison and her newly-found friend usually went walking or driving together over the heather-clad mountains, or along the loch-side, so remotely picturesque and silent.

One day she received an offer—through a firm of estate-agents in Edinburgh—from a well-known cotton-spinner in Oldham to rent Carsphairn furnished for a year. It was a most tempting offer, and Mrs. Morrison showed the letter to her friend.

"If I were you, I would accept it," Mrs. Pollen urged. "It would do you good to travel, to see London life a little, and go over to Paris and to Nice in winter. I could not vegetate always on a Scottish estate, much as I love the country."

"I confess I feel half inclined to accept. Lately I have felt very lonely and dull at Carsphairn, and now with winter in front of us I should, I agree, be far more happy with a little amusement."

"Of course," said Ena, as they were walking together near the hotel. "You are going to Edinburgh next week, so I would write to the agents and say that you will call upon them."

"Very well, I will," said Mrs. Morrison. "You are coming to Edinburgh, too, aren't you?"

"Just for a couple of days before I return to London."

"Then we will travel together, and stay at the Caledonian," said Augusta Morrison.

And so it was agreed.

That Ena had successfully ingratiated herself with Mrs. Morrison was proved by a letter she wrote that day to her niece at Brighton, in which she said:

"*I have met an exceedingly nice woman here—a Mrs. Pollen, who lives in Upper Brook Street, London. I will ask her down to Brighton while I am with you. She has persuaded me to spend a little time in London after I leave you, and I think the change will do me good. I am contemplating letting Carsphairn furnished for a year, and spending the winter first on the Riviera, and later in Egypt. I make few friends, as you know, but I am sure you will like Mrs. Pollen. She is very often at the Metropole, at Brighton. Next week we go to Edinburgh together, and after I have done my business there I shall come straight to you."*

Ena, with her innate cunning, had been quick to realise the open friendship which her companion had extended towards her. This somewhat surprised her, for a woman is the enemy of every other woman. Few women ever see beauty or good qualities in another.

Only a few days before Ena went north, she was discussing the point with Lilla Braybourne over tea in the latter's drawing-room.

"Women see in every other female thing a potential rival, my dear Lilla," she had said. "That is what makes my task so hard. Every woman defends herself against every other woman, fully confident that the hand of the female world is raised against her."

"I think I agree," was Lilla's reply. "I've hardly ever known a woman to admire the good looks of another of her sex. Curious, isn't it? But it's quite true what you say. Pussies lap tea and scandal everywhere, and even a female saint too often uses her crown of thorns to scratch."

"Yes," laughed the handsome adventuress. "I heard it said the other day that to the woman of thirty the girl of eighteen is a crime, and that to-day's fashion is to look sixteen if you're sixty, and to collar your daughter's lovers if they are not wide awake enough to prevent you. That's what makes it so hard for me."

"Few women can attract women, Ena. You are one of them. You deserve the O.B.E. for it."

"But it is a most difficult and often dangerous undertaking," she declared; "and, after all, the O.B.E. has been given for less."

By the least lapse of the tongue or a too eager appearance to scrape up an acquaintanceship would, Ena knew, alienate Mrs. Morrison for ever. The widow's reverence for her departed husband was the saving clause. She had professed deep sympathy, and in the delightful fiction she had told about her own life and "dear Peter," her late husband, she had attracted Augusta as one of the few women who were womanly.

Who was it said that modern love starts in Heaven and ends in the Sunday newspaper? Ena's philosophy was always amusing. She scoffed at love, at life, at beauty, at everything. Indeed, on that very day as she walked with Mrs. Morrison she had caused her to laugh heartily by referring to some woman friend of hers who lived at Surbiton as "one of those women who shine with virtue and the cheapest sort of complexion soap."

Ena Pollen had a caustic tongue as far as her own sex was concerned, yet she could assume such a suave, sweet manner towards women as entirely to disarm them.

It was so in Mrs. Morrison's case. As the warm, delightful days went on, they were inseparable, exchanging intimate details of their own careers, and fast becoming firm friends.

The arrival of the steamer from Balloch each afternoon was the chief excitement, and by it visitors to the hotel came and left.

One afternoon the steamer brought a short, round-faced little man, very well-dressed, whose speech showed that he came from Glasgow. He had a suit-case with him, and took the one room which happened to be disengaged, giving the name of John Greig. He was an alert-looking business man, probably a Glasgow merchant out for a few days' relaxation from the eternal bustle of Sauchiehall Street.

He sat alone at dinner, and once or twice glanced in the direction of the two ladies who sat together in the window, for Mrs. Morrison had now joined Mrs. Pollen. Both were better dressed than the other visitors, especially Ena, who wore a semi-evening frock and a jade-coloured velvet band in her red hair.

After dinner the visitor strolled alone in the garden until he found a man to chat with, the pair sitting smoking in the moonlight until it became time to retire.

When John Greig reached his room he flung himself into a chair, and beneath his breath, remarked:

"By Jove! She's a handsome woman, too! But she's not Joan Eastlake. That's my belief. Nevertheless, now I'm here, I may as well make quite certain."

And he took out a final cigarette from his case and smoked it reflectively before he turned in.

Next day he was about early at the loch-side, and though he contrived to arouse no suspicion in the minds of either those connected with the hotel or any of his fellow-visitors, he kept casual observation upon the pair. Now and then he would accidentally be so close in their vicinity as to be able to overhear scraps of their conversation. Yet so cleverly did he do this, and so utterly uninterested did he appear to be, that even Ena, who was ever suspicious of eavesdroppers and persons watching, failed to realise the intense interest which she had evoked in the little round-faced man.

The following day Ena accompanied her friend on a trip across to Loch Katrine, but the stranger idled about the hotel and wrote letters. After lunch, however, at the hour when the small establishment was quietest, the curiosity of anyone watching him would certainly have been aroused. His actions were truly a little peculiar.

At about three o'clock that afternoon, having ascertained that none of the servants were about, he slipped silently to Mrs. Pollen's bedroom, the door of which was unlocked, and, entering quickly, closed the door after him. Then, walking straight to a big dressing-case which lay upon a chair near the window, he took out a bunch of keys and tried one after the other in an effort to open it.

He failed, none of the keys would fit.

"If I force it she'll suspect," he murmured. "No, I must give it up for the present—curse it!"

Then he made a tour of the room, opened the wardrobe, and examined the contents of several drawers, but though some expensive jewellery was there, he cast it aside in contempt.

Mr. Greig did not want jewels. It was evident that he was in search of something else far more interesting. But that lock upon the dressing-case was an unusually good one, and had defied all his many keys.

There was but one course to pursue, and that was to retreat to his own room, which he did in great disappointment and chagrin.

That evening he watched the two women on their return. His movements were those of a practised watcher. He was unobtrusive, disinterested in everything save the picturesque surroundings, and behaved as though he had no interest whatever in any person in the hotel.

That evening, while in the garden after dinner, he found himself sitting on a seat beside Mrs. Morrison, and ventured to address a remark to her regarding the glorious sunset.

What more natural than in a few moments Ena and her friend were chatting affably with the new-comer.

"This is my first visit to Scotland," Ena declared, though it was a falsehood, "and I'm delighted with it. My views—those of a Londoner—have entirely altered concerning Scotland and the Scottish people. I don't agree now with the ridicule cast upon them."

"I'm very glad of that," declared Mr. Greig. "In the south you don't really understand us, I think. And perhaps we here don't quite understand you. National prejudices are very hard to break down."

"They are. But you see the majority of the English never come north. They view the Scottish people by the ridicule cast upon them by performers on our music-halls. It is unfortunate, but it is a fact."

"Never mind," laughed the pleasant-faced man from Glasgow. "Our national pride is never hurt by those amblers on the stage who wax fat upon the profits of their mimicry. We only laugh at it up here, I assure you," he declared to Mrs. Pollen.

The conversation drifted naturally to the fact that Mrs. Morrison told him her name, which was Scottish, and the identity of her late husband, so well known in Glasgow.

"Oh! I knew your husband quite well, Mrs. Morrison," declared John Greig, for no shrewder or more well-informed person was there between the Lowlands and Cromarty. "I knew him twenty years ago. Do you recollect Mr. Buchanan, who had an office in St. Vincent Street, Glasgow, and with whom he went into partnership? Mr. Buchanan died about four years ago. I went to visit him once at that beautiful house of his on Loch Rannoch."

"Then you knew Mr. Buchanan!" cried Mrs. Morrison. "He was a dear fellow. My husband was devoted to him. Together they built up the works."

"I know. Everyone in commercial circles in Glasgow knows how closely they worked together, and, Mrs. Morrison, I may tell you that not a worker on the Clyde has any but good words for your husband and his partner. The conditions of work in your husband's place at Govan were always ideal. We hear much of labour trouble in these post-bellum days, but if all works were like your husband's there would be little to grumble at."

"It is awfully good of you to pay such a tribute to my husband's regard for his employees," said Mrs. Morrison, much gratified. "He and I often discussed their welfare, and I always agreed with him that labour should be duly paid and there should be no sweating. We have Socialist propaganda on the Clyde to-day, but is it at all astonishing in view of the high prices, of Government muddle and waste, and the advancement into society by the King's favour in the shape of 'honours' of bare-faced swindlers and those who escape under the more euphonious name of profiteers?"

"Ah! I'm glad that you have realised the deadly peril of Britain, Mrs. Morrison," Greig said. "As a business man in Glasgow—I am an exporter to the East—I know much of what is transpiring among the Socialists, and I know the deadly peril of Britain to-day."

The fact that Greig had known not only her husband but his partner, Buchanan, appealed to Mrs. Morrison, with the result that he had frequent chats with her, and incidentally with her friend, Ena Pollen, whose belongings he had so carefully scrutinised in her absence.

The man from Glasgow, with his round, merry, well-shaven face, a countenance of prosperity, was a typical man of business, and he appealed to old Morrison's widow as a very nice man.

With her estimate Ena, any suspicion utterly disarmed, entirely agreed.

Pleasant, humorous, and careless in his relaxation from money-making in grim and grimy Glasgow, John Greig was an excellent fellow on holiday. His estimate of women—for he was a bachelor—coincided entirely with that of Ena Pollen.

To be frank, he had, in the course of conversation, gauged her views regarding her own sex, and he at once sought to cultivate her acquaintance upon her line of thought.

"Of course," she said next morning, as he found himself gossiping with her after breakfast, "woman ought not to work at all. No man really likes a woman who works for him. Work isn't woman's natural element, though trouble is. Work is an odious word to women."

"Really, Mrs. Pollen, your philosophy is quite upon that of my own thinking," laughed Greig. "Once a man I know declared to me that to girls business life would be a dull existence if it were not for its sly opening for an illicit romance."

"One woman writer has said, and with much truth, that petticoats, like time, were made for slaves, and that there is more virtue in a single pair of trousers than there is in a multitude of skirts," laughed Ena.

"True. Was it not the same lady author who told us that the wrong part of wrong-doing is being found out?"

"Ah! yes. And the same feminine philosopher went farther," Ena said. "She declared that the woman who thinks it wicked to buy silk petticoats and luxurious 'undies'—'because no one sees them'—is a fool; but the hedonist who frankly revels in the feel and *frou-frou* of silk and *crêpe de chine* and mysterious lace things is as wise as Eve, who wore leaves rather than nothing, and made a tantalising mystery of herself out of the poor resources at her command."

The man from Glasgow laughed immoderately. "Really," he remarked, "you have no great admiration of your own sex, Mrs. Pollen."

"No, I have not," declared the Red Widow frankly, as they both halted and leaned over a gate which gave entrance to a great green meadow beyond which was the edge of the loch, the water of which lay like a mirror in the morning sunlight.

Up there, far removed from the life and bustle of the outer world, with all its political bickerings and its labour troubles, life was very enjoyable, and the two women who had become so friendly had quickly discovered in John Greig a man whose ideas corresponded exactly with their own—a man who had formed distinct views upon life, and who was not afraid to admit them.

At last came the afternoon of their departure for Edinburgh. They bade Mr. Greig farewell on the Pier just before the steamer started for Balloch.

Then, going on board, they waved him a farewell as the paddles began to revolve, sending out long ripples over the glassy surface of the loch.

He raised his hat with a merry laugh, but as he did so, he remarked beneath his breath:

"After all—I'm not sure, *even now!*"

CHAPTER X
MORE MYSTERIOUS CIRCUMSTANCES

"Let's pull up here; it's so delightfully shady."

Marigold Ramsay, who spoke, lay back among the crimson cushions of the punt, with her eyes fixed upon the sky.

She loved the river. That Sunday afternoon was perfect, and she was enjoying the day on the river after a week's hard work in the bank.

Gerald, who was an expert with the punt-pole, was taking her up that pretty reach of the Thames which winds between Shepperton and Walton, with the long rows of poplars fringing the river bank.

They had lunched at the little riverside inn at Halliford, and were now making their way slowly up-stream. Gerald, in flannels, with coat off and sleeves upturned, placing his pole and withdrawing it without any apparent effort.

Since that adventurous night at Bridge Place they had become even closer friends. No day passed but they met. The previous two Sundays Durrant had spent with her, the first at Dorking, where they had wandered over Leith Hill and along the Surrey lanes, and the next Sunday at Brighton. This, the third Sunday, they had decided to spend together on the Thames.

As they were passing beneath a long row of trees which overhung the water, the girl, who was in white, raised herself from her couch of cushions and suggested that they should tie up the punt there.

"Certainly," he replied, and a few moments later he had secured the punt to a tree root, and, sitting down to rest, he lit his pipe.

"Do you know, Gerald, I've been thinking again about Mr. Boyne," she said. "I can't get the man out of my mind."

"Well, to tell the truth, Marigold, neither can I," replied the young man. "Ever since that night at Hammersmith I've been trying in vain to solve the mystery."

"About the person concealed upstairs," remarked the blue-eyed girl reflectively. "Yes, it's most curious."

"It's more than curious," her companion declared. "Though I haven't mentioned it to you, I've watched the house for several nights, but I must admit that I've seen nothing at all suspicious."

"Oh! Then you've been on the watch!" she cried excitedly.

"Yes, on four occasions, and all to no purpose. Last Friday I waited from nine o'clock till one in the morning, and got wet through. He returned about ten, but did not come out again."

"He was upstairs with his secret friend, I suppose," said the girl.

"No doubt. Whoever may be confined there could not exist without seeing a human face and conversing with him, even for five minutes each day, or he would certainly go mad," said Gerald. "You remember I said that Italians, who have abolished capital punishment for murder, have substituted solitary confinement. It is far more terrible. They confine the assassin in a cell in silence, without sight of a human face. Their food is placed upon a turntable which revolves into the cell, so that the prisoner never sees a face. Such torture was invented long ago in the Bastille, and in every case it drives the guilty one raving mad within five years."

"How horrible!" cried the girl.

"I admit it is, but surely the punishment is far greater than that of hanging, or even the guillotine. Both are instantaneous, yet in Italy the criminal suffers all the tortures of Dante's Inferno—and deservedly so."

"Then you saw nothing?" asked Marigold.

"I fancied a lot, but I saw really nothing to increase my suspicions. One thing we know—that he is concealing some person in that locked room. Now who can the person be?"

"It may be some relative who has done something very wrong and is afraid of the police," suggested the girl.

"Agreed. It may be. But we have discussed the matter so many times that I think we should not talk further—but act," he said. "We have proved beyond doubt that Bernard Boyne is a man of mystery. Your deaf aunt, a most worthy woman, acts as his housekeeper. Why does he retain her? Merely because she is stone-deaf. Why does he want a deaf woman to wait upon him? Because there are sometimes noises in the house which would arouse the curiosity of any who chanced to overhear them."

"We must discover the identity of the person concealed," remarked the girl with the big blue eyes, as she lay back lazily among the cushions.

"We must. At all costs I intend to solve this mystery. Marigold," he said, removing his pipe from his lips and looking straight into her eyes, "my own belief is that you have discovered some very strange and startling drama of our complex London life—one which, when investigated, will prove to be astounding."

"Do you really think so?" asked the girl, looking into his handsome face.

"Yes—I do. Up to the present all our efforts have been in vain," he said. "Only one fact has been established, and that is that there is a prisoner—whether voluntary or not we cannot tell—in that creeper-covered house. We both saw Boyne creep up with food to him, while I saw his light beneath the door. Somebody is living up there in secret. Is it a man, or is it a woman? His eagerness makes me think that it is a woman. Who is it?"

"Somebody he is shielding—somebody who has committed some serious crime, who fears to show his or her face lest it be recognised by agents of Scotland Yard."

"Really, Marigold, you are very acute," he exclaimed. "We have so many murder mysteries since the war, and in all of them the police confess their utter confusion, that the present situation fills me with great apprehension."

"I know," she said. "But why not let us begin again? Let us watch the house. I'll watch one night, and you watch the next. Surely we can by that means discover the truth. If the place is watched every night, this man Boyne must, in the end, be defeated."

"But I thought you liked Boyne?"

"Yes; he has been always very good to me. Remember that he is the owner of the place, and my aunt is his housekeeper," replied the girl.

"I quite appreciate your point," said Durrant. "But if we are to fully delve into the affair we must not be influenced by the fellow's open heart. The greatest criminals of the world have always been those who have been popular on account of their bonhomie and generosity."

The girl sat silent, her eyes fixed upon the rushes slowly waving in the stream. A motor-launch passed them, making a high wash against the bank, but she took no heed. She was still thinking of that strange occupant of the house in Bridge Place.

Three times during the past week she had, indeed, visited her aunt in an endeavour to discover something more. Boyne had been out, as usual, therefore she had been able to examine the place thoroughly. She had ascended to that locked room on each occasion, and had listened there. Once in the silence she had heard a distinct movement, a slight rustling, within.

Yet afterwards, as she had reflected, she wondered whether it had not been due to her imagination, or perhaps to a blind flapping at an open window. When one is suspicious, it is so easy to imagine queer circumstances.

"I only wish we could solve the mystery," she remarked wistfully. "It worries me. Auntie seems quite unconcerned."

"Because she has no suspicion, worthy old soul. She has no knowledge of Mr. Boyne's nocturnal visits with food to his friend."

"Why shouldn't we tell her, and then she'll be on the alert?" suggested the girl. "She might discover something."

"She might—but more probably she would be too eager, and thus put Boyne upon his guard," remarked the young fellow. "No. We must work together in strict secrecy if we intend to be successful."

"But who can he possibly be hiding?"

The young man in flannels shrugged his shoulders, and replied:

"I confess that the problem is getting on my nerves. The more I think it over the more inscrutable it becomes. Mischief is being worked somewhere. Of that I feel confident. All the actions of our friend Boyne point to it."

"But that shroud? Why does he wear it?" asked Marigold blankly.

"As a disguise, without a doubt. Perhaps the person upstairs has been confined there so long that his mind has already become deranged, as is inevitable after a long period of solitary incarceration, and Boyne now takes the precaution of adopting the simple disguise so that his friend should fail to identify him. He may have done his captive some great injury—or something."

"True; but, if he has, it was not in order to gain. Bernard Boyne is a comparatively poor man. My aunt says that he seems to have only just sufficient money to make both ends meet."

Gerald Durrant drew a long breath. Upon his countenance was an expression of doubt.

"He may pass as a poor man, and yet be rich," he remarked. "It may sound romantic, but there are many people living in the by-streets of London, successfully concealed beneath assumed names and unsuspected by their neighbours, who for years have lived a life of penury though they are really well off. And their motive is, for some reason or other, to cut themselves adrift from friends in their own sphere. Indeed, it is a well known fact that in the last days of King Edward an ex-Cabinet Minister lived for several years in seclusion in a meagre side-street near Kennington Park, as Mr. Benwell, his real identity never being suspected until, owing to his sudden death, an inquest was held, and the police, searching his papers, discovered that he was immensely wealthy and one of Britain's foremost statesmen, who was believed to be living in seclusion in Italy."

"Perhaps Mr. Boyne is some person who has sought retirement in a similar manner," Marigold suggested.

"No. If I'm not mistaken, Mr. Boyne is playing a very deep and rather dangerous game—how dangerous I cannot yet discover."

"But you could discover nothing when you watched—just as I failed to find out any fact," she said. "I had no idea you were on the watch."

"I saw you on Tuesday night," he laughed. "You arrived at the house about half-past eight, and had a great trouble getting in."

"Were you there?" she cried eagerly. "I never dreamed that you were in the vicinity. Yes, you are right. I rang and banged on the door half a dozen times before I could attract auntie's attention. She generally leaves the door unlocked in case anyone should call."

"Boyne returned about twenty minutes after you had left, but though I watched till midnight, he did not come out again."

"Couldn't you take a day off one day and follow him when he goes out in the morning?" the girl suggested. "I would do it, but I fear that he'd recognise me."

"I might. But I think I may be more successful at night. It is very difficult to keep observation upon a person in broad daylight. In the darkness it is much easier."

"Why not try again to-night?" suggested Marigold. "I'll go with you."

He shook his head.

"Sunday night is a bad night. We know his habits on week-days, but he may have gone out all day to-day," he replied. "No; to-morrow would be more likely."

"Then let's both go there to-morrow night, and if he comes out of the house we'll watch where he goes."

With this suggestion Gerald agreed, and after she had smoked the cigarette he handed to her from his case, they resumed their punting up-stream in the afternoon sunshine.

Next night they met by appointment at Hammersmith Broadway station at half-past eight, and after a consultation, it was arranged that Marigold should call on her aunt on some pretext, and having ascertained if Boyne had returned, she would rejoin Gerald at a spot in King Street.

Hence he lounged about the busy thoroughfare for a quarter of an hour until she returned with the news that Boyne had been home since six o'clock, he having returned unusually early.

"Ah! That's a good sign," said Gerald. "He'll certainly go out again to-night!"

As they strolled together they arranged that Marigold should loiter near the King Street end of the street, while Gerald should stand in an entry near the house which he had used in his previous observations.

"If you see me pass into King Street, don't follow me too closely," he urged, "and at all hazards don't let him see you. Remember that people who are engaged in crooked business keep their eyes skinned and are always full of suspicion."

"I'll take good care he doesn't see me," the girl answered him. "Trust me to be discreet."

Then they parted, and for about an hour Marigold waited in vain for a sight of her lover. It had now grown quite dark, and the street lamps in Bridge Place were none too brilliant. She was still loitering in the darkness, full of expectation at every footstep on the pavement.

At last she again heard footsteps, and a few moments later recognised Boyne's well-built figure passing within the zone of lamplight across the way. He was walking hurriedly in the direction of King Street, all unconscious that he was being followed. But a few moments later, with noiseless tread—for he wore rubber heels to his shoes—Durrant came along, his eyes searching eagerly for the girl he loved.

Suddenly he saw her in the shadow, and realised that she was discreetly following him.

The pair exchanged a few words in the crowded King Street, and while Gerald hurried on after Boyne towards the station, the girl followed a little distance behind.

They saw him buying a ticket at the station and also purchase a late edition of the evening paper. Then he descended to the platform of the tube and took a train going towards Piccadilly.

Gerald and Marigold, who had separated, travelled on the same train until, on arrival at Knightsbridge, the man they were watching alighted. Marigold, who had been on the alert at each station, saw him emerge from the next car, while close behind him was Gerald, with whom, of course, he was unacquainted.

Together they followed him along Sloane Street to Pont Street, where he ascended the steps of a smart-looking red-brick house and opened the door with a latchkey.

"Now that's curious!" remarked Gerald when he rejoined the girl. "Did you notice that he entered that house yonder as though it were his own home? I wonder who lives there?"

"We must find out," declared Marigold, highly excited at having tracked Mr. Boyne so far.

"Yes. But I shall be compelled to watch the house and see what happens now," he said. "I mean to follow him to-night wherever he goes. It almost seems as if he lives here—as well as in Hammersmith!"

"Well—he certainly has a latchkey, and this is not a street where they take in lodgers."

"No," he said. "Some of these houses are the legations of the smaller States of Europe. Over there is the Serbian Legation."

"Well, we'll wait in patience," she said. "Fortunately it's a fine night."

"The last time I watched, last week, it came on terribly wet about eleven o'clock," he said, "and I hadn't my mackintosh. When I started out it seemed a perfect night. But just now the weather is so changeable."

On the darker side of the street by the railings, the young people idled together, with a watchful eye upon the long flight of steps which Boyne had ascended. Though the blinds were drawn, it was evident that the comfortable West End house was well lighted, and it was, no doubt, the residence of someone of considerable means. Indeed, it requires a good income to run a house even in Pont Street in these post-bellum days.

The traffic had died down. Few taxis were passing, for as yet the home-coming pleasure seekers were not on their way from the theatres.

For half an hour the pair waited in the shadow, full of eager curiosity. The movements of the mystery-man of Hammersmith were, to say the least, suspicious.

Suddenly, from the basement a young footman appeared, and hurrying along to the end of the road, hailed a taxi and brought it to the door.

Then, as they watched, they saw, a few seconds later, the front door open, and a man in evening dress descended the steps and entered the taxi.

The light from the open door shone upon his face as he halted to speak to the servant, and then, to their amazement, they recognised the man to be Bernard Boyne.

His chameleon-like change staggered them both for a second, but Gerald, ever quick to act, whispered:

"Go home, Marigold. This is very funny. I'll try to follow," and a moment later he had sped away noiselessly into the darkness.

The fact was that his quick eyes had espied a taxi which at that moment had driven up on a stand a little farther down, and without delay he told the man that he wanted him to follow the taxi in front, and that he would give him treble fare for doing so.

"Right y'are, sir!" replied the young Cockney driver, who instantly entered into the spirit of the chase, and already his cab was on the move as Boyne left.

Gerald saw Marigold standing watching the departure, and knowing that she would make the best of her way to Wimbledon, kept his eyes upon the taxi, which was soon out into Knightsbridge, going in the direction of Hyde Park Corner.

Why Boyne, the humble collector of insurance premiums, should possess a latchkey to a house in Pont Street, and emerge from there dressed in evening clothes as a gentleman of means, sorely puzzled Gerald Durrant.

He felt instinctively that he was on the track of some very remarkable sequence of events. This man who disguised himself every night before he took food and drink up to his imprisoned friend, evidently lived a double life. In Pont Street he was a rich man, while in Hammersmith he was poor.

One point of satisfaction was that he was following the unsuspecting man, and would at least know his destination, even if that night he failed to discover the object of his visit.

That he was in a hurry was apparent. He seemed to have spoken excitedly to the young footman—who appeared to be a foreigner—before stepping into the taxi.

Up Park Lane they went, until suddenly the taxi conveying the man of mystery pulled up before a house in Upper Brook Street, while the vehicle in which Gerald had followed passed on for some distance before it stopped.

"'E's gone in that 'ouse, sir," said the taxi-man in a low voice.

"Yes, so I see. He may not be long. I'll wait," and he stepped out and strolled a little way in the opposite direction. Meanwhile Boyne had paid his man, who had turned his cab and left.

The house into which Boyne had disappeared was a block of flats, for as he passed he had caught a glimpse of the uniformed porter who had saluted him and followed him to the lift.

The mystery was thereby greatly increased, though many more startling circumstances were yet to be encountered.

Gerald Durrant idled there in the vicinity of the taxi, little dreaming into what a labyrinth of doubt and mystery he had now been drawn.

CHAPTER XI
SPREADING THE NET

Gerald Durrant remained outside the house in Upper Brook Street for more than half an hour. Much puzzled, he stood in a doorway opposite the block of flats into which Boyne had gone.

Marigold was on her way back to Wimbledon Park, and that night he intended to probe the mystery farther.

He waited, and still waited. A neighbouring clock struck the hours. The hall-porter at one o'clock closed the door and switched off the lights, yet Gerald still waited for the insurance agent of Hammersmith to emerge.

That he was known to the hall-porter was apparent, for the man had saluted him. It was strange, to say the least, that the man who was compelled to scrape for a living in Hammersmith should be guest in a fashionable flat in Upper Brook Street.

Bernard Boyne was certainly a man of mystery, for not only did he possess the latchkey of the smart house in Pont Street, but he was also known at that block of expensive flats.

The young fellow lit a fresh cigarette and, leaning against the deep portico of the house opposite, possessed himself in patience. Time went on. A police constable passed and repassed, but did not notice him in the shadow, for he hid his cigarette. All the windows of the great building he was watching were in darkness. It was evident now that Boyne would not come out again before morning.

Yet Durrant, with great pertinacity, waited there through the whole night until, at half-past six, the hall-porter threw open the outer door, and milkmen, the postman, and newspaper boys began to arrive in quick succession. Without bite or sup Gerald waited there till half-past ten, when, full of chagrin at being thus foiled, he was compelled to hurry to his office, getting a wash and a shave on the way.

At lunch he met Marigold as usual, and told her of his failure, whereupon she said:

"I have the afternoon off. I'll go at once and see my aunt, and ascertain when he got back."

This she did, and when that evening Durrant arrived home at Ealing he found a wire awaiting him which told him that when Boyne's housekeeper took him up his early tea as usual, her master had been in bed!

Durrant held his breath. The mystery-man had some means of exit from Upper Brook Street—a back way, without a doubt.

But what was the motive of it all? Why should he pose as penurious in Hammersmith, and wear evening clothes in Mayfair?

That night Durrant went again to Upper Brook Street, and, exploring the rear of the building, found that there was a servants' entrance to the flats which led into a mews, and through a back street. By that Bernard Boyne had, no doubt, walked out while Durrant had been keeping his night vigil.

This fact further impressed both Marigold and her lover that Boyne was not what he represented himself to be.

Durrant set out to probe the mystery, and by dint of ingenious application to the affair, he became on friendly terms with the hall-porter. Truth to tell, Durrant had represented himself to be a demobilised officer who had been in love with a lady who had rented one of the flats. He had discovered her name from the house-agent, and knew that she had married during the war.

From the hall-porter he learned that the man who had passed in was an occasional visitor, but to whom he did not know. He would try and ascertain. The lips of all hall-porters of flats are readily unlocked when their hands are "crossed with silver." And why not? In our post-war civilisation little is effected without a *quid pro quo*. Even the British Cabinet Minister looks for reward; alas! that it should be so. Patriotism in all the Allied Countries seems synonymous with personal ruin, and those who have realised the fact are the profiteers upon gallant men's lives.

Gerald's discovery at the back of Upper Brook Street brought the pair to a dead end as far as their investigations went.

They met as usual at lunch and discussed the situation. What could be done?

"All I can see, Marigold, is for you to continue your visits constantly to Bridge Place and learn all you can from your aunt," Durrant said. "There is evidently something extraordinary in progress. But what it is we cannot possibly tell without more thorough investigation."

"But what can we do further?" asked the girl.

The Red Widow | 85

"I can do nothing just yet, except to receive reports from you," replied Gerald. "You can visit Boyne's house and let me know from time to time what is in progress there."

"But the prisoner upstairs?" she asked. "How can I know more?"

"By watching," was his reply. "Do you know, Marigold, I've been thinking—thinking deeply over the affair. We are both agreed that we intend to fathom the secret of this man. Well, now could you not one evening, when you visit your aunt, be taken suddenly very unwell, and then remain there in the house and watch?"

"Really, Gerald, that's a splendid idea!" exclaimed the girl. "Yet it seems an imposition upon Mr. Boyne."

"I know that. He poses as a man without anything whatever save the commission he collects upon the premiums on the lives of the honest inhabitants of Hammersmith. Yet, as we know, he is in touch with certain people of a much higher class than himself. The house in Pont Street is a great enigma to me. We must elucidate the mystery. That is my object."

"I am ready to work at your orders, Gerald," was the girl's reply, with the genuine love-look in her eyes. "Yes, we will do our utmost to solve this mystery!"

In consequence of this conversation, a few days later Marigold went one afternoon to visit her aunt, old Mrs. Felmore, and in the evening was taken very unwell.

Mr. Boyne, who returned as usual about six o'clock, was told of the girl's illness and went down to the kitchen, where he saw her, and, speaking kindly, asked if he should fetch the doctor.

"No, thank you, Mr. Boyne," the girl answered, rather weakly. "It's awfully good of you, but no doubt I shall be better presently, and able to go home. I have a curious dizziness. It came on quite suddenly."

"Are you subject to it?" he inquired. And then in the next breath asked if he could get her anything.

"My aunt has given me a cup of tea," was her reply. "And I already feel better."

"Don't think of going to Wimbledon to-night unless you feel better," he urged. "Mrs. Felmore can make you up a bed in the spare room."

She thanked him, and though she assured him she would be well enough to go home in an hour or so, she had no intention of returning home that night.

Boyne, on his part, looked weary and worn. His clothes were shabby, and his cheap boots were down at heel and dusty after a long day's tramp in the meaner streets of Hammersmith.

Returning to his sitting-room, he took his bulky insurance books from his pocket. Then he threw off his jacket, sat down to tea in his shirt sleeves, and fed "Nibby," his pet rat.

Mrs. Felmore, like many deaf folk, could tell what was said by watching people's lips. When her employer had left the kitchen, she remarked to her niece:

"Isn't Mr. Boyne a dear nice man? Whenever I feel unwell he is always so ready to get me anything. You know how bad I was with my rheumatism last winter? He wouldn't let me work, but engaged old Mrs. Kirk from the Mall."

"Yes, auntie, he is," Marigold declared. "But I didn't tell him how bad I feel. I really don't know what has come over me."

"Why not let him call the doctor?"

"Oh, no. I'll be all right soon," she said cheerfully; and then she reseated herself in the summer twilight near the open window.

At half-past eight o'clock Bernard Boyne, having washed and changed his clothes, went out.

Marigold fell to wondering where he might be going. It had been arranged that Gerald should be on watch outside the house that night, but when they had met at lunch, he had told her that he was compelled to accompany his principal to Birmingham that afternoon, for a conference was to be held in that city on the following day.

"I may be away for a day or two, dear," he had said. "But in the meanwhile discover all you can."

Boyne went direct from Hammersmith to Pont Street, where he found that his wife had gone out to dinner. She would be back soon after ten, the young man-servant informed him.

Therefore he went to his room and put on evening clothes—a very smartly-cut suit with white waist-coat and mother-of-pearl and diamond buttons. As he stood before the long cheval glass, examining himself after he had tied his cravat and put on his coat, the transformation, he thought, was surely complete. Nobody meeting him in that luxuriously furnished house would ever have recognised in him the trudging, hard-working insurance agent of Hammersmith.

He descended to the drawing-room, but his wife did not return till past ten. She was in a strikingly handsome gown of black-and-gold tissue, with a shimmering ornament in her hair, while around her neck was a rope of splendid pearls.

"Well, Lilla!" he exclaimed pleasantly, as he threw himself lazily into a soft arm-chair. "I'm glad you're back early. Where are we to meet Ena?"

"At Murray's, at eleven. Then we go on to the Carlton to supper," was her reply. "Remember our name to-night is Davidson, and we live at Welsford Hall, in Northamptonshire. Ena wants to introduce us to Mrs. Morrison."

"But Mrs. Morrison is likely to meet one of us again, and it might be awkward," the man remarked, as he slowly lit a cigarette.

"She is not likely to meet us again—except at Ena's house—is she?" said his wife, with a curious expression in her narrow eyes.

"No, I suppose not—if all goes right, and there is no hitch," he said reflectively.

"Hitch! How can there be a hitch?" asked Lilla. "Ena will do her part, while you do yours."

"When does Ena propose that the little affair shall be done?" he asked.

"Next Saturday—if that suits you?"

"Saturday," he repeated again reflectively, as he examined his cigarette. "It will take about nine to ten days, so on the following Monday or Tuesday week it should be complete."

"It ought to be, Bernard. We shall soon be wanting more money, you know. We've been spending freely and investing a lot of late. Ena was here this afternoon. Mrs. Morrison came up from Brighton this morning in order to go to the theatre with her, and meet us at supper afterwards. You can tell her how you hunt with the Fitzwilliam and Lord Exeter's hounds. She knows nothing of fox-hunting, and it will impress her."

"Yes. Ena has told me the woman is just the widow of a Glasgow man who has plenty of money, but who knows practically nothing of English society."

"Why Ena is so keen that we should meet the woman, I can't think," Lilla remarked.

"Well, to tell you the truth, I suggested it," was his reply. "When she invites her to dine we shall be there. It looks better for Ena to have other guests, especially if—well, if anything happened."

"I hope nothing untoward will happen," she exclaimed quickly.

"No," he laughed. "Don't worry, my dear. It is all plain sailing. We shall cash a big cheque before long—depend upon it! But time is getting on. We ought to get along to Murray's and meet them on arrival."

Therefore the pair put on their coats, and a taxi being called, they drove to Murray's, where they awaited the arrival of Mrs. Pollen and her guest.

Ten minutes later they came. The red-haired widow was dressed superbly, and wore wonderful beads of Chinese jade. Her companion, handsome and also well-dressed, expressed delight when her hostess introduced her to her old friends, Mr. and Mrs. Davidson. The latter both became extremely affable, appearing very pleased when Ena told them, what they already knew—namely, that she had reserved a table at the Carlton for supper.

Then the four drove in a taxi to Pall Mall, where they had a very pleasant meal.

Mrs. Morrison, of Carsphairn, was a hard-headed and sensible woman. She cared but little for the so-called excitements of society, but that evening she had greatly enjoyed the play, and now as she gazed around at the smart crowd coming in and taking the tables allotted to them, the daring and often magnificent dresses, and the host of good-looking men, it was something of a novelty to her.

"Before my husband's death I travelled a good deal on the Continent," she explained to Mrs. Davidson. "But nowadays I remain mostly in Scotland. I entertain a few people at Carsphairn for the shooting, but beyond that I live very quietly."

"So do we," Lilla replied. "We are just country cousins. Our place is in the wilds of Northamptonshire, and my husband hunts a good deal."

"Ah! Northamptonshire and Leicestershire are the centre of fox-hunting, are they not?" said the Scotch woman, addressing Mr. Davidson.

"Yes. We have several packs within easy reach, though Welsford, where we live, is, strictly speaking, in the Fitzwilliam country. I love hunting," he added.

"My husband even goes cubbing at four o'clock in the morning sometimes," laughed Mrs. Davidson.

"Ah! He is evidently an enthusiast!" Mrs. Morrison agreed. "My husband was a fisherman, and I confess I had to go with him on some very dull expeditions in the north of Scotland and in Ireland."

"That's the worst of men," Lilla declared. "If they take up hunting, fishing, or golf, it becomes an obsession. They talk of nothing else."

And so the chatter about hunting and hunting men continued, apparently to the intense amusement of Ena Pollen—or "Mrs. Morrison" as she was known to the Manchester solicitor and the doctors who had pronounced her life to be a "first-class" one.

The orchestra was playing one of the latest waltzes, and the big restaurant was filled with chatter and laughter. Surely none who sat there that night and noticed the three ladies and their male companion as they drank their champagne, and ate that supper dish of the London restaurants, *mousse de jambon* served from the ice, would ever have dreamed that a most diabolical plot was in progress, a conspiracy the most subtle and fiendish that the evil mind of man could ever devise.

Ena Pollen was, of course, the life and soul of the party. Very handsome, with her auburn hair and her bizarre dress, she was regarded by half the people in the restaurant. Some of them knew her by sight as a regular habituée of the smart restaurants and dance-clubs, for it was part of the great game which the heartless trio was playing for her to be remarked and regarded as a woman of outstanding grace and beauty.

Men courted her society, and in more than one instance—if the truth be whispered—had been hurried to the grave in consequence.

The quartette, after a delightful meal, took their coffee and Cointreau at a little table set beneath a palm out in the hall. Mrs. Morrison had become as charmed with Mrs. Davidson as she had been with Ena Pollen.

"You must come up and see me at Carsphairn," she urged Lilla. "No doubt your husband, living in the country, shoots. I can give him some grouse in the season. We have a fair amount of game on our moor at Balmaclellan."

"I shall be delighted, Mrs. Morrison," was Davidson's reply; as he lifted his eyes to Mrs. Pollen they exchanged significant glances.

Then, after a merry chat, Ena suddenly said:

"Can't all three of you dine with me at home one evening? You are not going North yet, are you, Mrs. Morrison? Do come. What about next Saturday?"

"I'm going back to Brighton to-morrow," was her reply.

"But you can easily run up on Saturday. Do. Let us dine early and go to a show together, eh?" she suggested with her usual enthusiasm. "You'll come, Lilla, won't you?"

Mrs. Davidson hesitated. She replied that she feared that she had an engagement that evening, and her husband was certain that he had.

"Oh, now, do come!" urged the Red Widow. "If Mrs. Morrison will come, you really must come."

Then, after a few half-hearted arguments and protests, Mrs. Morrison accepted the invitation and the Davidsons did likewise. And so the quiet little dinner was fixed, Ena promising to get a box at some theatre.

"Then we will go to Murray's or Giro's afterwards," she added.

Later, when Boyne and his wife were together in a taxi on their way to Pont Street, Lilla turned to him, and said:

"It all seems to go well if you can be ready by Saturday. If you can't, then we shall be in the cart!"

"Leave it all to me," he said in a hard, changed voice. "We shall be at Upper Brook Street on Saturday, and I hope we shall be successful. It won't be my fault if we fail."

CHAPTER XII
THE PERSON FROM UPSTAIRS

Marigold Ramsay, still pretending her sudden and unaccountable illness, lay upon a narrow iron bedstead in the spare room of Bernard Boyne's house, listening, and unable to sleep. She was there as a watch-dog.

Time after time she heard the bells of St. Paul's, Hammersmith, chiming the hours, but there was no sound below. Mr. Boyne had not returned.

The night was sultry and her window was slightly open. As she lay awake, she wondered what strange secret could be hidden in that house of mystery. Her aunt suspected nothing. That was evident, or she would have mentioned it to her. To old Mrs. Felmore, Bernard Boyne was a good and patient master, the persevering honest man which all Hammersmith judged him to be. None dreamed that he led such a curious double life of dusty tramping by day, and enjoying himself in the gay haunts of the West End by night.

It was nearly half-past two when a taxi set him down at the end of Hammersmith Bridge, and he walked to that house covered with virginia creeper. Not recollecting the fact that Marigold might still be there, and knowing that old Mrs. Felmore would not hear him enter, he placed his key in the latch and entered, closing the door heavily, as was his wont.

Marigold, on the alert, heard him. He went along the narrow, stuffy passage into his sitting-room. The girl sprang from her bed, put on the dressing-gown her aunt had lent her, and opened the door noiselessly. She heard the click of a lock in the room below, and knew that Boyne was giving Nibby his food, as he did every night without fail. Mrs. Felmore always left him something, meat or biscuit, to give the tame rat each night before he retired.

"Nibby" was Mr. Boyne's weird obsession; Mrs. Felmore hated it, but it was in its cage living in the cupboard by day, and allowed to run about the room at night, nibbling the evening newspaper or the old-fashioned furniture, for it was as destructive as all its race. One day Mrs. Felmore found that it had gnawed the corner of the carpet, while on the next she discovered that it had made a hole into the door of the cupboard opposite that in which it lived. And rat-holes are unsightly, to say the least.

As Marigold listened she heard Mr. Boyne speaking to his pet.

"Now then, you've had enough, Nibby! Get back, you elusive little dear!" And she heard him chasing him across the floor.

Then he unlocked another cupboard, and a few minutes later he came out into the passage and ascended the stairs. In consequence she closed her own door noiselessly, slipped the bolt, and stood listening. He passed her door, and then ascended the next flight of stairs, therefore she reopened her door instantly and, looking out, saw his form disappearing round the corner of the next landing.

She held her breath. He was dressed in that long hooded cloak of white, just as she had seen him on that well-remembered night weeks ago. He was on his way to that locked room, and carried in his hand food for its imprisoned occupant!

Dare she follow him? She was there at Gerald's suggestion, and it was for her to discover all she could. As she listened she heard the key being put into the Yale lock of that strong door at the top of the stairs. She heard him enter, the latch clicking behind him.

Then she heard strange cries—cries of surprise and rage—human cries!

Summoning courage she crept noiselessly after him, listening intently. There were no sounds of voices—only those strange cries—though, having ascended the second flight of stairs, she could see a streak of light beneath the door, and could hear him moving about within. Suddenly, just as she was about to ascend the third flight, she heard him approach the door and open it. Instantly she drew back and flew down into her room. And none too quickly, for a second later they would have encountered each other face to face.

Boyne, unsuspicious of being watched, for so occupied was he that he had forgotten Marigold's presence in the house, returned to his sitting-room, divested himself of the hideous disguise which he always wore when visiting the locked room, and then reascended to bed.

The girl lay awake for hours until, wearied out, she fell asleep till her aunt brought her some tea.

"Don't let Mr. Boyne know that I've stayed here to-night, auntie," she said, getting up hurriedly. "I'll get away before he comes down. I don't want him to know I've been so ill."

The old woman read her lips and nodded, saying in a whisper:

"As soon as you're gone, dear, I'll make the bed."

"I don't want any breakfast. I'll get to the City early, and have it there."

And this she did.

When Boyne came down to breakfast he asked his housekeeper how her niece was, to which she replied that she had recovered at about ten o'clock on the previous night and gone home to Wimbledon.

Saturday was always an "off" day with Mr. Boyne. Working people did not pay their weekly insurance premiums till Monday. Saturday is the half-day with the working class as Wednesday is with the shop-keeping community. Now on that particular Saturday Bernard Boyne, at eleven o'clock in the forenoon, sent Mrs. Felmore to King Street to buy him a tin of tomato soup. He wrote down the brand on an old envelope. And he wanted nothing else.

"If one grocer has not got it, another has, no doubt. If you can't get it in Hammersmith go down to Chiswick or Bedford Park," he said. "You'll find it somewhere."

And the old woman, whose shopping successes were always marvellous considering her stone deafness, went forth, little dreaming that such a brand as that he had written down was non-existent.

So all the morning until well into the afternoon Bernard Boyne had the house entirely to himself. As soon as she had gone, Boyne put on his white disguise and, rushing upstairs to the locked room, opened it.

"Now then!" he shouted roughly. "Are you ready? Have you dressed yet? No—you haven't. Now put it on—quick. Come out and get some air. It's stifling in this place!"

He waited at the door, whereupon a white figure, dressed exactly the same as himself, emerged, and slowly and painfully came down the stairs.

The two weird figures, linked arm in arm, descended to Boyne's parlour, whereupon in an authoritative tone he ordered the strange creature to be seated.

"Sit there!" he said. "And I'll open the window. You want a bit of air and exercise."

"Food! Food!" came the words, weak and squeaky behind the hideous mask.

"Very well. I'll go and get you some. But you can't eat it yet. Not till you're back again in your own room. Food!" he said roughly, with a sneer. "You're always wanting food and water. Fortunately the cistern is up there, or I'd have to carry up every drop for you. But your food I never forget, do I, eh?" he shouted, as though the strange figure was as deaf as old Mrs. Felmore.

The hooded figure, huddled in the arm-chair, only shrugged its shoulders.

From the voice it was impossible to tell the sex of the individual. The tone was weak, squeaky, and quite unnatural.

"Now, tell me, what have you done?" asked Boyne. "How is it progressing? I know you must be lonely sometimes, but it can't be helped. You are not fit to mix with us, you know. And you exist upon my charity. I am always good to you! Understand that!"

"I—I know," squeaked the figure, whose white cloak was soiled and stained, while those two long slits for the eyes under the pointed hood gave it a most weird and forbidding appearance.

"I hope you appreciate all I've done for you," Boyne went on. "If I had not risked all this, where would you have been—tried and executed in the hangman's noose. But I have done my best—though often you don't appreciate it."

"I—I do!" cried the voice from behind that strange disguise. "And I do all that you tell me," it whined.

"Very well," laughed Boyne. "We'll let it rest at that. The failure you lately had put me right in the cart. We mustn't have another. Remember that! Let it sink into your brain. You are clever, I know. But a single slip and both of us will go where we don't want to!"

"I know! I know! Yes—yes," replied the huddled figure. "But it was the weather—always the weather. And it is so hot under that roof."

"Weather be hanged!" replied Boyne. "This is winter—cold winter!— and yet you believe it to be summer."

As a matter of fact, it was hot summer weather, yet Boyne was trying to impress upon his companion that heat was cold, and vice versa.

The two weird figures in white cloaks, with only slits for the eyes, like Brothers of the Misericordia of Mediæval Italy, only in white, instead of black, sat opposite each other. Boyne was giving to his prisoner a breath of air, and a change in his living room.

A few minutes later the strange occupant of the locked room uttered the single word:

"Nibby?"

"Oh, yes, dear little Nibby is here," was Boyne's reply.

Rising, he fumbled beneath his cloak, and with his key unlocked the cupboard and opened the cage, from which the tame rat darted down and across the room. A second later he was sniffing the cloak of the figure from upstairs, running around the hem of the cloak with his little pink nose, while the wearer of the cloak put down a hand to be smelt, saying:

"Nibby, my dear little Nibby, that I have lost so long!"

In all London no scene in broad daylight could have been more weird than that at noon on a summer morning in Bridge Place, Hammersmith.

Boyne, the mystery man, held in such high esteem from Addison Road to Kew, sat there with the poor crouching figure as his victim. Behind those long narrow slits in the white fabric showed a pair of dark, deep-sunken eyes—eyes that were inhuman and unnatural.

The voice from behind the mask was metallic and squeaky. Whether the person was a man or a woman could not be conjectured. The high-pitched note was feminine.

"Am I not good to you to allow you this little relaxation?" asked Boyne. "You don't often get it, I admit, for the old deaf crone is always about, and I can seldom get rid of her."

"I—I felt—I felt very ill—last week. Days ago!" croaked the mysterious occupant of the locked room.

"I go up to you every day. You never complained. You are usually asleep when I come up."

"You come up at night. But all day I look out from the window over the roofs towards the river."

"River! What do you mean? There is no river here. It is a desert—a desert of bricks and mortar. You dream."

"Yes—yes. I dream! I—I'm always dreaming," was the response.

It was evident that Boyne held his half-imbecile prisoner completely in his power, and that all the orders of the insurance agent were obeyed.

Into the room strayed a ray of summer sunlight across the threadbare green carpet, lighting up the dingy old place.

The stranger from upstairs saw it, and squeaked:

"Look! It's summer—summer!"

"Summer!" cried the man who held him enthralled. "You're dreaming! It's winter. We get sun in winter sometimes. Surely you know that—dense as you are."

"I'm not dense," came the protest. "I do all you ask—fine jobs, too."

"You're dense about sunshine," Boyne repeated.

"Ah! yes. But not about the rats. Where's Nibby?"

Boyne caught the little animal and gave it into the hands of the strange figure, who stroked its sleek coat.

Suddenly the weird form in the soiled white disguise sprang to its feet without warning, and, facing its jailer, shrieked:

"Ah! But who are you? Who are you? I'm beginning to realise the truth at last—*yes*—*at last*!"

CHAPTER XIII
RELATES A STRANGE CONVERSATION

"Who *are* you?" shrieked the weird, hooded figure in the white cloak in a fierce voice, standing up suddenly above the seated man who was in exactly similar disguise.

The pair, one seated, and the other having suddenly sprung up, faced each other. The smaller, and apparently weaker figure had assumed a distinctly offensive attitude. His eyes shone behind the narrow slits.

"Fool!" laughed Boyne, who was seated. "Sit down, you idiotic fool!" And he waved his hand in contempt. "If I had not looked after you, and hidden you here, you would long ago have been given over to the hangman. Just remember that!" he shouted loudly. "Sink that into your skull, sleepy brain!"

"But—but," faltered the figure. "But who are you? You are not Wisden!"

Boyne, disguised in his white cloak with hood—the two presenting the most weird spectacle in the light of day in that dingy room in Hammersmith—started, then hesitated for a second.

"Yes," he replied, in a hard voice. "I am Wisden! Now you know! Wisden, of Twywell! Do you recollect the name?"

"You—Wisden!" gasped the person whose countenance was disguised by that hideous hood. "I—I——!" And he sank back into his chair.

"Now you know, you accursed fool!" exclaimed the mystery man. "And let that also sink into your silly noddle. Further, keep a still tongue. Be silent when you are up there, for people may listen and hear you. If they do, then you'll be discovered, and your death will be quick. Recollect that they are waiting for you—the affair isn't forgotten."

"No," sighed the weird figure. "No—I know it hasn't been forgotten. My crime!—*my crime!*"

"Yes. But don't refer to it. Just keep a level head, my dear Lionel, as you always do. I will still look after you if you remain silent and do what I order. I will supply you with everything. But be very careful that when I carry you up your food you don't speak. Somebody might overhear. These cursed walls have ears, although the old woman Felmore is deaf. Do you understand me?" he asked in a more imperative voice, rising, taking him by the shoulders, and shaking him. "Now tell me—you understand—eh?"

"Yes, yes!" the other gibbered in a strange tone. "You—Wisden—Willie Wisden! Oh, yes! I—I see! Dear old Willie, who was with me at Monte Carlo. Oh, yes! *And that beautiful microscope?*"

"You've got it upstairs. Don't you recollect it? Why, I gave it to you in the Terminus Hotel, in Marseilles, three years ago. Are you growing foolish? Surely not!"

"Yes. Oh, yes! I recollect now—the beautiful mike—oh, yes! Oh, what that instrument must have cost—oh, what a lot!—what a lot of money!"

"It did cost a good bit. And it's yours. So don't worry. I'll look after you, Lionel. But don't play the fool, or you'll go to the gallows over that unfortunate little affair—I warn you! Scotland Yard is looking everywhere for you, and they would have had you long ago if I hadn't taken you in hand and had pity upon you."

For a few moments the strange figure huddled in the chair remained silent.

"Yes—I know. And—and Lilla?" he asked.

"She's dead—died a year ago," was Boyne's prompt reply.

"Lilla dead!" sighed the other. "Poor Lilla! She was a very good wife to you—just as Alice was to me! Poor Lilla!"

"Don't you bother about my personal affairs, Lionel. Just keep your own end up, and breathe the bit of fresh air now while you can before you go back to your own quarters. I don't like you getting up through that trap-door on to the roof. Somebody might see you one night."

"My quarters! My prison, you mean!" he retorted bitterly.

"Prison? Fool, what are you saying? Your room is surely comfortable, and I do my best for you. If you want to get out—do so. And you'll be arrested by the first police constable who comes along."

"But it is prison!" replied the mysterious figure in a voice asking for pity. "Prison!"

"Well—take your liberty, and take the consequences," the other responded roughly.

"Look what I do! I'm always working for you—always!"

Boyne laughed harshly.

"Very well! Give it up, and I'll fling you out into the gutter—now—just as you are! I shan't suffer," he added, "but you will! By gad you will!"

The man from upstairs cringed and drew his breath.

"No! No! Wisden! No!—don't do that! I'll do all you ask—all! Alice—my dear Alice—always said you were my best friend—my very best friend."

"And so I am, my dear fellow!" exclaimed Boyne. "I've done my best for you all along—all along."

"Look!" cried the lonely man who lived upstairs, and whose movements were never heard by deaf old Mrs. Felmore. "What's that?"

And with a shriek of horror he pointed to a corner of the dingy room.

"What? I don't see anything!" was Boyne's reply. "You've got one of those spooky fits of yours coming on again. You'd better go back."

"I don't want to go back," whined the person whose Christian name was Lionel. "Surely you won't send me back, Wisden?"

"Yes; for your own sake you must lie low. Try to understand what I say. We are mutually interested in each other. It is to the advantage of both that you should remain here. I am not your jailer, recollect. If you wish, you can walk out now. But I warn you that you will walk straight into the hangman's noose. Scotland Yard and the Old Bailey are awaiting you, and are ready, never fear."

"But where's Alice?" asked the squeaky voice.

"Alice is dead."

"Are you sure? How and where did she die?"

"In Avignon. In a house close behind the Pope's Palace. Surely you remember? You were there."

"I wasn't there. I swear I was not. When we were in Avignon we were all happy together. Alice with me, and you with Lilla."

"My dear boy, your memory is at fault. Did you not stay in Avignon while Lilla and I motored to Paris? Now think! Did you not take an apartment in the Rue Cardinale, and remain after our departure? Alice, your wife, died there! Why, only a few minutes ago you deplored her loss!"

"Yes. But how can I be certain that she is dead?" asked the other dubiously.

"Because I tell you she is. I'm not a liar!" cried Boyne fiercely, again assuming an overbearing attitude.

"But I want to go home—to see my home again—the garden—the flowers—and Alice."

"You'll never see her again. And you are safer here. So you had better go back to your room and keep a still tongue. And be careful not to make a noise. You made a horrible row the other night."

"I didn't!"

"Yes, you did. I could hear you moving about above me. You should move your bed across to the other side, near the trap-door that goes out on to the roof of which you are so fond."

"Ah! because I get air. But I only open it and go out after it's dark, I assure you."

"Well, you've got plenty of stores. I bring you bread and fresh meat and vegetables, and you've got the cistern full of water. Why, if I went away for for a month or six weeks you wouldn't starve. I always see to that. And look what it costs me!" exclaimed the humble insurance agent.

"Ah! Nibby. Dear little Nibby!" cried the weird man from upstairs in that inhuman, high-pitched voice, as he noticed the tame rat dart across the threadbare carpet.

"Yes, Nibby knows you!" laughed the man Boyne. "He's a dear little fellow, isn't he?"

"Yes. I miss him after so long," replied the man. "Can't I take him upstairs with me?" he asked piteously.

"No, he would gnaw through the door to get back to me, and old mother Felmore would find rats in the place. She knows of Nibby, but we don't want to arouse her curiosity. Women, deaf or not, are always dangerous when one has secrets."

"And how is Mrs. Pollen—eh?"

"Mrs. Pollen!" echoed Boyne. "Whom do you mean?"

"Why, Ena Pollen, the friend of Lilla. You know the woman—tall, handsome, red-haired. She worked a dirty trick upon some man she met. They had supper at the Ritz. He died, and nobody suspected. Ugh! Isn't it funny how one can lead a crooked life and everyone think one perfectly honest?"

"Well, you're not honest, my dear Lionel," laughed Bernard Boyne. "If it had not been for me I repeat you'd have been hanged for that affair two years ago."

The man in the hooded cloak shuddered.

"Yes," he replied in a changed voice. "You are right; I owe everything to you, and that's why I do all you ask of me. They say there is no genius without lunacy. So I suppose you think me a lunatic—eh?"

"I don't think, Lionel—I know you are," Boyne responded. "You've acted as a silly fool, and you made a serious slip in killing the girl, but I'm trying to save you from the police. They are still hunting over all Europe for you."

"But did I kill her, Wisden? Did I? I don't remember it!"

"Remember it. Why, you've got no memory. You only remember all your science and your wonderful knowledge—a knowledge unequalled. Yes! you killed her, and by an ace I rescued you from arrest. You recollect little Maggie?"

"Ah! yes. I—I know what you mean!" gasped the other. "Little Maggie! But I didn't kill her!"

"You did. Your damnable criminal instincts led you to kill her, and that's why Scotland Yard is searching daily for you!"

"Maggie! I—I killed Maggie!"

"Yes, you did—and you know it, you infernal hypocrite!" cried Boyne. "Now, don't try to argue. I'm in my right senses. You aren't! I haven't time or inclination to have a war of words over it. Besides," he added, glancing at his watch, "Mrs. Felmore will be back at any minute, so you must get upstairs again—and without delay."

"But can't I go home? I—I want to see my garden—the flowers——"

"No!" snapped Boyne. "You can't. You'll stay here."

"Do let me go—do," pleaded the other in that curious high-pitched voice. "I do want to see my garden again."

"You'll see the inside of a prison if you are not very careful," Boyne declared in a warning tone. "So don't think about going home."

"But am I never to go home?"

"At your own risk. Remember, I'll take no responsibility. Your description and photograph are in every police-station here and on the Continent, and, as I've told you lots of times, the moment you step outside into the street you will court danger. You'll be arrested by the first policeman who sees you!"

"Surely I may go home—if only for a day! You could take me there."

"Later on, perhaps," Boyne said encouragingly, in a tone which he would have adopted to a child. "For the present you must remain where you are, safe. And don't make a noise, otherwise somebody may hear you," he urged.

"I don't make any noise. I'm always so careful. And I only go out on the roof at night."

"The less you go out there the better," growled the insurance agent. "I run risks every time I come up to bring your food. Only the other day Mrs. Felmore was saying that Nibby seemed to have an enormous appetite. That's why I've brought you up that store of tinned stuff."

"I haven't had any tea for a week."

"But you've got your gas-ring and your kettle."

"The kettle leaks."

"Then why the deuce didn't you tell me that before? I'll bring you a new one to-day."

"And some fresh milk and some eggs. I've tasted none for weeks."

"Well, if you are in hiding you must put up with what food you can get," growled Boyne. "I do my best for you—and even now you're not satisfied."

"I want to go home."

"Home? For them to know that you're still in London? They all think you've escaped to Greece, and got clean away. That's what I told them."

The man so strangely disguised drew a long breath.

"Ah! if only I could have got away," he murmured wistfully.

"Yes, it would have saved me a lot of bother, wouldn't it?" snarled the other. "No; be patient, and be grateful."

"I am grateful, Wisden—very grateful."

"You're not! You're a dissatisfied hound who deserves no pity or consideration. I do my best and shelter you, and all you do in return is to grumble."

"Oh! but you don't know how lonely it is up there. I sit all day alone."

"And sleep your hours away! Look at me, trudging about all day long for next to nothing. True, I have freedom, but there's no charge against me as there is against you."

"No!" cried the man Lionel in his squeaky voice. "But there may be one day, remember! There may be!"

"Don't be a fool!" snapped Boyne. "Get back to your den, and lie low."

"I shan't!"

"What—you defy me—eh?"

"Yes. I know you—who you are!" shouted the mysterious man. "You're *not* Wisden. *Your voice is not his!*"

"Infernal idiot! So you've got another attack coming on, have you! Come, get up," for he had sunk into a chair again. Pulling him up, he shook him roughly by the shoulder, saying: "Get up, and come along."

"I won't!" he cried sullenly. "I tell you I won't go up there any more!"

"Very well then, I'll fling you out into the street now, just as you are. You'd cut a fine figure, wouldn't you?"

"I don't care!"

"All right. If you don't care, come along and get out of my house." And he took him again by the shoulder and hustled him out of the room towards the front door.

"What do you mean to do?" asked the mysterious prisoner in a frightened voice.

"Do!" Boyne echoed fiercely. "Why, kick you out! I'm sick of trying to help such an unthankful blackguard."

"I—I'm not unthankful," he declared. "I'll go back."

"Ah! I thought you wouldn't relish being put into the hands of the police—eh?" laughed Boyne. "Go upstairs."

The hooded man turned towards the stairs with a disconsolate sigh, but without further words. He saw that all argument was useless.

"Come!" whispered Boyne, whose quick ear had caught a sound in the kitchen below. "Mrs. Felmore is back! By gad! hustle up—quickly."

And the man painfully climbed back to his secret hiding-place, the door of which Boyne closed just as Mrs. Felmore arrived at the foot of the stairs in search of her master.

"Curse the fellow!" Boyne muttered beneath his breath. "He's growing defiant, and that means trouble for us—serious trouble!"

CHAPTER XIV
ON SATURDAY NIGHT

The events of that particular Saturday were of such portent that it is necessary to describe them in some little detail.

When the Man from Upstairs had safely escaped from Mrs. Felmore's observation, and Boyne had expressed regret that her shopping expedition had been fruitless, the honest insurance agent ate the frugal lunch which his housekeeper put before him, and then went out.

An hour later he returned with a large parcel, which he smuggled in away from the deaf old woman, and ten minutes later, pretending to have forgotten, he sent her out to buy some postage stamps.

So she put on her hat in calm obedience, and once more went forth into King Street.

As soon as she had gone, Boyne opened the parcel, which contained a new tin kettle and a quantity of groceries and provisions, and then sprang up the stairs, unlocked the door with his key, and entered the secret abode.

He was there for about three-quarters of an hour. He heard Mrs. Felmore come in, but took no heed. If she knew that he was upstairs, she would no doubt believe that he was looking out some of his insurance papers.

About half-past three Boyne came forth, and, locking the heavy door, descended to his sitting-room with a satisfied smile upon his smug countenance. What had happened in that locked room evidently pleased him. He went to the nearest telephone call-office, and ten minutes later was speaking with his wife in Pont Street.

"You, Lilla?" he asked, recognising her voice. "It's all right! I shall go to Ena's at six, and then come on to you. Have you heard anything?"

"Yes. She's come up from Brighton, and not being able to get a room in any of the big hotels, has gone into a private one at Lancaster Gate. Is all correct?"

"Yes. See you after I've seen Ena," was his reply, and he rang off.

Back again he went to Bridge Place, and at half-past five left for Upper Brook Street. He, however, did not pass the inquisitive hall-porter, but entered by the servants' way, for he was by no means well-dressed.

Inside Ena Pollen's flat, he walked to the drawing-room, where the Red Widow joined him, asking anxiously:

"Well, how goes it, my dear Bernard?"

"All progresses as we would wish. I thought I'd run up here before I go to Lilla's to change. Where is Mrs. Morrison?"

"At Lancaster Gate. At a private hotel I recommended. I urged her to remain in town for a week or ten days, and she's consented."

"Excellent. What's the place like?"

"Oh! quiet and eminently respectable. Mostly rich old fogies from the country go there. I thought it would be better to remain in touch with her, you know."

And the Red Widow laughed grimly.

"I've got the table set ready. Come and see it," she urged. And she took him into the adjoining dining-room, a handsome apartment, with carved oak furniture and several old and valuable paintings upon the walls. Upon the circular polished table the plates were set upon small mats in the latest vogue, while both the silver and glass were ancient. Covers were laid for four, the decorations consisting of only two long-stem glasses of pale-pink carnations. Taste and delicacy were displayed everywhere, especially in the antique Georgian plate, with the genuine Queen Anne "montieth" as a centre-piece.

"Will it do?" she asked. "I laid it myself."

"It is perfect! It will impress her with your sense of the artistic, Ena," he declared. "I hope the meal you will give us will be as refined."

"I hope so," she laughed. "In a sense—a certain sense—it will be more so."

He laughed at the hidden meaning contained in that remark. Then he glanced around the room, and recollected the great expense which the preliminaries of that single meal had entailed.

"I've asked her for half-past seven," Mrs. Pollen said, "so you'd better go over and dress, and get here a little late. She'll settle down before you come. Then you can both apologise. Of course, we've not met since that evening at the Carlton."

"Right, I quite understand," he said. "Where is she to sit?"

"There—with her back to the sideboard."

Boyne nodded approval.

The Red Widow opened the cupboard on the left-hand of the sideboard, where he saw in a row four beautiful liqueur glasses, delicately cut, with square stems. His quick eye examined them, and he took out one. It was exactly the same as the other three except that it had a round stem.

He held it in his fingers for a second, and a sinister smile played about his lips.

"Yes—I see!" he remarked. "She likes liqueurs. Most women do."

"Especially Cointreau. They like the subtle flavour of tangerine orange," laughed Ena. "Don't you recollect what she said about it at the Carlton—that it is her favourite drink with coffee?"

"Yes. And we, of course, indulge her!"

"Indulge!" echoed the woman. "A nice word, truly!"

Boyne was twisting the liqueur glass he had selected in his fingers.

"I wish you'd get me a cocktail, Ena," he said. "I'm dying for one."

"Then I'll get you one at once. There's none here. I'll go into the kitchen and mix one—gin and French vermouth, with a dash of anisette and lemon—eh?"

"Exactly. That's what I want. You're a dear," replied the man, and the widow left to prepare it.

A few minutes later she returned with a small glass on a silver tray. He took it, and swallowed the contents at two gulps.

"By Jove! Excellent. Johnnie at the Ritz couldn't make a better, Ena. But you were always famed for your corpse-revivers!"

"Glad you like it. Now get away at once, or you'll have no time."

"Mind the glass!" he said in a serious voice.

"I'll see after it all right, never fear. You do your work and I do mine—eh? Now get away, and don't arrive before a quarter to eight or so."

"Yours to obey, Ena," was his response, and he at once slipped out by the servants' entrance into the mews, and, hailing a taxi a few minutes later, drove to Pont Street.

On arrival he at once met his wife, who was anxiously awaiting him in the drawing-room.

"All right, Lilla! Don't worry. Things all go well," he assured her. "I've seen Ena, and we shall have a very delightful dinner. We go to the new revue at the Hippodrome afterwards, and then on to Giro's for supper—a very delightful evening."

"And then——?" asked his wife, looking him straight in the face.

"Well—and then a little affair of business—eh?"

Lilla laughed at the grimace her husband made.

Boyne left her at once, and ascending to his bedroom, shaved, exchanged his clothes for a smart evening suit, and carefully brushed his hair, until, when he descended, he presented the ideal man-about-town whose evening clothes were well worn and who wore his soft-fronted shirt as one accustomed to it every night. The man unused to the claw-hammer coat is always to be noticed in a crowd, just as is the woman who, putting on an evening frock occasionally, hitches it up on the shoulder and is palpably uncomfortable in it.

Bernard Boyne wore his clothes, whether the dusty suit of the Hammersmith insurance agent or the smart evening clothes in which he pursued his nocturnal peregrinations in the West End, with equal grace and ease.

When he rejoined his wife in the pretty drawing-room he presented a very different figure from the man who had sat in that ugly white cloak with the slits for eyes in that dingy, creeper-covered house in Hammersmith.

He rang the bell, and, ordering a taxi, lit a cigarette, and awaited it.

Lilla was splendidly dressed in a gown of navy blue and gold brocade, cut very low, with shoes and stockings to match. In her hair was a long osprey which well matched the gorgeous gown, the latest creation of Petticoat Lane—the writer begs pardon of his lady readers for such irreverent mention of Dover Street, Piccadilly, that street in which the latest fashions of feminine frippery have their birth, and to which the mere man sends his cheques in consequence of recurring crazes.

When together in the taxi, Lilla said:

"Now be extremely careful. This Scotch woman is very canny. Remember that! If we made a slip it would land us all in—well, at a very dead end."

"Don't be anxious, Lilla. I never like you when you grow anxious, because anxiety always brings us bad luck. And we don't want that to-night—do we? Eat your dinner and think of nothing—only of the revue at the Hippodrome. Leave Ena and myself to it. Don't bother—or you may arouse suspicion."

Later, when they alighted in Upper Brook Street just before eight o'clock, the uniformed hall-porter touched his cap as they entered and took them up in the lift.

"Oh! my dear Ena," cried Lilla, as the two women met in the drawing-room. "Do forgive me—do! Bernard came in late from the club. It's all his fault! It really is not mine! I waited for him half an hour."

"Yes, Mrs. Pollen," said Boyne penitently, "I take all responsibility upon myself. I had to see a man on business at the club, and the brute was half an hour late. So I had to rush home and dress—and here we are. Do forgive me—won't you?"

Ena Pollen laughed, declaring that she had overlooked the offence, whereupon Mrs. Morrison shook Lilla's hand warmly, and they sank into chairs until two minutes later dinner was announced by the smart maid.

Dinner! Bernard Boyne and Ena Pollen had given dinners before, artistic and perfect meals which would have delighted any gourmet, even though he had tasted the pre-war gastronomical delights of the expensive restaurants of Moscow, Petrograd or Bucharest.

When they sat down, Ena directed Mrs. Morrison to her seat with her back to the sideboard, saying:

"You won't have any draught there, my dear. This room is so full of draughts. I don't know where they come from!"

"I hope you are staying in town a little while, and that we shall see something of you," said Lilla to Mrs. Morrison as they tackled their asparagus soup. "You must not go back to Scotland yet, you know."

"Well," replied the other, a handsome figure in her discreetly décolleté gown, "Ena has been urging me to remain in London for a few days, but I couldn't get a room anywhere. All the hotels are full up, but I at last got in at a place in Lancaster Gate—quite comfortable, though it's a bit expensive."

"All hotels are terribly dear now, though, after all, hotels are cheaper than one's household expenses," Lilla replied.

"Well, I've taken my room for a week. I may be in London longer, but I have to visit my sister-in-law at Aviemore on the twentieth of next month, and then I go over to Arran to my niece."

"Stay with us as long as you can, Mrs. Morrison," Boyne urged warmly. "You must dine with us at Pont Street one night next week."

"Thanks! I shall be delighted. I've got appointments with the dressmaker."

"And the dentist, of course," laughed Boyne. "All ladies have appointments with their dentists. It is the best excuse a wife can have for the deception of a too inquisitive husband."

"Not in my case, Mr. Davidson," declared the widow of Carsphairn, with a merry smile. "I have no one to whom I need make excuses. But, as it happens, I am going to a dentist!"

"There you are!" laughed Ena. "He divined it."

The meal went on merrily to its end, after which the maid handed round the black coffee in exquisite little china cups, the spoons having handles shaped like coffee beans. Then she retired.

Ena, glancing at the old chiming clock upon the mantelshelf, suddenly exclaimed:

"Oh! it's getting late! And Evans hasn't put on the liqueurs. I'll get them myself."

And rising she obtained from the sideboard four liqueur glasses, together with bottles of old brandy, Benedictine and Triple-Sec.

"Now, dear, you'll have your favourite Cointreau," she said, addressing Mrs. Morrison, and pouring out a glass of the clear water-like extract of Tangerine oranges.

"No—no thanks!" was the prompt reply. "I really don't want it."

"Oh, but you must!" declared her hostess, pressing her. "I'm going to have one, and so will you, Lilla, I'm sure."

"Oh! yes. I love it," declared the other woman, while Boyne glanced eagerly to satisfy himself that the stem of Mrs. Morrison's glass was *round and not square*.

"Come, you must have half a glass, dear," declared Ena, and she poured it out disregarding her guest's half-hearted protests.

Then, the others being served, the big silver box of rose-tipped cigarettes was opened, and they took one each.

Bernard Boyne watched the widow from Scotland sipping her small glass with the utmost satisfaction, while the other two women were excited, though they seemed quite cool, engaging her in conversation.

"Do you know," exclaimed Mrs. Morrison, "I grow more fond of this liqueur each time I take it. We can't get it in Scotland, so I order it from London. It is the purest of all the liqueurs, that is my belief."

"It is," declared Boyne, with a meaning look towards Ena. "It is never injurious as so many of these green, red and yellow alcoholic and sugar concoctions are."

"No," replied the wealthy owner of Carsphairn. "I quite agree." And she drained her glass with undisguised satisfaction. "It has a most exquisite flavour, and it does one no harm."

Boyne smiled grimly across to his hostess and suggested that they should be going if they wanted to be there at the opening of the revue.

The quartette sat in a box, and greatly enjoyed the medley of songs and dances until, at the close, they went off to a gay supper at Giro's, which they did not leave till nearly two in the morning.

Just before Boyne dropped his wife from a taxi at the corner of Pont Street, he said:

"Well, Lilla! It all went well, didn't it? No hitch. We ought to have some news from Lancaster Gate about Wednesday or Thursday."

"Good!" replied the woman. "We'll wait in patience. Only I do hope it will turn out as we expect."

"It will—never fear! Good-night."

And she stepped out to walk down the street to her own house, while he continued in the taxi to Hammersmith Broadway, where he also alighted.

Then, as he walked home, he muttered to himself:

"It can't fail this time. On Wednesday next we shall hear how beneficial to the health is that most excellent liqueur."

CHAPTER XV
CARRIES THE MYSTERY FARTHER

On Monday, according to a previous arrangement, both Gerald and Marigold obtained leave of absence for the afternoon from their respective principals, and after lunching together as usual, went on the top of an omnibus to Kew, where they walked for an hour in the celebrated gardens. Then they went to Hammersmith to take tea with Mrs. Felmore. The deaf old woman welcomed them warmly, and they sat together in the kitchen, though Gerald could not talk with Marigold's aunt.

The girl, who could speak with her aunt with ease, put to her several questions concerning Mr. Boyne's movements, but learned nothing unusual. She feared to tell the old woman of that uncanny disguise which he adopted when he visited that locked room upstairs, or of that weird, but certainly human cry which she had heard above.

Personally, Gerald suspected the cry to be the result of her vivid imagination. The theory that somebody was imprisoned in that upstairs room was fantastic, but highly improbable, therefore he had dismissed it. Yet presently the old woman made one remark which struck him as curious. In the course of conversation Mrs. Felmore said:

"Poor Mr. Boyne! He does all the good in the world that he can. Only yesterday I found hidden in one of the cupboards in his bedroom a whole lot of tinned stuff—tongues, fruit, jam, biscuits—a host of things that he's got up there on the quiet. I asked him what he was hoarding them up for, and he said that he was sending a big parcel of groceries to a poor widow he knew at Notting Hill Gate."

"Curious to have a store of tinned stuff in his bedroom!" remarked Gerald, at once recollecting the suggestion that somebody might be in hiding upstairs.

"Yes, sir," replied the old woman. "But Mr. Boyne is very eccentric sometimes—very eccentric!"

"In what way?" he asked eagerly.

"Oh! he gets up in the middle of the night and goes up and down stairs—I often see the light under my bedroom door."

Marigold and her lover exchanged glances.

"I wonder what he does?" asked the girl.

"Ah! That I can't say," was the old housekeeper's response. "I asked him one day not long ago, and he simply told me he had woke up, and as he couldn't go to sleep again, he went down to do his accounts."

"Well, this store of food shows him to be of a philanthropic turn of mind," remarked Gerald, with a smile. And then, disregarding the fact that Boyne might return at any moment, he succeeded in getting Mrs. Felmore's permission to slip upstairs and view the collection of preserved foods which was going to the poor widow.

Marigold quickly found it stored in the bottom of a cupboard, covered by an old overcoat and some worn-out shirts, which had apparently been flung in at haphazard.

Gerald's quick glance saw something which further aroused his curiosity—a small brand-new tin tea-kettle and a little enamelled basin. With them was a new roll of absorbent cotton-wool and a quart bottle of cheap port wine, which from its label had been purchased of a local grocer.

"Funny that he should send her a tea-kettle and basin!" remarked Durrant, as he handled them. "And look! What's this?" And he took out a small wooden box about three inches square, such as is used by jewellers to send watches by post. He opened it and within, carefully packed in cotton wool, was a small lens surrounded by a threaded brass ring evidently a portion of some optical instrument.

"Part of a telescope!" the girl exclaimed. "Surely a widow would not require that—however poor she might be!"

"Yes, dear," said her lover, holding the box in his hand and reflecting. "This is a curious hoard, and I am wondering if it is intended for the unknown person who is living in seclusion above."

"Well, Mr. Boyne's explanation to auntie is quite clever, if what you suggest is the solution of the mystery."

"But is not Boyne always clever?" he asked. "That he is leading a double life we have already established. It is now for us to solve the problem of the reason of this locked room upstairs."

"Then you think this has been bought in order to feed somebody who is living up above in silence and seclusion?" she asked.

"It seems like it. But if we watch carefully and see in which direction it disappears, whether inside this house or outside, then we shall begin to penetrate the mystery."

"But how shall we do it?"

"This requires very careful consideration, dear," was his reply. "My own feeling is that you should by some means or other endeavour to spend the next few days here with your aunt, so that you can keep daily watch upon this strange collection of provisions. But we mustn't remain here, for Boyne may return at any moment."

So they descended the stairs to the kitchen, and hardly had they reached it when the heavy tread of the man of mystery was heard in the hall above.

While Mrs. Felmore was upstairs interviewing her employer as to what he required for tea, the lovers held hurried consultation.

When the old woman returned, Gerald rose and motioned to her that he intended to go as perhaps Mr. Boyne would not like to discover him there. He placed his finger upon his lips, shook hands with the deaf housekeeper, and stole out and up the area steps, keeping well out of sight of Boyne's window.

"Mr. Durrant was in a hurry, eh?" asked the old woman.

"Yes, auntie. He was afraid that Mr. Boyne might not like him calling here, so he's gone. But I'm here, and—well, to tell you the truth, auntie, I don't exactly know what to do!"

"Do—why?" asked the old woman, her eyes starting as was her habit when surprised.

"I'm at a loose end, auntie. They want my room over at Wimbledon— but only for a week. Hetty and Jack have come home from their music-hall engagement in Paris, and they've asked me to give up my room for a week. So I've no place to sleep. I've been wondering if Mr. Boyne would mind me coming here. Do you think he'd object?"

"No, I'm sure he wouldn't mind, dear!" she declared. "I'll ask him now—when I go up. He's often inquiring after you."

So when she took up her master's tea a quarter of an hour later, she said:

"Marigold's downstairs, sir. She's in a bit of trouble, sir."

"Trouble! Why?" asked Boyne sharply. "What's the matter? Has she left the bank?"

"Oh, no, sir. It's only because she's turned out of her room at Wimbledon for a week for her brother-in-law and his wife, so she wants to come here and stay with me. Would you have any objection?"

"Of course not, Mrs. Felmore. Tell her to come up and see me now."

Then, when the old woman had gone, his genial attitude instantly changed.

"So the girl wants to come here—does she? Yes, she shall come. Oh, yes!" he growled grimly. "She and that fellow are playing a very pretty game. But I shall win, never fear!"

A moment later Marigold entered the room, saying:

"It's awfully good of you, Mr. Boyne, to put me up again! I fear I'm a terrible nuisance, but I was in such a difficulty that I came to auntie, and asked her if she knew of anyone who could give me a room. She then said that she thought you might allow me to stay here."

"My dear Miss Marigold," he said quite genially, "you are welcome to stay with your aunt. I've told you so over and over again, haven't I? How are you getting on at the bank?"

"Oh, quite well, thanks! It is rather monotonous—figures always—but still it's better than at that motor dealer's where I was before. People who deal in motor cars have no conscience, and are, I believe, the biggest liars on earth."

Boyne laughed. He had an appreciation for the smart young lady clerk, whose quick wit and ready repartee always appealed to him. But two days before he had made a discovery which had aroused his suspicions.

It was, however, arranged that Marigold should occupy the same room which she had had when taken suddenly ill a short time before, and Boyne added:

"Just do as you like, my girl. I have a great regard for your aunt, as you know, and you are quite welcome here, I assure you."

The girl, believing that he was unsuspicious, thanked him and, leaving the room, descended to the kitchen, where she told her aunt all that had transpired.

Personally she liked Mr. Boyne. It was only the discovery of that weird disguise of his that had aroused her curiosity, which, indeed, was but natural.

She left the house half an hour later and travelled to Wimbledon Park, returning with her leather blouse case containing a few necessaries.

Eight o'clock had struck ere she arrived at Bridge Place. At the corner of the street Gerald confronted her. He had kept watchful vigil upon the house to see whether Boyne had brought out any parcel for the poor widow. But the man of mystery had not come forth.

She told her lover with enthusiasm how Boyne had invited her to stay there, and promised to keep a watchful eye upon things.

"Excellent, dear," Gerald declared. "You go in, and I'll still remain here, and follow him if he goes out to spend the evening."

"Be careful that he doesn't notice you," she urged. "He has awfully quick eyesight."

"I know that. He very nearly spotted me the other day. In fact, I was afraid that he had."

"I see you've got a cap on," she laughed. "Where is your hat?"

"I've left it in a shop in the Broadway to be renovated and ironed, and I bought this cap to wear meanwhile. Does it make any difference?"

"Certainly it does. And you've got a new jacket, too."

"The same. I bought it at a reach-me-down shop in King Street an hour ago, and left my own there. Does it fit?"

"Not very well around the collar, but nobody would really notice it," she declared.

Gerald Durrant was both shrewd and determined. When he set his mind upon a thing, he carried it through at all costs. He intended to penetrate the veil of mystery which enveloped this good go-to-meeting collector of insurance premiums.

"Well," he said at last. "Be watchful, and be careful, dear, that you don't arouse his suspicion. He's a mystery, and all men of his calibre are ultra-suspicious, and masters in the art of concealing their own feelings."

"Don't fear, Gerry," she laughed. "I shall be as clever as he is. You do your watching outside, and I'll do mine within. I shall probably telegraph to Mr. Kenyon to-morrow and make excuse that I'm ill. Then I shall have a day in the house to examine things a little more closely."

"That's a good idea! Watch those things in his bedroom—that tea-kettle and the other things. Find out when they go—and where," were his parting injunctions.

Five minutes later Marigold went down the area steps into the kitchen, where her aunt was cooking Mr. Boyne's succulent steak.

"He says he's very hungry to-day—hasn't had any lunch, so I went out and got him this!" exclaimed the old woman. "If he eats it all, then he ought to do well, eh?" she remarked, in her somewhat high-pitched and rasping voice.

"Yes. I suppose he'll go out afterwards," said Marigold.

"He said he'd got to go out at nine—to a meeting somewhere," was her aunt's reply. Therefore her niece took from her bag a postcard, scribbled something upon it, and in pretence of going to the post she went out to Gerald and told him what she had learned.

This afforded Durrant time to go along to the "Clarendon" for dinner and a rest before resuming his patient observations.

On her return, Marigold put on an apron and helped her aunt. Indeed, she carried up the tray into Mr. Boyne's room.

"Ah! I see I've got a new parlour-maid, eh?" he laughed merrily. "And an unusually smart one, too!"

Marigold laughed, and set the table, saying:

"Well, I thought I'd just give auntie a hand, Mr. Boyne. Half an hour ago she complained that her leg hurt, because of the stairs, so I thought I'd help her."

"Very good of you," he said, lounging in the frayed old arm-chair in his shirt-sleeves, a different figure indeed from that he so often presented at night in the West End. There, in the smart restaurants and in theatres, he wore his evening suit and nodded acquaintance with many well-known people, who little suspected his obscure abode.

Marigold waited upon him as though she were a waitress instead of a ledger clerk, but he was reading the evening paper as he ate his meal, and spoke but little more.

"Yes, you're a pretty miss, you are!" he growled to himself after she had left the room. "If you don't mind you'll be very sorry that you entered my house."

At a quarter to nine, having washed and changed into a rather seedy suit of blue serge, he went out. Marigold heard him bang the door, and knew that Gerald was on the alert outside.

The evening passed quietly until at ten Mrs. Felmore went to bed, and her niece also retired. She bade her aunt good-night, went into the spare room and closed the door.

She shook out her thin summer dressing-gown, and placed it upon the rail of the narrow bed. Then she reopened the door and stood listening on the stairs, her ears strained to catch any noise from the locked room on the next landing of the frowsy old house.

No sound reached her ears, save the noise her aunt made moving about in her room. Downstairs the cheap old clock in Boyne's sitting-room ticked loudly and suddenly struck the half-hour. Beyond that all was silent.

Marigold, after a long vigil, at last turned off the gas and, throwing herself on the bed, dressed as she was, soon fell asleep.

Meanwhile Boyne re-entered the house noiselessly and, taking off his shoes, crept in silence up the stairs to her door. He listened, and could hear by her deep, regular breathing that she was asleep.

Slowly he turned the handle of the door—which he had purposely oiled before going out—and, flashing a pocket-torch to the ceiling, saw her lying there, still dressed!

Without a sound he withdrew and crept back down the stairs.

"I thought so, young lady!" he muttered to himself, when he was back in his sitting-room. "You don't know much—neither does your young man! But I must take steps for my own protection, that I can see!"

He stood with his back to the fireplace, his eyes staring at the sideboard in front of him for some moments. Nibby was scuttling about in the cupboard, so he let him out and the little rodent sniffed his hand.

"I wonder what makes the girl so inquisitive?" he thought. "Surely the old woman knows nothing! If she does, then she would, of course, confide in her niece, who, in turn, would tell this young fellow Durrant."

The lovers were unaware that Boyne had been making the most careful inquiries concerning both of them, for the instant he realised that he was being watched, he had laid certain diabolical plans by which to triumph.

"It's their lives—or *mine!*" he whispered to himself, with a strange hard look in his eyes. "I can't afford to be watched by such inquisitive folk. I was a fool not to take Lilla's advice concerning this girl."

He walked across to the sideboard and poured himself out a liqueur-glass full of brandy, which he tossed off at a single gulp.

"I'll test her and see what happens," he said aloud, with a chuckle. Then, slipping on his shoes and going to the front door, he opened it, and, having banged it, walked heavily back along the passage to the room.

The noise awakened Marigold, who, all unconscious that Boyne had seen her there, instantly jumped up and listened.

She heard footsteps on the stairs and saw a passing light beneath her door.

She heard him ascend the next flight of stairs towards the locked room, and then carefully opening her door, peered out after him.

Suddenly he turned and descended, as though he had forgotten something, but his quick eye, as he flashed his lamp upon her door, detected that it was noiselessly closing.

In pretence of ignorance he passed down to his own room, and entering it, closed the door heavily.

"Yes," he whispered to himself. "Ah! I was not mistaken! The girl is here in my house to spy upon me! She's dangerous—just as dangerous as the man. And in my game I allow no enemies to confront me!"

Then, laughing grimly, he clenched his bony fists and set his teeth.

Afterwards he retired to bed, leaving the girl listening attentively to noises he purposely made.

CHAPTER XVI
BAITING THE TRAP

Next day Boyne remained in the house until Marigold had left to go to the City—for she was anxious to report the result of her vigil to her lover and then, instead of going out upon his daily collection of insurance premiums, he went to Pont Street.

He arrived at the fine red-brick house about eleven, opening the door with his latchkey. He found his wife in her bedroom, and closing the door, he exclaimed in an unusually excited voice:

"Lilla! there's trouble brewing—*very serious trouble!*"

"In what direction?" gasped the handsome woman, starting from the long mirror before which she was arranging her blouse.

"That girl Marigold—the old woman Felmore's niece—is suspicious, and she has established herself in my house in order to watch me!"

"Why is she suspicious?"

"I don't know. That's the mystery of it. How much she knows I can't tell."

"One thing is plain," said the woman. "If we are to save ourselves, her lips must be closed. Surely that will be easy—just a nice box of chocolates, tied with ribbon, or something like that—eh? We did it before with little Louise, at Cheltenham."

"Yes—but I don't like doing it. She's really an awfully nice girl, and I haven't the heart to give her a 'dose.'"

"She's watching you, you say! Therefore she's a danger to us all. Didn't I warn you about her weeks ago? If you don't want to court trouble, just give her a box of those beautiful expensive sweets, and then good-bye to all our worries."

Boyne made no answer.

His wife saw his hesitation, and went on:

"It was a rotten trick at Cheltenham, I admit, but it had to be done—just as it must be done in this case. We surely can't afford to take any risks, my dear Bernie! What a good job that you've found out that she suspects—eh?" she remarked. "So she must fade out—and very quickly, too. It's up to you to do the necessary!"

"But the man—this clerk in Mincing Lane—Gerald Durrant. He's a most pertinacious person, it seems. We have, I think, more to fear from him than from the girl," Boyne said.

"Didn't I express doubt a week or so ago, but you assured me that it was all right?" retorted the handsome woman. "Well—what are you going to do?"

"Do! Why, there's only one way—put an end to their inquisitiveness," he replied.

"Do be careful."

Oh, I will be—never fear. But I shall want your assistance, Lilla, and perhaps Ena's too. Neither the man nor the girl is acquainted with either of you, which is one point in our favour."

"Have you thought out any plan?" she asked anxiously.

"I've not completed it yet," he answered.

"There must be no failure, remember," said his wife, betraying considerable anxiety. "What could have aroused the suspicions of this accursed girl, I wonder?"

"Ah! I can't tell. I'm always most careful. But I have confirmed my suspicion that while the girl is in the house the fellow watches outside. He followed me last night, and I led him a pretty good chase up to Hampstead, where I called to see Ted Lyons."

"Ted might be useful—eh?" she exclaimed quickly.

"No. We must keep this affair to ourselves. It's far too dangerous."

"Well, Ena and I will help you. But something ought surely to be done as soon as possible!"

"I quite agree, Lilla. But the question is how shall we act for the best?"

"It's easy to deal with the girl—especially as she's living in your house for a week—but how shall we tackle the man?" she asked.

"That's the difficulty. I don't want anything to happen while she's in my house," was his reply. "I allowed her to stay because I wanted to satisfy myself that she was really spying. Now I've confirmed my suspicions, and we must act."

"Well, at any rate, it's a good thing that we know the truth," the woman answered. "You must have blundered in some way or other, so it is up to you to wriggle out of a very awkward situation."

"It is awkward, I admit," he said, gazing blankly out of the window. "If they got to know the true secret of that upstairs room, it would mean that we should at once be in Queer Street, in more senses than one—shouldn't we?"

"They must not know!" said the woman in a hard, fierce tone. "You will know how to deal with them, Bernard. People who have tried to pry into our private affairs before have, all of them, bitterly regretted it—haven't they?"

Boyne grunted, but made no reply.

"Will you tell Ena?" she asked.

"Not yet. It may only frighten her unduly. When I want her help I'll see her—perhaps to-morrow," was his reply.

"I suppose we ought to have news from Lancaster Gate very soon," she said. "Mrs. Morrison went to tea with Ena yesterday. To-day she has gone back to Brighton, but is due here again to-morrow."

"Yes, we ought to hear of some development soon," he said with a grim smile. "That affair is going all right. It's this girl and her man who are so confoundedly dangerous to our plans."

"You had similar trouble with Aitken a year ago, and you found an easy way out of it, Bernard. No doubt you'll soon think of some means by which an end can be put to their infernal inquisitiveness."

"I have a call to make," he said, rising from his chair suddenly. "I'll be back again this afternoon. I'm going into the City."

And he went out.

At lunch time Marigold met her lover, and it was arranged that, as he would be at the office late that evening, he should not resume his watch until the following evening, neither of them, of course, suspecting that Boyne knew they were keeping him under observation or that he was busy laying a most devilish plan for their undoing.

Gerald Durrant had grown fonder of Marigold than ever, and the pair were now inseparable. He disliked the idea of the girl living in that house of mystery, but she told him that she was in no way afraid, and that she was determined to solve the curious motive of Boyne's double life.

When, at six o'clock, she returned she sat down to tea with her aunt, and later, while she was laying Mr. Boyne's table, he came in, greeting her cheerily, as was his wont.

His attitude towards her was distinctly friendly, for he gave no outward sign of suspicion.

The evening passed uneventfully, for Boyne went out about eight o'clock, and he did not return until long after the old woman and her niece were in bed.

Marigold listened, but only heard him go up to his bedroom and close the door. After that there was no other sound.

Boyne spent part of the following day with Lilla at Pont Street, where he held a long and secret consultation with her, after which he took a taxi to Upper Brook Street and sat with Ena for half an hour, explaining what he had discovered concerning the unwelcome attention which young Durrant and the girl was paying to him.

The Red Widow at once became greatly perturbed.

"But how much can they know?" she gasped, leaning forward in her chair, pale and agitated.

"Very little."

"They know nothing of your upstairs friend—eh?"

"No. But they may suspect."

"Then their suspicion must be at once removed, my dear Bernie!" said the woman, in a decisive voice. "We are, I see, confronted with a very grave peril."

"I agree. Lionel will be wondering why I've not been up to see him since Sunday. I shall go up this afternoon, before the girl comes back from the bank. I've got a lot of stuff to take up to him. He's got no kettle, poor chap!"

"Ah! What a life he must lead," said the woman.

"It is his own fault. He was too curious—and he got the worst of it, as they all do!"

"But he was quite harmless. This fellow Durrant is our enemy."

"And he must be treated as such. I've found out a lot about his movements," said Boyne.

"You quickly find out about people, Bernie. You're really wonderful."

"Not very wonderful, Ena," he laughed. "I simply went a few days ago to Chalmers, the private inquiry agent in Regent Street who has done work for me often. I told him I had lent young Durrant money, and wanted to know something of his habits and of his friends. This morning I had a long confidential report about him. He lives out at Ealing."

"A pity you allowed the girl to stay with her aunt. Why ever did you do so?"

"Well, if she wished to walk into a trap, then it surely wasn't my business to keep her out of it—was it?" he asked, with a sinister smile. "I knew the reason why she had so suddenly been deprived of her room at Wimbledon Park, and allowed her to think that I was a fool."

"She'll no doubt know different ere long," laughed the Red Widow.

Then, opening the door, Boyne satisfied himself that there was no servant in the passage, and returning to her, he began to speak rapidly in a low, tense voice.

"What?" she asked breathlessly, when he had finished. "To-night?"

"Yes, to-night—why not?" he asked. "Wear one of your smartest black dresses. Come round and see Lilla. Then you and she can arrange things."

"But, Bernard! It's a most desperate game!"

"Not more so than any other," he laughed. "A dangerous situation always calls for drastic measures."

"But will the trap be sufficiently well-baited?"

"I'll see to that—never fear! Just act as I tell you and to-morrow we shan't have much to fear from at least one of this inquisitive pair!"

For a few minutes she seemed lost in thought.

"Ah! I see you are hesitating, Ena!" he laughed again.

"I am. It's a terrible plot!"

"Bah! Fancy you saying so—you! who have assisted to bring off so many little affairs that have brought us big money. Surely you're not growing squeamish now, at a moment when we are all in distinct peril?"

"No," she answered with an effort, for it was evident that the plan which he had placed before her had held her horrified. "No, I—I'm not—not at all squeamish, but—well—I'm wondering if we couldn't find some other way out of it."

"None. We're in danger, and we must take precautions to defend ourselves—at once—to-night!"

"Very well," she answered somewhat reluctantly. "I'll go round to Lilla about six."

"When we meet we shall do so as strangers, of course," he said, with a sinister smile. "Look your best—won't you?"

"Very well," she laughed, and five minutes later he sat down at the telephone in the room and spoke to his wife.

"All right, Lilla," he said. "Ena will be with you about six. I've told her exactly what we've arranged. I'm now going back to Hammersmith," and, after hanging up the receiver, he took leave of the Red Widow and went direct to Bridge Place.

Mrs. Felmore was surprised that her master should return so early, for he was at home before five. Marigold had not come in from the office, therefore he sent the deaf old woman out to the post, and, putting on his long white gown, took up to the attic the new tin kettle and some other things. But he did not obtain them from that cupboard in his room. He had purchased duplicates on his way home.

He was not upstairs for more than five minutes—just sufficient to reassure the weird recluse and hand to him the necessities required. Then he came down again, and calmly read the evening paper till his meal was ready.

Marigold did not return before seven, but she left her lover to resume his vigil outside.

At eight o'clock Bernard Boyne went out as usual, and Marigold spent another quiet evening with her aunt, confident that Gerald was keeping a very vigilant eye upon the man of mystery!

Next day at the lunch hour she went eagerly to the little restaurant, but he did not put in an appearance. She wondered why.

On returning to the bank she at once rang up his office, but was informed that he had not been there that day! He had sent his principal a telegram stating that he had been suddenly taken ill, and apologised for his absence. The doctor had said that he could not return for several days.

Making excuse to Mr. Kenyon, the assistant manager, she left the bank at four, and at once went over to Ealing, only to find that his sister had received a telegram late on the previous night, which had been handed in at Charing Cross Post Office and read:

"*Don't worry! Am all right. Returning in two or three days. Writing.—* GERALD."

Further mystified, she at once went back to Hammersmith, where she found a telegram which had arrived for her at eleven o'clock that morning. It had been dispatched from Knightsbridge, and read:

"*Am all right, dear! Do not worry. Have discovered something, but am not returning for a day or two.—*GERRY."

"Is it from Mr. Boyne?" asked her aunt as she watched the girl's face.

"No. Why?" she asked.

"Because Mr. Boyne hasn't been home all night," was her aunt's reply. "I can't think what's happened to him! When I went up this morning to wake him, because I thought he had overslept himself, I found that his bed had not been slept in!"

CHAPTER XVII
"NEWS" FROM LANCASTER GATE

Marigold was naturally much puzzled.

What had her lover discovered? What did he know?

By the varying forms of the telegrams she saw that he had excused himself from the office upon a plea of illness, while really he was working in secret to elucidate the mystery of the hooded man of Hammersmith.

The fact that Boyne had been absent that night and had not yet returned, did not arouse her curiosity, for she concluded that Gerry had been following him ever since the previous evening.

She relied upon her lover's cleverness and ingenuity. The changing of his clothes showed her that he was resourceful. She admired him for it.

So she took her tea with her aunt, and afterwards laid Mr. Boyne's table in eager readiness for his return.

He came in and greeted her as cheerily as usual.

"Tell Mrs. Felmore that I expect she's been wondering where I've been all this time. But I went out to Loughton, in Essex, to see a friend last night, and I stayed there. Tell her so, Miss Marigold, will you? And now for my supper! I'm horribly hungry!"

He ate his meal, yet not by any means in the manner of a hungry man. He only toyed with it, for, a matter of fact, he had left Pont Street half an hour before, having taken leave of the Red Widow and his wife, whose faces had borne grim smiles of complete satisfaction.

That night as Marigold lay awake, unable to sleep, she became obsessed by the one idea that she ought to leave the house of mystery and return to Wimbledon Park.

Gerald, by his mysterious message to her, had evidently got upon the track of something, therefore it was useless for her to remain any longer in that strange atmosphere of doubt and fear.

Boyne had retired, and though she remained on the alert until the first streak of dawn shone through the blinds, she heard no movement to arouse her suspicion.

Next day, when she came down into the kitchen, she told her aunt that she was returning home. So, taking her blouse-case, she left before Mr. Boyne came downstairs.

"Marigold has gone to the bank, sir," said Mrs. Felmore when she placed Boyne's coffee and kippers upon the table. "She left word that she thanks you very much for allowing her to stay here, but she couldn't encroach on your kind hospitality any longer."

"Oh!" exclaimed Boyne in surprise. "She's gone—eh?"

"Yes, sir. She went out a quarter of an hour ago. She waited to see if you came down—but she had to go."

Boyne grunted, and remarked something beneath his breath—words that the deaf woman, even with her expert lip-reading eyes, could not understand.

Marigold had slipped safely out of the way. The fact filled him with intense chagrin. What did it portend?

"At least Durrant's activity is at an end!" he growled deeply to himself. "Now we have to deal with this girl. For the present nobody can know of the whereabouts of Gerald Durrant. When they do—I hope the peril will be over!"

And he swallowed his coffee with the gusto and satisfaction of a man who had made a most complete coup, and from whose mind some great weight had been lifted.

An hour later he entered the Hammersmith Post Office and telephoned to the Red Widow.

"Any news, Ena?" he asked as he sat in one of the boxes.

"Yes. Augusta spoke to me half an hour ago. I'm going round to Lancaster Gate at eleven. She's taken ill. A pity, isn't it?"

"Sorry to hear that!" he replied in a grim voice. "I'll see you at Pont Street at seven—eh?"

"Yes. I'll run round," Ena answered. "I've just been through to Lilla. I wonder what can be the matter with poor Augusta? A chill, perhaps—eh? Poor lady! But I hope it isn't serious."

"I hope not. Good-bye for the present."

And then the honest, hard-working collector of insurance premiums of the poor of Hammersmith went forth upon his daily round, trudging from street to street, knocking or ringing at the doors of the insured.

He made a call in Dalling Road, just beyond the railway arch, and then, proceeding up the thoroughfare, consulted his pocket account-book. Close to Chiswick High Road he made a further call, where he signed the book for the weekly premium.

Presently he halted at a small and very poor-looking house in the Devonport Road, a turning off the Goldhawk Road, where he rang at the door. At the windows were curtains blackened by the London smoke, for the whole neighbourhood was one of genteel poverty, but of despair.

An ugly, but cleanly dressed old woman answered, and, seeing him, knit her brows.

"Ah! Come in, Mr. Boyne!" she said, and the collector of premiums entered.

Five minutes later he came out, the old woman following him. He was evidently not himself, for usually his was a kindly nature towards the poor. But that day his manner was rough and uncouth. Something had upset him.

"Well, I'm sorry, Mrs. Pentreath," he said in a loud voice. "But, you see, it isn't in my hands. I'm only a humble servant of the company—an ill-paid servant who gets just a living wage upon the premiums he collects. You've had time to pay, you know, and if you can't pay up this week— well, the policy must lapse. You've been given notice of it for six weeks. The company has been very lenient with you. Other companies wouldn't have been so lenient."

"But my poor Bertha! She's come home from service, and is in bed with consumption. I have to look after her and try to give her the nourishment Doctor James orders. It isn't my fault that I haven't paid you. It really isn't."

"I can't help that," replied Boyne roughly. "Your insurance policy must lapse—that's all.

"And after fifteen years that I've paid regularly each week!" exclaimed the poor woman in dismay.

"Well, it isn't my fault, I tell you. I'm not the company," was his harsh reply.

"And my poor Bertha so ill. It's cruel—it's inhuman, I say!" she shouted in a shrill voice.

Boyne only smiled grimly. He was not the kindly man of other days.

"It probably is so," he replied, turning away from the door. "But it's our insurance business; and business is business, after all!"

"Yes!" retorted the poor woman. "You people are robbing the poor— that's what it is! And after fifteen years! Why, I've paid your company more in that time than what they would have paid to bury my Bertha!"

At a small house in the Loftus Road he knocked three times, and a dwarfed, red-eyed girl at last opened the door.

"Poor mother's dead, Mr. Boyne! Didn't you see the blinds?" she asked.

"Dead!" he exclaimed, looking at the little window of the sitting-room. "Get your book."

"I'll go and get it," was the girl's reply. "Mother died late last night. The doctor says it's heart disease."

"All right. Give me the book," he said brutally. "I suppose we'll have to pay. You paid up last week, didn't you?"

"Yes, sir, I paid you—and you'll find it down," the girl said, and, disappearing, she presently returned with the insurance book.

The house-to-house visits of the insurance collector of those fat dividend paying companies who insure the lives of the lower classes are truly fraught with many strange dramas and stirring tales of poverty and misfortune.

While Bernard Boyne was on his weary round, Ena Pollen alighted from a taxi at the private hotel in Lancaster Gate, a big, old-fashioned house which for years had been known to country visitors to London as a quiet and excellent place in which to stay.

The young man-servant who opened the door told her that Mrs. Morrison was upstairs. The proprietor's wife met her in the hall, and, in response to the Red Widow's inquiry, said:

"Mrs. Morrison hasn't been very well for a couple of days. She was taken ill last night, so I called my doctor—Doctor Tressider—and he came to see her. He seems puzzled. He can't make out at present what's the matter with her. He's calling again to-night. She came over very ill when she returned from Brighton."

"I'll go upstairs," said Mrs. Pollen. "It is most unfortunate, isn't it? She's only here in town for a short time, and now she's taken ill like this. I do hope it's nothing serious."

"Oh, no. I asked Doctor Tressider, and he thinks it is simply a little stomach trouble. To-morrow she'll be better," was the woman's reply.

So Ena ascended the stairs, and, after tapping at the door, entered the neat little bedroom on the second floor.

"Well, dear!" she exclaimed cheerily as she entered. "I couldn't let the day pass without coming to see you. Whatever is the matter?"

"I really don't know, Ena," replied Mrs. Morrison of Carsphairn. "I felt so ill in the train coming up to Victoria that I had great difficulty in getting back here."

"But the doctor says you'll be all right to-morrow," said Ena.

"I feel awfully ill," replied the other feebly. "I seem so feverish—hot at one moment and cold at another."

"No, no," said Mrs. Pollen cheerily. "You'll be all right, never fear. When one feels feverish one's temperature is generally below normal. I do hope these people are looking after you all right?"

"Oh, yes, they do. I have no complaint to make on that score. You recommended me here, and I must say that I'm most comfortable. But what worries me is my visit up North."

"Don't bother about that," laughed the other. "Get well first. Write and tell them you can't come."

"I wish you would do it for me. Pen and paper are over there," said the sick woman, whose eyes glistened strangely.

"No; you must do it," replied Ena quickly. She had a reason. "If I were to write to them they might think it strange. You are not too ill to write. I'll get you the pad."

And, carrying it to her on the bed, she induced Mrs. Morrison to write two letters to her friends—letters which she duly posted when she got outside.

"The doctor doesn't seem to know what is the matter with me," the invalid said in a weak voice after she had laid down her fountain pen. "My head is so terribly bad—and my throat too."

"What time is he coming again?"

"To-night, I think. I hope so."

"My dear, it's only a chill," Ena said with comforting cheerfulness. "You'll be all right in a day or two. You've been in a draught, perhaps."

"Ah! but my head! It seems as though it must burst. At times I can't think. All my senses seem blurred."

"Did you tell the doctor that?"

"Yes. And it seemed to puzzle him more than ever. I hope I'm not going to have a bad illness."

"Of course not," laughed Ena. "You'll be better in a day or so. Remain quiet, and I'll run in to-morrow morning to see how you are. If you're worse, tell them to ring me up. I'm just going round to the Davidsons. They will be most distressed to hear of your sudden illness."

The widow of Carsphairn turned over on her pillow and moaned slightly. Her face was flushed, and it was evident to Ena that the last words she had uttered the sick woman had not understood.

So she took her leave, and on descending the stairs to the wide hall, again encountered the proprietor's wife.

"My friend Mrs. Morrison seems very unwell," said Ena. "I can't make it out at all. I do hope the doctor will discover what is the matter with her."

"Doctor Tressider is my own doctor," replied the woman. "He'll be here again before dinner time, and I hope he won't find anything really very wrong."

"Well, whatever he says, would you mind letting me know over the 'phone?" asked Ena, taking out her visiting-card, upon which was printed her telephone number.

"Certainly I will," was the reply.

"And if there is anything serious I'll come round at once," she said.

So they parted, and Ena hailed a taxi outside, and returned to Upper Brook Street well satisfied with her morning's work.

CHAPTER XVIII
THE COUP AND ITS CONSEQUENCE

Next day passed, but though Ena remained at home in a high state of anxiety, she received no message from Lancaster Gate.

At eight o'clock she rang up, and spoke to the proprietress of the hotel.

"Mrs. Morrison is certainly not quite so well as she was yesterday, but though Doctor Tressider has been twice to-day he has not yet been able to diagnose the complaint."

"Is she in pain?" asked Mrs. Pollen sympathetically.

"No. She does not complain. But no doubt we shall know more to-morrow."

"Very well. Please tell her I inquired, and to-morrow, about eleven, I'll call and see her again."

And, having rung off, she spoke to Lilla, telling her of the conversation.

"You'll go to-morrow and see her, my dear," urged Boyne's wife. "Bernard is here. I'll tell him."

"What about the girl?" asked Ena.

"Oh, for the present she's all right. She's gone back to Wimbledon. The telegrams have satisfied her."

"Right! Then I'll see you to-morrow after I've been to Lancaster Gate," said the Red Widow, and then they broke off the conversation.

"Well, the doctor doesn't know yet what's the matter," Lilla afterwards said to Boyne, who was sitting in the handsome drawing-room.

"Oh! he will to-morrow—never fear!" was the man's grim reply. "He must be a duffer if he doesn't recognise the symptoms. I expected him to know yesterday."

"You thought we should have had news on Wednesday, and it's now Friday."

"Yes. But delay is rather a good sign," he said. "Did you tell Ena about the nursing home?"

"Yes; I did so yesterday."

"I've heard that Miss Propert's, out at Golder's Green, is quite a good place. Nobody connected with it has any knowledge of us."

"I told her that. And she agreed. She is rather afraid that some of Mrs. Morrison's friends may come up from Brighton, and she is in no way anxious to meet them."

"No! She mustn't do so!" declared Boyne. "She must take good care that no friends are at Lancaster Gate when she calls."

"Good! I'll tell her that over the 'phone presently."

"And also tell her not to take a too eager interest in her—I mean, no interest further than that of a comparatively freshly made friend," he said; and afterwards they went out to a theatre together.

Next morning, just before eleven, as Ena Pollen was contemplating speaking with Mrs. Morrison's hotel, the proprietor's wife rang up.

"Mrs. Pollen," she said, "I'm very sorry to give you bad news about your friend. Doctor Tressider has just been here, and says that she is suffering from diphtheria!"

"Oh! I'm so sorry!" cried the Red Widow. "How very unfortunate! Are any other friends there?"

"No. But I believe somebody is coming up from Brighton this afternoon."

"Very well," said Ena. "I'll take a taxi and come round now."

This she did. Pleading that she might become infected, she did not ascend to Mrs. Morrison's room, but sat in the little office of the proprietor's wife.

"Of course she can't remain here," said the woman. "It isn't fair to my other visitors."

"Of course not," Ena agreed. "She must go at once to a nursing home. A friend of mine had diphtheria about a year ago, and went to a place somewhere at Golder's Green. I think Prosser or Potter was the name of the person who runs it. We might perhaps find it in the telephone directory. I think that was the name—but I'm not quite sure. Poor Augusta! I'm so sorry, but I really think it would be unwise of me to go in and see her—don't you?"

"I quite agree," replied the proprietor's wife, and, taking down the telephone directory, she began to search for the name, but could not find it.

At last, after some minutes, she exclaimed:

"Ah! Here it is. Miss Propert's nursing home. Yes, Golder's Green! Here is the number. I'll telephone and ask if they have a room vacant."

Five minutes later it was fixed. Miss Propert had promised to send an ambulance at once, and soon afterwards the Red Widow was round at Pont Street reporting to Lilla all that had taken place, while early that same afternoon the patient had already been transferred to the nursing home, where she had been promised by the unsuspecting matron "every attention."

As the days passed Marigold Ramsay travelled each morning from Wimbledon Park to the City, and sat each luncheon hour in the same little restaurant, but alone.

She was sorely puzzled why Gerald did not write to her. Without doubt he had gone somewhere to follow up a clue concerning the mystery man of Hammersmith, but she felt hurt that he had not written to tell her of his whereabouts.

Time after time she took out his telegram, which she carried in her big bag-purse, and re-read it:

"*Am all right, dear. Do not worry. Have discovered something, but am not returning for a day or two.* —GERRY."

The "day or two" had elapsed. He told her not to worry, therefore she tried to obey him. Still, it was strange that he did not send her a line.

Twice she called at his office in Mincing Lane, but she was told by a female clerk that Mr. Durrant had not returned. Nothing more had been heard of him, except that he was away at home ill.

Marigold smiled within herself at the excuse her lover had given for his absence, and wondered hour by hour what he had discovered concerning Mr. Boyne.

She went over to Hammersmith and had tea with her aunt. From her she learned that her employer had been at home each night. The only night he had been absent was the night of Gerald's disappearance.

She even contrived to get a glimpse of the interior of that cupboard in Mr. Boyne's bedroom, but the groceries intended for the poor widow of Notting Hill Gate were still there intact, as well as the tea-kettle and the bowl.

What had taken Gerald away?

For three days her anxiety increased, when on the fourth evening, on her return to Wimbledon, she found a telegram from him. It had been dispatched from the post-office in Bristol Road, Birmingham, and read:

"*Returning very soon, dearest. Remain patient. Tell my sister. Love.*— GERRY."

Time after time she read it with complete satisfaction, and afterwards she went out to Ealing and showed it to her lover's sister.

"That takes a great weight off my mind, Marigold," said Gerald's sister. "Still, his sudden disappearance seems very strange. I wonder why he's gone away—and why he's in Birmingham?"

"Yes," replied the girl. "It does seem curious, but think I know the reason."

"What is it?" asked his sister anxiously.

"A secret reason," was Marigold's reply. "I'm sorry that I can't tell you—not unless he gives me permission."

"What—is anything wrong?" asked the young woman.

"Oh, nothing wrong with Gerald—not at all. Only he is trying to find out something—that's all. And until he is successful I don't think he wants anyone to know his intentions."

"Well, I hope he's made it right at his office. Employers don't like men who pretend to be ill at home and go away."

"No doubt he has. Gerald isn't a fool," the girl replied, a little piqued at his sister's words, and very soon afterwards she left for home.

The message from Birmingham allayed her anxiety to a very great extent. When once Gerald took up any matter he never left it until it was complete. He was the very essence of business, and his principal held him in high esteem on account of his method and his pertinacity. Marigold knew that. He was following some secret clue concerning the hooded man of Bridge Place, and it seemed as though he feared to put anything concerning it into writing.

That night as she lay awake she reflected that the message was indeed very gratifying, yet at the same time, she found herself wondering why he had not written her just a few brief words.

She, however, kept her own counsel, feeling confident that Gerald would as soon as possible return to tell her what he had found out.

The fact that the store of food in Boyne's bedroom was still there negatived the idea that it was intended for any person concealed in the locked room above. On thinking it all over, she began to doubt whether that curious cry was really human, or did it only exist in her imagination?

Next day she went to the bank as usual, but life was very dreary without Gerald's smiling face. He was her ideal of the fine courteous man, strong, and devoid of that effeminacy which, alas! too often characterises the temporary officers who so gallantly assisted in winning the war. He had neither pose, drawl, nor affectation, as is so common in and around Fenchurch Street. He dressed quietly, and his manners were gentlemanly without being obtrusive. He spoke little and listened always. In Marigold's eyes he was the type of a perfect modern gentleman—as indeed he was.

City life, with its morning rush to business from the suburbs and its evening scramble for a seat in 'bus, train or tram, is to the business girl a wearing existence. The tubes, with their queux, the trains with their packed compartments, the 'buses with their boorish attendants, and the trams crowded to suffocation with either rain-wet or perspiring humanity, are part of the life of a London business girl. Yet she is always merry and bright, for she takes things as they come and thrives upon a gobbled breakfast or a belated home-coming.

Marigold Ramsay was typical of the London female bank clerk—eager, reliable, assiduous at her work, which consisted of poring over big ledgers all day beneath a green-shaded electric light until the figures—units, tens, hundreds, thousands, tens of thousands, and hundreds of thousands—danced before her tired eyes ere she closed her book and put on her hat to return home.

On the night following the receipt of that gratifying message, she rushed back to Wimbledon wondering if any further telegram awaited her.

But there was none. In disappointment she sat down to her evening meal, the one problem in her mind being the whereabouts of the young man who was her lover and who had so mysteriously left her side and disappeared.

He could not be following Boyne, for the latter was living quite calmly his usual uneventful life, therefore, if he were not following him, why could he not write to her and explain?

That point sorely perplexed her.

Meanwhile Ena Pollen telephoned twice a day to Golder's Green to inquire how her friend Mrs. Morrison progressed, and on each occasion the matron would answer her, but the news was of increasing gravity.

She sent kind messages, but the matron expressed regret that the patient was too ill to be given them.

On the evening when Marigold had sped back to Wimbledon hoping for a further telegram, Miss Propert had, after telling the Red Widow how critical was Mrs. Morrison's condition, added that some relatives had come up from Brighton.

"Unfortunately, the doctor will not allow anyone to see her," she went on. "Only this evening I have had a telegram from her sister in Scotland saying she is on her way to London, but as she gives no address, I am unable to stop her, so her journey will be useless."

"Useless? Why?" asked Ena.

"Well—I'm sorry to tell you that the doctor who saw her an hour ago holds out but little hope of her recovery. She has diphtheria in its most virulent form."

"Oh! How terrible!" cried Ena. "But is it really so very serious?"

"Yes. There is no use disguising the fact. It is a most critical case."

"But, surely, there is no immediate danger?" she asked, full of concern.

"The critical period will be within the next twenty-four hours," came the reply. "If she gets over to-morrow night, she will probably recover."

Ena Pollen held her breath, while her brows narrowed, and she made a strange grimace.

"Well, Miss Propert, you won't fail to let me know how my friend is—will you?"

"Of course not," was the reply. "I hope she will be better to-morrow morning. But—well, personally, I entertain but little hope. I have never seen a worse case of diphtheria."

Ena hung up the receiver, and crossing the room, took a long sniff at her smelling-salts.

Then, going back to the telephone, she rang up Lilla, and said briefly:

"Our poor friend is very bad indeed. I'll let you know how she is in the morning. Is Bernard there?"

"No; he's just gone back," answered her friend.

"Well, I want you both to dine here to-morrow night. Will you?"

"Why?"

"You know the reason—*surely*!"

"Oh, yes—yes! Very well, dear. At half-past seven."

So that was agreed.

Next morning, just before noon, Boyne called at Pont Street and learned from Lilla—who had just spoken to Ena—that Mrs. Morrison of Carsphairn was in an extremely critical condition.

"H'm!" grunted her husband. "Then all goes as it should—eh? No other acute disease presents so great a liability to sudden death as diphtheria. I suppose the doctor, whoever he is, has been all along examining the patient's heart for any indication of an approaching catastrophe."

"But sudden death can't take place—can it?" asked Lilla.

"Oh, yes," replied her husband in a voice of authority. "The more insidious forms of sudden death from diphtheria take place through the nervous system and heart. In such a case the pulse beats only twenty or thirty a minute—and that is probably what has aroused the doctor's fears."

"But, according to Ena, she hasn't a very bad throat."

"That may be so," he said, speaking in the way of a medical man. "She may have an extension of the false membrane into the air passage, which would block the larynx trachea or bronchi, which is always gradual, and may be fatal. But if the doctor has come to the conclusion that she's in a very bad way, I should think that the end will come this evening."

"You'll dine at Ena's—eh?"

"Of course I will. I'll be there just after seven," he said, and, after leisurely finishing a cigarette, he left her.

Just before half-past seven he entered Ena Pollen's flat, where Lilla was already seated in the drawing-room. He wore a simple blue serge suit, for that night he had come straight from Hammersmith, and had not dressed to go to a restaurant or the theatre.

"Well?" he asked the Red Widow. "Anything fresh?"

"Nothing. I telephoned to Golder's Green an hour ago, and found Miss Propert was most despondent."

"Poor dear!" laughed Lilla. "What a pity! Her bill will be paid all right—so she needn't fret!"

Presently they sat down to a very pleasant little dinner, where, with sardonic laughter, the trio of death-dealers lifted their glasses of champagne to "dear Augusta's speedy recovery."

After dinner they returned to the drawing-room, where they took their liqueurs and coffee, all three being in excellent spirits.

The only serious moment was when the Red Widow suddenly remarked:

"I don't half like the situation concerning that young fellow Durrant! Do you know, I feel some strange presage of evil—I mean that we may have made a slip there."

"Slip!" laughed Boyne derisively. "Nothing of the kind, my dear Ena! I saw to that all right. And surely you can trust me?"

"But suppose we have?"

"No need to worry further about him. He won't trouble us any more."

"The next person to be silenced is that girl," Lilla said in a hard voice.

"Yes," was Boyne's slow reply. "I think I've formed a plan which will be just as successful as that we carried out concerning her too inquisitive lover."

And as he spoke, he blew a cloud of smoke from his lips and watched it curl towards the ceiling.

Suddenly—it was then about ten o'clock—almost as the words fell from his lips, the telephone bell rang sharply.

All three started.

"Ah!" gasped Ena, springing up. "There you are! At last!"

"Yes," she replied, taking up the receiver. Then, listening, she exclaimed: "Oh! you, Miss Propert—well? Oh! How dreadful!—how very sad! She passed away ten minutes ago! Thank you so much for telling me. I'm so sorry—so very sorry!"

And she replaced the receiver.

"You look sorry!" laughed Boyne. "Really, it is most distressing to think that we shall very soon draw ten thousand pounds!" he added mockingly, whereat the two women laughed gaily, for the coup so elaborately prepared had at last been brought off!

CHAPTER XIX
WHAT HAPPENED TO GERALD

The days passed, and Marigold, hearing nothing further from Gerald, called again at Mincing Lane, and there learned that they had not heard again from young Durrant.

A clerk had been sent over to Ealing to inquire about him, but had returned with the information that, instead of being ill, he had not been seen by his sister.

"The firm at once suspected something wrong with the books," said the female clerk of whom she made the inquiry, "but Mr. Durrant was such an honest, straightforward young man that we all ridiculed the idea."

"Have the books been examined?" asked Marigold breathlessly.

"Oh, yes; and nothing has been found wrong."

The girl drew a sigh of relief.

She then showed the clerk the telegram she had received from Birmingham, and she, in turn, promised to show it to the principal when he came in.

Marigold Ramsay walked down Mincing Lane to Fenchurch Street in gloom and despair. She returned to the bank and sat at her books, unable to work, unable to do anything, save to wonder why Gerald had so suddenly left her. Yet he had bidden her not to worry over him and had promised to return.

That evening she went over to Hammersmith, and her aunt, noticing how pale and worried she looked, inquired the reason, asking:

"Have you heard yet from Mr. Durrant?"

"No, auntie. Unfortunately, I haven't, but I'm expecting to hear every day."

"Funny he went away like that, wasn't it?" the deaf old woman remarked, though inwardly she suspected that there had been some quarrel between them, and that he had left her in consequence.

"Yes," replied the girl faintly. Then she asked after Mr. Boyne.

"Oh! he's been away four days now. He said he was going into Wales on some insurance business, and would be away a week or perhaps ten days."

"Unusual for him to go away, isn't it?" Marigold remarked.

"Yes. He's never been away for more than a week together in all the time I've been with him."

The girl left Hammersmith early, and, returning to Wimbledon Park, sat at her window and wept for a long time before retiring to rest. To her the world was empty and hopeless without Gerald.

What had she done, she wondered, that he should have left her in that fashion. That he was following Boyne was a mere excuse, she felt sure. It irritated her to think that he should try to deceive her. What was he doing in Birmingham? If there were reasons why he did not wish to return to London, then why did he not give her his address, and then she could easily have run up to see him.

The more she thought it over the more mystified did she become.

The mystery was increased three days later when, on returning from the City, she found a telegram on the table in the narrow hall.

Her heart leapt as she tore it open.

It had been sent from Paris, of all places, and read:

"*Sorry could not write, dear. Do not worry. Shall be back soon. Have wired to the office. Love.*—GERALD."

"Love!—Gerald!" she repeated aloud to herself. "Oh! why does he not give me an address, so that I can write to him? It's cruel—very cruel of him to keep me in suspense like this!" she cried in a frenzy of despair.

She ate sparingly in the little dining-room of the jerry-built villa—for nowhere is the jerry-builder more in evidence than in Wimbledon Park, with his white-painted gables and his white-painted balconies to his six-roomed houses. But let us not misunderstand. It is best for the workers—the brains and backbone of England—to live in smiling houses, even though jerry-built, than in many of those grey, rain-sodden houses of the Midlands and the North, where the "knocker-up" pursues his calling each dawn and the factory hooter sounds all too early.

Personally, the writer here declares that he has no love for the capitalist. The latter has too often, ever since the Early Victorian days, been either a swindler or an aristocrat of bad intentions, and the jerry-builder was the natural outcome of his parting with his estate.

Poor Marigold! She could go no farther in the maze of doubt and uncertainty.

A dozen times that night she re-read the mysterious, but unconvincing, message. She was a girl of high intelligence, or she would not have been employed by the bank. The whole affair puzzled her, as it would indeed have puzzled anybody.

Next day after her luncheon she went round again to Mincing Lane, and made inquiry regarding the missing man.

The same girl told her that the principal had received a mysterious wire from Paris.

"I saw the telegram," she said. "It was from Paris, and was quite abrupt, saying that he would probably return in a week or so."

"But what does it all mean?" asked the distressed girl.

"I really don't know," replied the other girl. "Mr. Durrant's gone away, and that's all!"

That night Marigold went over to Ealing, and to Gerald's sister she showed the telegram. It puzzled her sorely.

"Whatever can Gerald be doing in Paris?" she exclaimed. "Why could he not write to us, eh?"

"I don't know," was the reply of the unnerved girl. "I think he ought to send us some address."

"But he may do so later," replied his sister. "Gerald is a man of business. He would realise how troubled we all are."

"He seems to have faded out of existence," said the girl, seated in the front parlour of the neat little villa of the neat suburban road.

"Yes," said his sister. "He certainly does. I await a letter each morning, but none comes."

"But what can he be doing in Paris?" queried Marigold. "Without a doubt, he has lost the confidence of his firm. He pretended to be lying ill here, and they have found out that he isn't ill at all!"

"Yes. The other day a middle-aged man came to see him, but I was forced to admit that he wasn't here—that he was missing," replied Gerald's sister.

Marigold went home utterly dispirited. What could she do? It was useless to go to the police and raise a hue and cry regarding a man who, from time to time, telegraphed to his employers and to her that he was on the point of returning. So she was compelled to wait.

Gerald Durrant had disappeared. He had sent her messages, it is true, messages of comfort, yet when she argued within herself, she saw that he ought, at least, to have given her some address to which she could reply by letter or by telegram.

True, Boyne was absent. But he had only been absent for a few days, while her lover had been missing very much longer.

Four more days of blank despair crept slowly by. Seated beneath her green-shaded light at the bank, with her great ledger before her, Marigold reckoned up the columns of figures mechanically, and handed them to be checked. They were accounts of all classes of merchants, mostly of profiteers, firms who had made fortunes out of the valour and blood of the gallant fellows who had given their lives for Britain. She felt so unhappy without her lover. Gerald, who had directed those investigations concerning the hooded man who was her aunt's employer, had disappeared with startling suddenness, yet he had assured her that he was following some mysterious clue.

The latter she had proved, by reason of the knowledge of Boyne's movements, to be non-existent. Was her lover deceiving her? That suspicion caused her the greatest irritation and annoyance.

That evening she sauntered along Pont Street, and looked up at the red-brick house which Boyne had entered on that well-remembered night. But the place was in complete darkness, save for a light in the servants' quarters.

Then again she went to Bridge Place, and learned from the old deaf woman that her master had not yet returned.

"He's having a very nice long holiday," said Mrs. Felmore. "And he deserves it, too—a-tramping about Hammersmith all day and in all weathers, as he does."

Three weeks went past, but no further word had come from Gerald, either to his principal, his sister, or to his well-beloved.

Gerald Durrant had, truth to tell, met with some strange and startling adventures since the night of his disappearance.

In the darkness on that well-remembered night he was walking along the Kensington Road towards Knightsbridge, following Boyne at a respectful distance, and keeping a wary eye upon him, without arousing any suspicion as he naturally believed.

While passing the railings of Kensington Gardens, close to Queen's Gate, he saw a female figure lying upon the pavement with a lady bending over her concernedly.

Hastening up, he found both ladies to be well dressed, and inquired what had occurred.

"Oh, dear!" cried the elder lady, in great distress. "My sister has just slipped down on a piece of banana peel, I think, and she's broken her ankle. She can't move, and she doesn't speak. She has fainted. I—I wonder, sir, if you would be so kind as to call me a taxi."

"Certainly I will," replied Gerald, with his usual gallantry. "If you'll stay here, I'll go back to the rank. I passed it a few minutes ago, and there was a taxi there."

So he dashed back, got into the cab, and was soon on the spot where the lady, who had recovered consciousness, was standing on one foot, unable to put the other to the ground.

"It's so extremely kind of you," said the elder lady, while the injured one expressed faint thanks. Then, assisted by the driver, the lady was seated in the conveyance.

"I really don't know how I shall get her up the stairs," exclaimed the elder woman. "We live in a flat up at Hampstead and we have no hall-porter."

Gerald reflected a second, and suddenly recollected that Boyne was now out of sight, so that by that unfortunate accident he was prevented from further following him.

"I shall be very pleased to accompany you, and give you what assistance I can," he said. "May I get in?"

"Certainly. It's too kind of you," the injured lady declared. "I fear we are encroaching upon your time, but the taxi can bring you back to wherever you want to go."

So Gerald got in, while the elder lady gave the man an address at Hampstead—some mansions, the name of which he did not catch, for, at the moment, he was in conversation with her sister. All he recollected were the words:

"It's close to Hampstead tube station."

Next moment they drove off, whereupon the elder lady introduced herself as Mrs. Evans, and her sister she said was Miss Mayne.

"We live together," she went on. "My husband was unfortunately killed on the Somme, so we are companions for each other."

Meanwhile Miss Mayne was evidently suffering extreme pain.

"I'm so sorry, dear," her sister exclaimed. "But as soon as we get home, I'll ring up for Doctor Trueman. He'll no doubt soon set it right."

"Can you move your ankle, Miss Mayne?" asked Gerald, who had, in turn, already given the two ladies his name.

"Unfortunately, no—not in the least. To try to move it causes me excruciating pain. I really don't know what I shall do."

"Oh! Surgeons nowadays are wonderful," exclaimed Gerald cheerily. "Probably it is only a simple sprain. At least, let us hope so."

So completely engaged in conversation was Gerald, that he did not notice along what thoroughfare they were travelling. Indeed, the driver had taken an intricate route behind Regent's Park, a district quite unknown to the young man.

From the ladies he learned that they had been dining with a lady living in Phillimore Place, and were on their way back to Knightsbridge tube station on their return home when the accident happened. That they were refined, well-bred ladies was unquestionable, therefore he was genuinely concerned.

At last the taxi stopped before the entrance to a large block of inartistic-looking flats, and with difficulty Miss Mayne descended. Then, assisted by the driver and Gerald, she, with great difficulty, ascended to the first floor, while her sister opened the door with her latch-key, and switched on the light.

Within it was a cosy, well-furnished abode, just as one would expect to be the home of two refined women of good position.

Mrs. Evans paid the driver, giving him half a sovereign over his fare, and saying:

"I shall want you to take this gentleman back to the West End presently. So wait!"

"Very well, mum," replied the man, pleased with his tip, who then retired.

Then, turning to Gerald, she said:

"You'll stay a few minutes, won't you? I'll telephone to the doctor." This she did, the telephone being out in the hall, and while he sat with Miss Mayne in the small drawing-room, he heard her sister in conversation with Doctor Trueman.

"He'll be here in about a quarter of an hour!" she exclaimed, as she re-entered the room. "How fortunate, dear, to find him in!"

"Yes. I—— Oh! I do hope he'll give me something to dull this terrible pain'" replied the other.

"No doubt he will," said Gerald encouragingly. "It is too bad of people to throw fruit peel about the pavements. I've had more than one narrow escape from falling myself."

"It's positively criminal!" declared Mrs. Evans, with warmth. "Of course you'll stop now, and see what he says. Mr. Durrant," she went on, "I'm only too happy to have been of service to you."

"You'll have something?" she suggested. "I'm just going to get my sister a little brandy, and I'll get you a whisky and soda."

"No, thanks—all the same," Gerald replied. "The fact is I never drink whisky."

"Then a glass of port wine," she laughed gaily. "You won't refuse that—have it, to please me, won't you?"

He tried to protest, but she overruled him, and in the end he was forced to accept the glass of wine which a few minutes later she brought him upon a small silver salver, together with her sister's liqueur glass of old brandy.

She took nothing herself, but stood chatting as Durrant and her sister sipped their glasses.

"That's some very old port that was lately given to me by a friend," she explained. "Being a woman, I know nothing of wines, but we had a man dining here with us the other night who pronounced it first-class."

"Yes," Gerald said. "It is excellent, though I, too, have no knowledge of wines, which I always think is generally pretended save in the case of men with acute palates who are in the import trade. The man who to-day can sip a glass and tell its vintage is a *rara avis*," he declared.

Mrs. Evans agreed with him.

She watched him drain his glass with satisfaction, and then urged him to have a second one. But he refused, for, as a matter of fact, he found a strange sensation creeping over him. Though he did not mention it, being too polite, he felt across his eyes a slow, but increasing, blindness. Objects seemed to be receding from his gaze. The muscles of his throat seemed to be contracting, and he felt his cheeks hot and flushed.

He tried to stir himself in his chair, but he seemed paralysed. He could not move!

He endeavoured to speak, to tell the two ladies of his sudden seizure, but his tongue refused to articulate a word.

In his desperate efforts to ask them to call assistance, his hands pawed the air convulsively, and then, of a sudden, he felt himself collapsing, and all became blank.

Meanwhile the two women were watching him intently, and the instant they satisfied themselves that he was unconscious, Miss Mayne—who was really Lilla Braybourne, sat where she was, while Mrs. Evans, who was Ena Pollen, the Red Widow—jumped up from her chair, saying eagerly:

"All's well up till now! I must tell Bernie."

She dashed to the telephone, and, asking for a number, spoke rapidly:

"Lilla speaking," she said. "Bernie. He's here, and he's been taken suddenly ill. You'd better come round at once."

She listened. Then she said:

"Right—you'll get here in a quarter of an hour. He's asleep now!"

Then the pretended invalid and her pseudo-sister, leaving Gerald in the drawing-room, where he had collapsed so suddenly after drinking the glass of "doctored" port, went into the dining-room and mixed themselves a stiff brandy and soda each.

Afterwards the Red Widow, descending to where the taxi was waiting, gave the man another ten shillings, and said:

"The gentleman has changed his mind. He's staying here."

"All right, mum," the man replied. "Thank you very much. Good-night."

Starting his engine, he drove away well satisfied.

CHAPTER XX
THE ROOM OF EVIL

A quarter of an hour later Bernard Boyne stood in the room where Gerald Durrant lay back in the arm-chair, pale as death, quite unconscious.

"So you tried to get the better of me, my young friend, did you?" he laughed, as he stood before the inanimate figure. "But you dropped into the trap just as I intended. I could easily put you out of the way, you infernal young prig, but it might be dangerous."

"No, no!" cried Ena anxiously. "The body would be found. And Scotland Yard may possibly find traces of us. No! Carry out your plan—telegrams, a motor-car journey, a pretty story—and good-bye-ee!"

"Yes. But this fellow, and the girl who is in love with him, are distinct dangers, remember!"

"True. But it was the girl who aroused his suspicions. Send her underground, if you like, and as soon as you like, for none of us have any love for her, have we?"

"Ena," he said, his manner suddenly changing; "an idea regarding the girl, Marigold, has just occurred to me—one that cannot be investigated, and nothing can be brought up against us. Leave her to me!"

"Oh, we will, Bernie! But recollect, she must have a dose—and go out. That's the only way to put the tombstone over this affair. We don't want any unwelcome inquiries, or any resistance by the insurance company."

"Don't fret, my dear Ena. We shan't have any real trouble, I assure you. We are now dealing with it in advance." Then, turning to his wife, he exclaimed: "Those necessary telegrams? You have them all ready. Get busy, and send them. I've arranged with Jimmy, in Birmingham, and Hylda, in Paris, to send others at certain times."

"Great Scott, Bernie! Your brain is wonderful!" exclaimed Ena in admiration. "How can you think out all these details in such a short space of time?"

"When one is in danger one takes due precaution—and at once. I always do so," he laughed. "This fellow and his girl have tried to spy upon us—and we have to deal with them as they would deal with us. If they discovered anything they would at once tell the police, and very soon our game would be up. Hence, we have to put matters square at the least possible risk to ourselves," he added.

He took up the glass from which Gerald had drunk the excellent port, and carried it into the small kitchen, where he carefully washed it. Afterwards Ena handed him a small phial which he also carefully washed, and then half filled it with something he took from his pocket. The bottle was full of that cheap, but pungent, perfume—oil of verbena. When he had half filled the small bottle, he corked it and placed it in a cupboard in the kitchen, thus removing all trace of the deleterious liquid which the little phial had previously contained.

Lilla had gone out, but half an hour later she drove up to the door in a small open car. The manner in which she pulled up showed her to be a good driver.

The inhabitants of the whole block of flats—those houses piled upon one another, which are admittedly cheap to run, but which are so very expensive from a health point of view—were asleep when, assisted by the two women, and treading softly, they placed Durrant in the car, heavy and unconscious owing to the drug which had been given him.

Lilla then mounted to the driver's seat, and, leaving Ena to close the flat and return to Upper Brook Street as best she could, Boyne and his wife, with their unconscious victim in the bottom of the car, sped out across Hampstead Heath, and northward upon the Great North Road.

Not till forty-eight hours afterwards did Gerald Durrant slowly and painfully awake to a knowledge of his surroundings. By that time Marigold and the others had been reassured by the telegrams.

Gerald's first impression was of a strange, rather healthful smell—a smell of tar. He looked around. The ceiling of the room was low—a ceiling which badly required whitewashing. Before him was a small square window—a very small window. And he was lying fully dressed upon a narrow iron bedstead.

Apparently the house was an old cottage, but quite unfamiliar. He tried to think, but his brain was addled. His memory refused to serve him. The sun was shining in at the window, and the little room seemed close and stuffy. It was the sunset, he gathered.

Try how he would, he could recollect absolutely nothing. All he could recollect were the faces of those two women whom he had assisted in their distress.

He strove to think. At last, he recollected how Mrs. Evans had given him that glass of good port, and how afterwards they had chatted together. Then all was blank.

Of time he had no idea. What, he wondered, would Marigold think of his absence? And what would they think at the office?

His first impulse was to wire to Wimbledon Park and to Mincing Lane. Yes, it was imperative that he should do so.

Yet he knew not where he was, for as he raised himself upon his elbow from the bed, he saw that the only look-out from the small window was a high brick wall, apparently the wall of a warehouse. The room was dusty and uncleanly. There was no carpet—nothing save a very ragged square of black-and-white linoleum. He got up and, dazed as he was, he tried the door. It was strongly bolted from without!

He shouted—yelled at the top of his voice, but nobody came. Upon the little deal table he saw something which told him that he was a prisoner—a jug containing some water, and a plate with some unwholesome-looking cooked meat and some bread.

He examined them with a rising feeling of indignation. Then, in a fury, he raised a heavy wooden chair, and savagely attacked the door. Time after time, he took it by its leg and banged it upon the door, making a tremendous noise. Yet the strong oak resisted every attempt, until, piece by piece, the chair was broken up. Then he looked around for something stronger. There was a rusty iron fender. This he took up, and using it as a battering ram struck the door repeatedly. But the fender being of cast iron broke in half, but made no injury to the door.

He crossed to the window and, smashing the glass, tried to open it. But outside were strong iron bars. He was indeed a prisoner!

In desperation he flung the mattress from the bed, and, taking down the bedstead, attacked the door vigorously with one of the iron bars. He used the end—for it was hammered out—as a crowbar and succeeded after long effort in inserting it between the door and the lintel, but so well was it secured by bolts that he had no power to force it open, and in the end the thin iron bent, and thus became useless.

Presently he hammered on the floor, and tried to awaken somebody, still all to no purpose. In the meanwhile, darkness was falling and soon he would, he knew, be without light. Notwithstanding that his head was aching terribly, and there was a feeling as though his skull was slowly being crushed in a vice, he set to work to liberate himself in another way.

He tore aside the old linoleum, and succeeded in forcing up one of the dirty floor-boards. This he followed by another, and yet a third, until below was revealed the plaster of the ceiling of the room underneath.

Then, taking a heavy piece of the bedstead, he struck down with all his might.

The iron struck the plaster, but, contrary to his expectation, he was unable to force a hole through the ceiling. Then, suddenly, to his dismay, he discovered that what he had believed to be plaster was concrete—that the floor was a fireproof one, and that being so, any attempt to penetrate it without proper tools was foredoomed to failure.

He gazed about him, utterly bewildered.

What could have happened after he had drunk that glass of port so kindly offered him by the handsome Mrs. Evans? That he was in the hands of enemies it was plain, but who were they? He wondered whether his incarceration in that place had any connection with his inquisitiveness concerning Bernard Boyne.

He reflected. Boyne had not been cognisant of being followed. He was convinced of that. Had he been so, he would not have paid those nocturnal visits to Pont Street and Upper Brook Street.

In the evening light he stood utterly perplexed. At his feet he saw that the boards were discoloured by a large brown stain some three feet in diameter. One part of it was thick, as though dark paint had been spilled there. He bent to examine it more closely, and from the wood scraped a portion of the thick substance with his finger-nail.

The stuff seemed curiously sticky, very much like paint. He took it across to the window, and there examined it minutely in the light, rubbing it between his thumb and forefinger.

Next moment a cry of horror escaped him. "Great Heavens!" he gasped. "Why—it's blood!"

Apparently there had been a pool of blood there, but it had nearly all dried up, save that portion which had not yet become completely hardened.

What could it mean?

He returned to the spot which had been immediately beneath where he had lain upon the bed. Had some previous occupant of that barred room been foully done to death while sleeping? It certainly seemed that such was the explanation.

"Who brought me here, I wonder?" he said aloud to himself, as the ghastly suggestion crept over him. "What is Marigold thinking of my disappearance? What can they think of it at the office?"

Across the narrow room he paced in frantic anger at having been so entrapped without the slightest motive. The dead silence of the place oppressed him. Without knowledge of where he was, either in London or in the country, he set his teeth and regretted the moment when he went to the assistance of the two women. Yet, surely, they could have nothing to do with his detention there? The absence of motive held him completely perplexed.

In the fast-fading light he made a complete and minute inspection of that chamber wherein he had made the gruesome discovery. If someone had really been done to death in that place recently, then there might be other traces of the tragedy. Further, how was he to know that he, in turn, would not fall a victim!

Hastily, because the light was going, he turned out a cupboard, but found nothing save a quantity of newspapers. Some rubbish in the rusty fireplace he examined, but his search there was also fruitless.

Then he turned his attention to a long, narrow double-doored cupboard let into the wall close to the bed. One door was bolted from within, and the other locked. To force it open was only the work of a few moments. Within he found a quantity of feminine apparel of good quality, a skirt, shoes, and other things.

One object which he took up caused him to ejaculate another cry of horror, and to hold his breath.

He carried it across to the broken window, and there bent to see if what he suspected was the actual truth.

Yes! He satisfied himself that it was. What he held in his hand was a woman's cream *crêpe-de-chine* blouse, prettily trimmed with lace, but the neck, chest, and all over the left sleeve were stained with blood!

"Then the victim was a woman!" he gasped aloud.

Quickly he examined all the other articles of attire, but found no traces of blood upon any other. He decided to keep his knowledge to himself, so that when he escaped, as he intended to do, he might at once inform the police of what he had found. Therefore he instantly set to work to replace the floor-boards, and recover them with the old piece of linoleum which hid the great ugly stain. Then, restoring the room to order in the best way possible, he replaced the blouse and the other feminine garments where he had found them, and was able—after a great deal of difficulty, for it was nearly dark—to place the two doors of the cupboard together in such a way that they closed, so that all trace of them being forced was thus removed.

That some unknown woman had recently lost her life in that place was now quite certain. After he had put the place in order again—all save re-erecting the bedstead, for this could not be done, neither could he mend the broken chair—he stood in the darkness pondering. It was impossible to remain in that horrible place all night. If he slept he might be attacked, as the poor woman had probably been. And in his half-dazed condition he needed sleep badly.

His one thought was of Marigold.

"What will she think, poor girl!" he cried aloud in his anguish. "What has she done now that I am missing?"

He listened. There was no sound save the chiming of a church clock in the distance, followed by the shrill whistle of a locomotive. Then he heard the long-drawn siren of a ship repeated three times, but some distance away. Evidently the place was near a river, or perhaps by the sea. That would account for the smell of tar.

Then all became quiet again. The silence and darkness began to get upon his nerves until he could stand it no longer. The thought that a dark tragedy had been perpetrated upon that very spot where he stood filled him with horror.

Therefore at last he again went to the window, and began to send up some unearthly yells in a fierce endeavour to attract the attention of somebody outside.

Time after time he repeated his shouts, but nobody answered. He could hear the voices of two common women gossiping, and though he could not see them he shouted to them. But they only deigned to yell back.

"Oh, shut up! Do shut up—whoever you are!"

Suddenly he recollected that drunken brawls and cries for help are only too frequent in lower-class neighbourhoods, therefore his cries for assistance, though they must be heard, were being disregarded.

So he desisted, and resolved to remain patient a further quarter of an hour, and then resume his cries for help.

He was standing in the darkness near the window when a slight and curious movement behind him caused him to turn sharply.

Beneath the door he saw a light, but whoever was there wore rubber soles to their shoes, for they made no sound. The slight noise which had fallen upon his strained ears was the slow and stealthy drawing of a bar outside the door.

Someone was creeping noiselessly in!

On tiptoe he crossed, and, seizing the bar of iron, sprang behind the door, his hand raised ready to fell any person who entered.

The handle of the door was very slowly turned, but next second—ere he became aware of it—a strange thing happened.

CHAPTER XXI
LOST DAYS

As the door of the room in which he was imprisoned slowly opened, and he stood ready to attack the new-comer and fight for his liberty, he became suddenly blinded and rendered utterly powerless by a burst of heavy grey smoke.

He drew one whiff of it, and, reeling, fell senseless upon the floor.

Then, as the fumes which had rendered him unconscious slowly cleared, there stood in the dim light a form wearing an exact replica of the white cloak and hood which Bernard Boyne used when he visited that upstairs room in Hammersmith. The window being broken, and now that the door was open too, the fumes quickly dispersed, yet Gerald lay there where he had fallen, pale as death, and breathing only slightly.

"A heavy dose!" laughed the hooded man grimly. "He won't get over it for quite a long time!"

And then he turned and left, leaving the door still open, so that all trace of the poisonous vapour which he had released from a heavy iron cylinder should be removed.

An hour later he returned, but without his cloak, for the gas-mask was no longer needed. He carried an electric torch, which he flashed into the white face of the unconscious victim.

"You'll soon go away—never to return!" growled the mysterious man aloud; and then suddenly by the reflection of the light his face became revealed.

It was Bernard Boyne.

"The fellow knows too much—and so does the girl!" he muttered to himself. "We must deal with her next. But she's not yet dangerous. Still, as Lilla says, in our business we can't afford to take any risks. So stay there for the present, my friend," he added.

And bending he felt the prostrate man's pulse in the professional manner of a medical man. Then, apparently well satisfied, he crossed the room, closed the window and, after locking the door outside again, descended the stairs.

When young Durrant at last began to slowly recover his senses, he awakened to find himself seated in an arm-chair in a small and not uncomfortable cabin on board a ship. The vessel was rolling heavily, and ever and anon the waves swept up past the porthole, partially obscuring the light.

He drew his hand across his fevered brow and endeavoured to think. But all was hazy, uncertain, and unreal. Was he still dreaming? he asked himself. He placed both his hands upon the arms of the leather-covered chair and felt them. No! It was no dream! He was on a ship at sea!

Suddenly across his brain swept recollections of that room in which he had been imprisoned—that gruesome chamber with its unmistakable evidence of a tragedy—the place in which some unknown woman had been foully done to death. He remembered his meeting with those two ladies outside Kensington Gardens, their hospitality and its dire result. At any rate, there was one satisfaction, that his enemies, whoever they were, had spared his life.

He rose, his limbs feeling very sore and stiff. How long had elapsed since he had so suddenly met that mysterious burst of smoke he had no idea. Nor had he any knowledge of where he had been, or where that room of tragedy was situated. All remained a complete blank.

In rising to his feet he nearly fell owing to the heavy roll of the vessel—a steamer evidently, for he could feel the vibration of the engines. Unsteadily he opened the door, and found himself in a narrow gangway, with several cabins on either side. Opposite him a door stood open, revealing a burly, dark-bearded man in uniform lounging in a chair, smoking a pipe and reading a book.

Hearing Gerald's footsteps he turned his head.

"Hulloa!" he cried roughly. "Got over your drunk then, Mr. Simpson? Come in here!"

"Thanks," was Durrant's reply. "But I never drink, and my name is not Simpson."

"Ah! I thought you'd say that! Sit down, anyway," the captain remarked, with a good-humoured laugh. "Yesterday when we had a chat, you didn't deny that your name was George Simpson, did you?"

"I don't remember having had a chat with you yesterday," replied Gerald, amazed at the captain's words.

"Ah! You don't remember much, do you? Got a very bad memory, I know."

"No, I've got a pretty good memory, and to my knowledge I've never seen you in my life before."

"And yet you spent last night with me, and drank more than you ought to have done. Whisky is a bad thing for you, young fellow. You should leave it alone. Never drink till you're forty-five. That's what I say."

Durrant sank into the chair, and gazed around the captain's cabin absolutely bewildered.

"What ship is this?" he asked at last.

"You asked me that yesterday. This is the *Pentyrch*, of Sunderland, bound from Hull to Singapore," was the reply.

"And we are on our way there!" gasped the young man in blank dismay.

"Yes. Three days out."

"Where are we now?"

"Off Finisterre."

"Will you tell me your name, Captain?" Durrant asked quite calmly.

"Bowden—John Bowden. And I live at Empress Villa, Queen Street, Sunderland. Aged forty-one; married; two kids. Anything more?"

"Yes, a lot," was the other's reply.

"You asked me a lot of questions about the ship last night, and I told you. We've got a general cargo, and after Singapore we go to Batavia, then to Wellington, New Zealand, and back home."

"How long shall we be away?"

"Oh! perhaps nine months—perhaps more if I get other orders," was Bowden's breezy reply. "This old tub ain't very fast, you know. She isn't one of your slap-up liners. We never have passengers. I don't like 'em. Only Mr. Morton asked me to take you out for the benefit of your health, and I consented."

"Mr. Morton! Who's he?"

"A friend of yours, isn't he?"

"I don't know anyone of that name," declared Gerald astounded.

Captain Bowden looked straight into the young man's face for a few moments in silence, and then, nodding his head, said:

"Ah! Of course!"

"Why of course?" asked Gerald in annoyance at the captain's tone.

The other only shrugged his shoulders, and continued puffing at his big briar pipe.

Gerald was utterly mystified.

Since that moment when he had lost consciousness in the presence of the two ladies he had assisted until the present, all his recollections were blurred and indistinct. Bowden had accused him of drinking heavily the night before. Yet he felt certain that he had never previously set eyes upon the black-bearded man before him. His unknown enemies had spared his life, but they had sent him out upon a nine months' voyage, evidently to get rid of him for some reasons known to themselves.

Was Bernard Boyne at the bottom of it all? He wondered. Yet Boyne could not know anything of his efforts to unravel the mystery of his life. How could he possibly know?

"Look here, Captain Bowden," he said firmly at last. "Let us be frank with each other."

"I'm always frank, young man—too frank for some people!" was the bluff seafarer's reply.

"Well, be frank with me. Tell me—do you know any man named Boyne—Bernard Boyne?"

"Never heard the name before," snapped the other. "What about him?" And he crossed his legs encased in his heavy sea-boots.

"Well, I thought perhaps you might know him," Durrant said. Then, catching sight of the coat he was wearing, he was surprised to see that it was unfamiliar—a heavy blue-serge suit, such as he had never before possessed. The mystery increased as each moment passed.

"No. I don't know any man named Boyne. Who and what is he?"

"He's an insurance agent at Hammersmith."

"That's somewhere in London, ain't it?"

"Yes. I'm a Londoner."

"Oh, are you? Yes, I thought so."

"Why did you think so?" asked Durrant.

"Because I know you come from Liverpool."

"You're trying to be funny!"

"Oh, no, I'm not! It's you who always tries to be funny, young fellow. You sat with me here, in my cabin, last night, and yet to-day you deny having done so."

Gerald rose from his chair, intending to firmly withstand the black-bearded fellow's ridiculous allegations, but at that instant he felt that same half-intoxication creeping over him, and he subsided.

"Captain Bowden, I'm sorry to tell you that I honestly think you are lying to me," he said a moment later.

"Thanks for the compliment, Mr. Simpson. I won't retort because you'll be ill if I do. We're in for bad weather in the Bay, I'm afraid. Glass falling with a run."

"I've never been to sea before," remarked Gerald hopelessly, yet surprised that the captain should take his challenge so mildly.

"Well, you'll get your sea-legs on this voyage, I can tell you," laughed the heavy-jowled captain.

At that moment the first mate came in, holding himself as he stood against the heavy rolling of the tramp steamer.

"Cargo is shifting a bit in number four hold, sir," he said. "Shall I tell Jenkins to call the men and see to it?"

"Yes. Do what the devil you like, Hutton," snapped the captain. "I see we're in for hellish weather. Look at the glass!"

"I noticed it half an hour ago, sir. We shall catch it strong after sundown."

"Yes, we shall. Better make everything tight now."

Then, turning to Durrant, Captain Bowden, refilling his pipe, remarked:

"That's the worst of these cursed old tubs. But you see, after the war they can't get new ones. All those labour troubles on the Clyde have interfered with shipbuilding. I was promised a brand-new boat a year ago. But she's still on the stocks. When she goes out I shall do the ferry trade from the Levant to London—four weeks out and home."

"But, now tell me—who put me on board this ship?" asked Gerald.

"Who put you on board? why, your friend, Mr. Morton."

"My friend? Why, I don't know the man!"

Bowden smiled, and showed that he was not convinced.

"What was this fellow Morton like?" inquired Durrant eagerly. "Describe him to me."

"Oh! a rather tall, lean, herring-gutted chap, with a baldish head, and narrow little eyes," was the reply. "But you can't tell me that you don't know him. Why, you were with him when I promised to take you on this trip."

"With him!" echoed Gerald. "I certainly was not."

"Ah! The worst of you, Mr. Simpson, is that you're so forgetful," exclaimed the breezy captain.

"I'm not forgetful!" cried Durrant resentfully, rising to his feet again, and steadying himself from the slow roll of the ship. "How did you come to know this mysterious friend of mine—Morton, you say is his name?"

"That's my affair! You don't believe me, so why should I bother to answer your questions?"

"I don't believe you when you say that I was here with you yesterday," was Gerald's frank reply.

"No, because your brain is addled," laughed Bowden deeply, knocking the ashes from his pipe. At that moment the ship's bell clanged loudly, marking the time. It was eleven o'clock in the forenoon.

"Yes, it is addled, I admit," said Durrant. "I've been the victim of a foul plot. I—well, let me tell you."

"Oh! I don't want to hear it all over again. You've already told me twice how you assisted two ladies in Kensington, how they took you to their house, and gave you a dose of drug. Then, how you found yourself imprisoned in a house, and all that long rigmarole. Spare me again—won't you?" the captain begged.

Durrant stood aghast.

"But I've never told you anything about it!" he said. "I've never told a living soul about my strange adventure."

"Look here, Mr. Simpson," said the captain, rising from his chair with slow deliberation. "I'm beginning to think that you're not quite in your right senses. You told us all about it last night in this very cabin—how you had been entrapped, drugged, and taken away."

"Yes. That is quite true, but I have never told anyone of it."

"Well, the less you say about that affair the better, I think. Nobody will believe you."

"But don't you think I'm telling the truth?"

"No. I know you are not. Morton told me that you were obsessed by the belief that you've been the victim of some very cunning plot, and that you were drugged," said the captain. "Now, just forget all about it, and enjoy your trip!" he added good-humouredly.

"Ah! This person, Morton, has told you, has he? He told you so as to discredit me when I explained to you the truth," cried Durrant. "But what I have told you are the true facts."

"Oh, of course they are!" laughed the captain.

"But don't let us discuss it any more."

"Where did I come on board?"

"Why, at Hull, of course. Four days ago."

"At Hull!" gasped Gerald. "I have no recollections of ever having been in Hull."

"Neither have you any recollections of ever having been born, eh?" remarked Bowden, with biting sarcasm.

"Did Morton bring me on board?"

"Certainly."

"And he paid you to take me on this trip?"

"No, excuse me. We pay you. You've signed on as steward at a bob a day wages. We're not licensed to carry passengers. The Board o' Trade don't like such old tubs as the *Pentyrch*. Yet she's a good old boat, I'll say that much for her. You'll see England again all right, never fear—unless the bloomin' boilers burst. They're none too strong, I'm afraid."

"You're not over cheerful, Captain Bowden," the young man remarked, more puzzled than ever at the extraordinary situation.

"Oh, I'm cheerful enough. It's you who seems to be a-worryin' over things."

"Well, and wouldn't you worry if you were drugged, waking first to find yourself locked in a strange room, and then again wakening a second time to discover yourself at sea?"

"You want rest, my dear young fellow—rest! And you'll get it here on the old tub. The weather will be better when we get along the West Coast."

"How can I send a message to London?"

"We ain't got wireless. Too expensive for such a hooker as this. It means an operator with lightnin' round his cap. So you'll have to wait till we get to Singapore, and then you can cable."

Wait for five or six weeks till the vessel arrived at Singapore! What would Marigold think? What was she thinking now?

He was, of course, in ignorance of those cleverly worded and reassuring telegrams.

"Can't I get a message ashore anyhow—by signal to one of Lloyd's stations?" he begged.

"No, you can't, for we're going straight out. Usually we go up the Mediterranean and through the Canal, but this trip we're going round the Cape."

"But surely you will allow me to communicate with my friends, captain!" he urged in distress.

"You certainly could if we had orders to put in anywhere. But we haven't. I can't send a letter to my missus, for instance. She'll know of our arrival at Singapore because the owners will send her a line, as they always do."

"All this is maddening!" declared Durrant, angrily stamping his foot.

"Yes, Morton said you were a bit eccentric, and it seems that you are!" remarked Bowden, taking down his shiny black oilskin which had borne the brunt of many a storm.

"I must go on the bridge—or Hutton will be cursing," he added. "Get your oilskin—you've got one in your cabin—and go and have a blow on deck. It will do you good—blow out the cobwebs, and freshen up your memory a bit."

Gerald returned to his cabin and found a black oilskin hanging behind the door. He put it on and, taking an old golf cap, ascended the hatchway to the deck, which was, ever and anon, being drenched with salt spray.

A glance around showed the *Pentyrch* to be a dirty old tramp, which was loping along in the teeth of a northerly gale.

"See yonder!" exclaimed the captain, pointing to a little line of land. "That's the last bit of Europe we'll see! To-morrow the weather will be a lot better. Have a look round the ship before dinner. And don't you trouble about that marvellous plot against you. There's nothing at all in it—take it from me! Your friends are all aware of your hallucinations, and they are much pained by them. So just keep quiet—and rest all you can."

While Bowden ascended to the bridge to relieve the first mate, Gerald explored the ship. He came across one or two rough sailors, who either wished him a sullen "Good-day," or stared at him as though he were some new species.

As a matter of fact, Bowden had given it out to the crew that their passenger was an eccentric, but harmless young man, who was labouring under the delusion that an attempt had been made to kill him. Hence the men's curiosity.

Gerald Durrant was unused to the sea, and in his present unstrung condition, he was indeed scarcely responsible for his actions.

But what the captain had told him had astounded him. The description of his mysterious "friend" Morton—a man who was evidently his enemy— certainly did not tally with that of Bernard Boyne.

Yet he could not erase from his mind the suspicion that Boyne had had a hand in that plot by which he had been carried away from London—just at a moment when his presence there was so much needed.

Again, as he stood against the hatchway gazing wistfully at the distant French coast that was fast disappearing, the thought suddenly occurred to him that if his disappearance was actually due to Boyne, then the latter must have, somehow or other, discovered the fact that he was keeping him under observation.

If Boyne had really found it out, then he would also know that Marigold had been assisting him. This would, no doubt, lead him to suspect the real motive of her two stays at Bridge Place.

Bernard Boyne would entrap her—just as he had been entrapped!

In his despair he saw himself powerless, either to warn or to assist the girl he so fondly loved!

CHAPTER XXII
FROM OUT THE PAST

After Boyne, his wife, and Ena Pollen—the trio of death-dealers—received the news of the death of Augusta Morrison, the go-to-meeting insurance agent of Hammersmith had left the flat and gone forth into Upper Brook Street. He had to meet a man in the smoke-room of the Carlton.

Suddenly, as he passed beneath a street lamp on his way towards Park Lane, a well-dressed girl accosted him, exclaiming with a strong French accent:

"Ah! M'sieur Bennett! At last! I have wanted to see you for—oh! for so long—long time!"

Boyne started. The maid, Céline, for it was she, was the very last person in the world that he desired to meet at that moment. All had been successfully conducted concerning Augusta Morrison, but here arose the aftermath of a very ugly affair—the death of old Mr. Martin in Chiswick.

At first he pretended not to recognise the girl who had been paid off by Ena, for he hoped to wriggle out of the precarious situation by bluff.

"No, no, m'sieur," cried the girl. "Surely you recollect me! I am Céline—who was maid to madame—your friend! You remember poor Mr. Martin—who died so suddenly—eh?" she asked.

He tried to extricate himself, but instantly it occurred to him that she was resuming her blackmail, and that if they were to save themselves, she must be paid more money. She knew something concerning old Martin's sudden end. That was plain. Therefore, she would have to be silenced. In every walk of life to-day the blackmailer of both sexes is to be found in one guise or another.

"And are you really Céline?" he laughed, halting beneath the next lamp, for she had joined him and had walked beside him.

"I am. Madame lives in the house you have just left. I saw her in Melun a little time ago. She so kindly called upon me."

As the girl uttered these words a man joined them, a tall, rather cadaverous-looking stranger in black, evidently a Frenchman.

"This is Monsieur Galtier—Henri Galtier," she explained, introducing them.

"Ah! I recollect. Madame told me that you are to be married—eh, Céline? I congratulate you," said Boyne in an affable manner. "Pardon my foolishness, but at first I did not recognise you as my friend."

The latter word was intentionally diplomatic.

"Yes, I thought you would recollect!" said the girl. "Is Madame upstairs? I want so much to see her."

"No," replied Boyne. "She isn't. I've just called, but she's out."

"There are lights in her windows," remarked the man Galtier in very good English.

"Servants, I suppose," said Boyne carelessly. "I myself went to see her upon some business—about some shares upon which she has asked my advice. She's gone away for the week-end, it seems."

"H'm!" grunted the Anglo-Frenchman. "How are we to know that?"

"Well, I tell you so," was Boyne's blunt response.

"Do you know, M'sieur Bennett, that Madame told me that you were dead? That you died of influenza, and here now you are coming from her house!" said the good-looking French girl.

"Yes; she believed that I was dead. I was away on business in Italy, and some fool spread the report that I had died in a hotel in Naples," laughed Boyne, yet inwardly full of concern. "But it was a shock to her when one afternoon I called."

Céline Ténot was not convinced. She had already received thirty thousand francs to keep a still tongue, but as a matter of fact her lover, Galtier, saw that it would be interesting, in more ways than one, to probe the mystery of the death of old Mr. Martin.

The ill-assorted trio walked together as far as Park Lane. At the corner the man Galtier halted, and addressing the girl in French, said:

"We'll go back, Céline, and see if Madame is really absent, as M'sieur Bennett alleges."

"She is away!" exclaimed Boyne angrily. "Haven't I told you so? Don't I want to see her myself?"

The Frenchman laughed in his face.

"No, no, my dear m'sieur! Do not tell any more lies. We saw you go in a long time ago. You dined there, and Madame is there. We both want to see her—on—on some important business!"

Bernard Boyne held his breath. He was cornered. He had successfully put Gerald Durrant out upon the high seas, but here was Céline, with her lover, watching them enter Ena's flat in order to await the news of the death of their latest victim!

"It's surely late to do business with a lady," remarked Boyne, for want of something else to say. In his excitement over the successful conclusion of the Morrison affair, he was now met with a very unexpected and serious contretemps.

Ena believed that she had successfully settled with the girl, but it was evident that Galtier was a blackmailer who intended to bleed them to the utmost.

Indeed, he had not been long in revealing his hand.

"I think, Mr. Bennett—or whatever your real name may be—you had better drop this mask," the Frenchman said, with a sardonic grin. "Let us come down to the same plane. The fact is you're a crook—and so am I, perhaps. Now then! What about it?"

"Let's walk along," the girl suggested in French.

The trio walked together, Bernard Boyne between the pair. They strolled down Park Lane to Hyde Park Corner, but their conversation was mostly in monosyllables.

Boyne was wondering how he could extricate himself from the highly perilous situation. It was evident that this shrewd Frenchman, who had so suddenly risen in the placid firmament of their future, knew something concerning the death of old Martin.

How much did he know? That was the question.

At first Boyne tried to fence with the pair, but soon he saw that it was of no avail. They both laughed at him openly, and it was clear that they had been watching him for several days.

"Now," slid Galtier, as they halted upon the pavement opposite the Hyde Park tube station "what are you going to do? Will you take us back to Madame, or are you going to lie to us further? Now then!"

Boyne saw himself at a dead end.

He had never dreamed that the smart French girl of Melun, who had been paid so handsomely by Ena, would again resume her claims. But, of course, the man Galtier was behind her and had, no doubt, prompted her. Fortunately, they could know nothing of the Morrison affair—or, indeed, of the clever plots which they were conducting against other perfectly innocent victims. Life assurance is always a gamble, but when one can guarantee death within dates then one holds a winning hand every time.

"Madame isn't at home," repeated Boyne sulkily. "Call there on Monday. She'll be back then."

"No, my dear M'sieur Bennett," replied the clerk from the Mairie of Chantilly. "If we call then she will have gone, and so will your wife." And he laughed lightly. "You see, I haven't been in London all these weeks without discovering something about all three of you!"

"But I don't see why you should come over from France to pry into our affairs. What can it benefit you?" asked Boyne, who, though excited, kept cool with difficulty.

"Oh! never fear, it will benefit us. We know how and why old Mr. Martin died so unexpectedly in Chiswick. We shall also know, ere long, how other insured persons have died, *mon cher ami*. So we had better turn back and have a little business chat with Céline's late mistress, and with your wife. That, perhaps, will clear the atmosphere."

"Ah! I see you want money! Both of you—eh?" snapped Boyne.

"Possibly," was the hesitating reply. "But perhaps it would be to our better advantage to tell the police what we know."

"That's a threat!" cried Boyne indignantly. "I allow no man to threaten me!" he declared boldly. "Go back to Madame's house. You are welcome. I am not her keeper."

"I would prefer to deal with you first, M'sieur Bennett."

"I don't want to have any dealings with a person who holds out threats," was his answer. "Madame paid Céline because she dismissed her without notice," he went on carelessly. "Just act as you wish. And I wish you joy. But please don't bother me further."

He was turning away when the Frenchman rushed after him, and stood on the pavement before him.

"Is this your final decision?" he asked fiercely, as he barred Boyne's way.

"Yes. You've come here to blackmail me," replied Boyne; "but you'll not get a sou out of me. Why should I pay you anything? I don't know you! I've never seen you before in my life!"

"But you will be very pleased to settle," snarled the fellow in English.

"I shan't, and if you are not very careful I'll give you in charge of the police for attempted blackmail."

"You swine!" cried Galtier between his teeth.

"The same to you, my dear friend—and a size larger; a bigger breed!" laughed Boyne defiantly.

Both the man and the girl were silent for a few moments, when the latter suddenly broke out into a torrent of abuse and vituperation.

Her companion tried to calm her, but in French she cried loudly:

"These people are assassins! I know what I overheard on the night when poor Monsieur Martin died. They killed him! And he was always very good to me—poor M'sieur! Madame is a fiend!" she went on. "I do not want her dirty money. I want to see her pay the penalty which all those who murder should pay!"

Boyne saw that his bluff had not succeeded. He had to deal with a very perilous situation. A false step might lead them all to the Old Bailey. The pair had evidently been watching them, and were aware that his wife and Ena were both in the flat.

"Well," he laughed harshly, "you both appear to be on the wrong track. Céline has, it seems, suspicions about something which she once overheard. What it was, I do not know, because I wasn't there; but I tell you, both of you, that as far as I care you can go to the devil! I've nothing to ask of you— nothing to fear!

"You really mean that—eh?" cried the lank, bony Frenchman.

"Certainly I do. Clear out—and now at once, otherwise I'll call the first constable and give you in charge for attempted blackmail!" said Boyne, standing erect before him. "We've had foreign blackmailers here before— lots of them—but we've no use for them in London."

"But Madame paid me to say nothing," urged Céline.

"What Madame did does not concern me in the least," he snapped. "She generously gave you something, I believe, because she considered that she had treated you shabbily. That's all!"

An awkward pause ensued.

"Very well," exclaimed Galtier. "We are enemies. Let it be so!"

"Of course we are enemies!" Boyne cried in a defiant tone that rather nonplussed the Frenchman.

"Très bien!" he exclaimed.

"Excellent," said the wily Boyne. "Let it be so, as you say. We are enemies. So go back to Upper Brook Street and find madame. Go and try to blackmail her. Meanwhile I shall call the next constable I meet and give you both in charge as undesirable foreigners."

The Frenchman, however, only laughed in his face, saying:

"Yes, do so, *mon cher ami*! I fancy you would regret such an action. But we are enemies, and at any rate, I intend to see madame, your friend."

"You want money, eh?" growled Boyne, as they stood together on the kerb.

"Perhaps we do—and perhaps we do not. It all depends upon your attitude—and madame's!" he replied, with mock politeness. "The mystery of the death of Monsieur Martin requires elucidating, and Céline can do that—when it becomes necessary."

"I don't understand you," Boyne said. "What about the old man's death?"

"Now, that's quite enough!" cried Galtier, in impatient anger. "It's no use you, of all men, pleading ignorance, Mr. Bennett. Céline has already had a little present from madame to keep a still tongue, and——"

"And you want a bit more, eh?" asked Boyne bluntly.

"No. That's just where you are mistaken, my friend!" was the Frenchman's reply. "Monsieur Martin died in mysterious circumstances, of which both madame and yourself are well aware, and it is but right that the police should know the truth, *otherwise we may have other people dying in a similar manner!*"

Those last words of his caused Boyne to wince. For what reason, if not with the object of blackmail, had Henri Galtier and Céline Ténot come to London and tracked them down?

He knew that Ena had been indiscreet in her conversation after old Martin's death, but he had believed that her visit to Melun and the payment to the girl had put matters quite right. It seemed to him, however, that Céline was entirely under the influence of that municipal employé from Chantilly, whose attitude was decidedly hostile.

"Well," Boyne asked of the man, "if you don't want money, what in the devil's name do you want?"

"I want to prevent you from playing any more of your hellish tricks upon innocent people. That's what I want!" was the Frenchman's hard reply, in a tone which left no doubt as to his firm intentions.

CHAPTER XXIII
THE CRY IN THE NIGHT

Marigold, hoping against hope, went each day from Wimbledon to the bank, where she sat adding and subtracting figures—always wondering. Each morning, after a hurried breakfast, she dashed to the station and hung upon a swaying strap till she got to the City. Each evening she repeated the same experience home.

Gerald was missing. No further word had come nom him. She waited as each day passed—waited eagerly, but he gave no sign. Each day she went to eat her frugal meal at the same little place, but his familiar figure never appeared in the doorway, as she knew it so well. His sister had heard nothing, and at Mincing Lane they were beginning to think that he had simply left his post without notice, perhaps in order to better himself.

For Marigold the days passed wearily enough. Where was he? True, he had sent her reassuring telegrams, but even they had ceased! He had given no address, therefore she was unable to reply.

She was, of course, in utter ignorance that her lover was on the high seas bound for the Far East, and that the reassuring telegrams she had received were forgeries.

The abnormal brain of Bernard Boyne worked quickly, and ever with criminal intent. He was possessed of the criminal "kink," and was also possessed of a super-mind for the evasion of any attempt at detection. Such men, "Jack the Ripper" of London, "Romer" of Madrid, "Lightning Lasky" of New York, and the "Ermito" of Rome—all of them famous criminals who have never been discovered by the police of Europe, though traps were set for them by the dozen—were exactly on a par with the humble insurance agent of Hammersmith, the highly popular "Busy Boyne."

One evening, three days after the news had been forthcoming concerning the death of Mrs. Morrison, Marigold went over to see her aunt at Hammersmith, arriving there about seven o'clock.

"Hulloa, my dear!" shouted old Mrs. Felmore, when she entered the downstairs kitchen. "Well, and how have you been, eh? Heard anything of Mr. Durrant yet?"

"Not a word, auntie," replied the girl wearily.

"And funny enough Mr. Boyne's gone away. I haven't seen him these last three days. I can't think where he can be. I have a kind of feeling that something must have happened to him," said the deaf old woman.

"Why, auntie?" asked the girl, placing her hand-bag upon the table and sinking into a chair.

"Well, he's never gone away like this before. He always tells me when he intends being away."

"When was he at home last?"

"Three days ago. He went out in the evening, and he's not returned. I've had to feed poor little Nibby, or he'd be starving," replied the woman.

"Yes, auntie, it is curious that Mr. Boyne isn't back."

"It's so lonely here. I get such creepy feelings at night, dear," said the woman. "It's bad enough to be here all day alone, but—well, I don't know, but I have a feeling that something is going to happen."

That feeling would have been greatly increased had she but known that, not ten minutes before, Boyne had stood at the corner of the street and watched the girl enter his house. Indeed, he had waited outside the bank, and had seen Marigold come out. Then he had followed her, and with satisfaction, when she had taken the underground to Hammersmith.

As he followed her in the crowd along the street, he muttered some sinister words beneath his breath:

"I have dealt with your lover, young lady," he growled to himself. "Now I must lose no time in dealing with you. You have only yourselves to blame for trying to poke your noses into my private affairs!"

Then he watched her disappear down the area steps, and afterwards crossed the bridge, and made a call upon a man he knew who lived in Castelnau Mansions.

Old Mrs. Felmore got her niece some cold meat and tea, for the girl had taken off her coat and hat, having decided to spend the evening with her aunt.

Much of their conversation concerned Gerald Durrant. The abrupt manner of his departure was, of course, a complete mystery, but the old woman inwardly had her doubts. What more likely than that Durrant, like so many other young men, had grown suddenly tired of Marigold and had "faded out," sending those reassuring telegrams in order to lighten the blow which he knew the poor girl would receive? This, indeed, was her fixed opinion, though naturally she said nothing of it to her niece.

"Auntie," said the girl presently, "I can't help feeling that something serious has happened to Gerald. I seem to become more apprehensive day by day, until I can't work—I can only sit and think—and think!"

"No, no, dearie," exclaimed the old woman cheerfully. "You mustn't let it get on your nerves. Those telegrams he sent told you not to worry. And I wouldn't—if I were you! It will all come right in the end."

"Ah!" sighed the girl. "Will it?—that is the question. Time is going by, and we hear nothing."

"He's probably in Paris—or somewhere—on some confidential business for his firm."

"But his firm know nothing of his whereabouts."

"Well, if he had gone on some secret business they would naturally profess ignorance," the woman pointed out.

"Do you know, I'm half inclined to go to the police and consult them," Marigold said.

"Ah! That's not a bad idea!" her aunt replied. "Go to the head police-station just outside the Broadway, and ask their opinion. They would take his description and advise you what to do, no doubt. I'd go to-morrow."

"I shan't have time to-morrow," the girl said. "I'll go round now. It's only nine o'clock." And, putting on her hat and coat, she went along to the headquarters of the T Division of Metropolitan Police.

But as she passed along the streets a dark figure went noiselessly behind her—the sinister figure of Bernard Boyne. She was going in the direction of the Underground Railway station, hence he concluded that she was on her way home.

He, however, received a rude and sudden shock when he saw her halt beneath the blue lamp, and ascend the steps of the police-station.

"Phew!" he gasped aloud. "Whatever is she there for? To give evidence against me—to put the police upon my track! By Jove! There's no time to lose. It must be done to-night!"

Next instant he turned, and going to the railway station he obtained a leather handbag from the cloak-room, and hastened with it back to his house. He wore rubber heels to his shoes, and moved swiftly and almost noiselessly.

In the darkness he ascended the steps, and opened the front door with his key. There was no light in the hall, and he could see through the Venetian blind of the kitchen that Mrs. Felmore was below.

Without passing into the sitting-room, he went straight upstairs to the mysterious apartment in which the hooded figure lived in secret. First, he placed his handkerchief over his mouth, and then, opening the door, passed in and switched on an electric torch which he produced from his pocket.

Without hesitation he unlocked the heavy bag, and took therefrom a long narrow deal box, which he opened, apparently to make certain that nothing was broken within, and then, placing it upon a table, drew down a little electric switch which was fitted at one end of the box.

Afterwards, scarcely looking around, he left the room, relocked the door, and crept out of the house without anyone having seen or heard him, old Mrs. Felmore being quite unconscious of her master's secret visit.

Back at the end of Hammersmith Bridge, Boyne glanced at his watch; then, chuckling to himself, he hurried to the police-station, in order to watch Marigold farther in case she had not already left.

When the girl had told the sergeant on duty the reason of her visit, she was passed upstairs into a room, where she was seen by the Inspector of the Criminal Investigation Department attached to the Division, a clean-shaven, fresh-complexioned man, who listened to her story very attentively.

From time to time he took notes of names and addresses.

"Have you any of the telegrams which the missing man sent you?" he asked presently.

From her handbag she produced two of the messages, which he read carefully.

"And since the twenty-third of last month you've not seen him?" he asked.

"No," replied the girl.

"And in Mincing Lane they have heard nothing since the receipt of the last telegram?"

"Nothing—neither has his sister."

The inspector looked her straight in the face, and said:

"I presume, Miss Ramsay, that this gentleman was a particular friend of yours, eh?"

Marigold blushed slightly and responded in the affirmative.

"Is there any reason you suspect why he should have gone away so suddenly? Did you—well, did you quarrel with him, for instance?"

"Not in the least. We were the best of friends," she answered. "I came here to ask whether you could assist me in finding him."

The clean-shaven man drew his breath, and gravely shook his head.

"I fear that we shall be unable to help you," he replied.

"Why? He is missing. Surely the police can trace him!" she cried in disappointment.

"No. He is *not* missing," was his answer. "The fact that he sent those telegrams is sufficient to show that he is keeping out of the way for some purpose best known to himself. He has, no doubt, some secret from you."

"Secret from me?" she echoed in dismay. "No, we both had a secret."

The inspector only smiled. He, of course, thought she alluded to the fact that they were lovers.

She saw his amusement, and wondered whether she dare be frank and tell him of their suspicions concerning Mr. Boyne. Yet the thought flashed across her mind that the story of his visits to that upstairs room, clothed in that strange garb, would never be credited. The London police hear strange stories from hour to hour, many of them the result of vivid imaginations, of hearsay, or deliberate attempts to incriminate innocent persons. Malice is at the bottom of half the fantastic stories told by women to officers of the Criminal Investigation Department, and Marigold saw that even though she told the truth, it would not be believed. Yet could she eliminate the real reason why her suspicions had first been aroused? She resolved to be frank, therefore after a brief pause, she said:

"The secret shared by Mr. Durrant and myself was concerning a certain man, resident close by here."

"Oh! And what is it?" asked the officer eagerly.

"Well, we have certain suspicions regarding a gentleman named Boyne, who lives in Bridge Place."

"Boyne? Why, not old Bernie Boyne the insurance agent?"

"Yes. Do you know him?"

"Oh—well, he's well known about Hammersmith," was the inspector's discreet reply. "What about him?"

"There is something about him that is mysterious," declared the girl. "Very mysterious."

"And what's that?"

"Well, Mr. Durrant was helping me to watch his movements when he suddenly disappeared!"

"Ah! That's interesting. Did Boyne know you were watching?"

"No. He had no suspicion. We watched him go to two houses, one in Pont Street, and the other in Upper Brook Street," Marigold said. "At night he dresses smartly and goes into the West End."

"A good many men do that, miss. By day they earn their money honestly by hard work, and at night fritter it away up West. I don't really see what there is in that. Isn't there anything else you know?"

Marigold hesitated. She feared to tell him of the strange disguise.

"Well, my aunt is Mr. Boyne's housekeeper, and I know that a room at the top of the house is kept locked."

"A good many upstairs rooms are kept locked. There's nothing much in that, I think."

"But I heard noises inside—a human cry!"

The inspector looked at her with disbelief written upon his rosy countenance.

"Are you quite sure of that, Miss—er—Miss Ramsay?" he asked seriously.

"Yes. I heard it," was her firm reply.

"Ah! Then, because of that you and Mr. Durrant believed that Boyne has somebody in hiding upstairs. Is that so?"

She replied in the affirmative.

"And you don't think Boyne discovered that you were watching him? If he did, I think he would have resented it very much, for I've met Boyne once or twice. Indeed, I passed him in King Street an hour ago."

"You passed him! Perhaps he's back then. My aunt hasn't seen him for three days."

"Well, I saw him in King Street to-night, but he didn't see me." Then, after a pause, he added: "I think, miss, you're mistaken regarding Mr. Boyne. I only know him slightly, but I know in what respect he is held in the neighbourhood, and how his praises are upon everyone's lips—especially the church people."

"Then you don't think that he has anything to do with Mr. Durrant's disappearance?"

"Not in the least. I should dismiss that idea from my mind at once."

"But how about that locked room?"

"Your aunt will be able to fathom that if she keeps her eyes open," he said. "And as for Mr. Durrant, you'll no doubt hear from him very soon. To me it seems perfectly clear that he has some hidden motive for keeping out of the way. Are his accounts at the office all right, for instance?"

"Quite in order."

"Blackmail may be at the bottom of it. That accounts for the mysterious disappearance of lots of men and women."

"But who could blackmail Mr. Durrant?"

"Ah! you don't know. A little slip, a year or so ago, and the screw is now being put on by those who know the truth. Oh! that is an everyday occurrence in London, I assure you, Miss Ramsay."

"Then you can't help me to find him?" she asked eagerly, after a brief silence.

"I don't see how we can act," was the officer's answer. "Had he disappeared without a word we would, of course, circulate his description and a photograph—if you have one?"

"Yes, I have one," she said anxiously.

"Good. But that is useless to us, for the simple reason that, after leaving you, he has sent you messages telling you not to worry. In face of that, how can we assume that anything tragic has happened to him? No, my dear young lady," he added. "I fear we cannot help you officially, much as I regret it."

Five minutes later Marigold descended the stairs, and walked out into the dark road utterly disconsolate and disappointed. Gerald was missing, yet the police would raise not a finger to assist her in tracing him!

Yet, after all, as she walked back to Bridge Place, she saw quite clearly that there was much truth in the detective-inspector's argument. Gerald had not suddenly disappeared and left no trace. He had urged her not to worry, and the inspector had advised her to keep on hoping for his return.

Later she sat in the kitchen with her aunt, and related all that had passed at the police-station.

"I quite agree with the inspector," declared the deaf old woman. "The police can't search for every man who goes away and sends telegrams saying he has gone. You see, Mr. Durrant hasn't committed any crime, for instance. So there's no real reason why the police should act. If he hadn't sent telegrams the case would be so different."

With that view the girl, greatly distressed and broken, had to agree.

It was then nearly ten o'clock, and at her aunt's suggestion Marigold resolved to stay the night and keep the old woman company.

"You can have the same room you had a little time ago," she said. "It is aired, for I always keep hot-water bottles in it in case it may be wanted. If you went home now, you wouldn't get there till half-past eleven. Besides, it's more cheerful for me. I'm beginning to hate this place now Mr. Boyne never comes near."

"The inspector said he saw Mr. Boyne in King Street to-night," Marigold said.

"Bosh! my dear," was old Mrs. Felmore's prompt reply. "He wouldn't be in King Street without coming home. It was somebody else he saw, no doubt." And that was exactly what Marigold herself thought.

Soon after half-past ten, Mrs. Felmore put out the light, and they both went to bed.

For half an hour Marigold lay awake thinking it all over, and thinking of the last occasion she had slept in that room, and of the mysterious chamber upstairs whence had issued those strange human cries. Then, at last, tired out, she dropped off to sleep.

How long she slept she knew not, but suddenly she was awakened by men's shouts, and next instant found the room full of smoke. There was a roaring noise outside. Half suffocated she groped her way to the door frantically, only to find the staircase above in flames.

"Auntie! auntie!" she yelled, not recollecting that her aunt was deaf, but by dint of fierce courage she got to the old lady's room. As she entered the door, Mrs. Felmore, half choking, met her in the red light thrown by the flames, and together they sprang down the staircase, along the hall, and, after fumbling with the chain upon the door, dashed out of the house to where a number of people, including three police constables, were awaiting the arrival of the fire brigade.

Meanwhile the top floor of the house was burning fiercely, the flames going up through the roof for many feet, and as there was rather a high wind, the sparks were flying everywhere.

Bernard Boyne's long deal box had sent petrol about the room of mystery at the time to which it had been set, and already all evidence of what was contained there, and of the mysterious origin of the fire, had been obliterated.

The insidious death-dealer had hoped to include Marigold and his housekeeper in that relentless plot to destroy all that might incriminate him.

But he was mistaken. Marigold Ramsay, though in her night attire—and who had fainted in the arms of a constable—had escaped unscathed!

CHAPTER XXIV
HARD PRESSED

When Céline Tènot and Henri Galtier so suddenly appeared outside Ena's flat as the dark shadow of menace at the very moment of the diabolical triumph of the death-dealers, Bernard Boyne realised that, in order to escape, he would have to summon all his wits. The death of old Mr. Martin in Chiswick was an ugly affair—a very ugly affair—and Céline more than suspected—she knew that somehow by the old man's death all three had profited.

At first Boyne was furious to think that Ena's visit to Melun, and the payment of that respectable sum, had been of no avail. But next second, he had seen that the only means of escape was to keep up his identity as Mr. Bennett, to temporise with his pursuers, and then to effect an escape. He saw that, at all hazards, he must prevent the pair of blackmailers from facing Ena and Lilla.

Therefore, when the Frenchman had expressed that hard determination that he wanted to prevent him from playing any more of his "hellish tricks" upon innocent people, he had stood in his path upon the pavement and replied:

"Now, Monsieur Galtier, just pause for a moment—and think! Aren't you a fool? Céline's late mistress has been very good to her, and now you come here and create trouble."

They were standing together against the railings of Hyde Park, not far from the taxi-men's shelter.

"I wish to create no trouble," declared the Frenchman in very good English. "Only trouble for *you!*" he snarled.

"That is extremely kind of you," Boyne retorted. "But if you still continue to threaten me, I shall take measures to protect myself, and also to retaliate."

"You have denounced me as a blackmailer!" the Frenchman snapped.

"I was wrong," said Boyne apologetically. "I withdraw those words. Naturally at first I believed you wanted more money!"

"Then you believed wrong," was the reply. "Our object in coming to London is to see madame and yourself—and to investigate further the death of Monsieur Martin."

"Well, that you are perfectly at liberty to do," Boyne said, with affected carelessness. "I have nothing whatever to fear. If you like to waste your time and money, do so."

"Céline knows the truth," retorted Galtier.

"Then let her go to the police and tell them. The London police pay little heed to the statements of discharged servants, especially if they are foreigners."

"Yes, I will go!" cried the French girl excitedly. "You are assassins!—assassins! You—both of you!—killed poor Monsieur Martin!"

"I think you will have to prove that," replied Boyne, remaining very calm.

"Hush, Céline!" said her lover. "We do not want a fracas in the street!"

"Bah! The man thinks we are afraid of him. But we are not! We are here to get at the truth about poor monsieur."

"Well, mademoiselle, you are at perfect liberty to institute inquiries," Boyne replied. "But before you go to the police as you threaten, just pause and ask yourself what all this storm in a teacup will profit you and your friend."

The vivacious girl shrugged her shoulders.

"Remember that madame is your friend," he went on. "She told me that she has recently been in Paris, and called upon you in Melun. Madame, since you left, has several times expressed regret to me that she was abrupt."

"Because she believes that I know your secret!" cried mademoiselle, interrupting.

"Let us walk on," suggested Boyne, turning purposely towards Knightsbridge. "There are some people trying to overhear our conversation."

Galtier saw a man and two women who had halted close by, probably attracted by the loud tones in which they were conversing. Strange conversations go on in the London streets at night, as every police constable knows. The night-world of London is an amazing world, of which the honest go-to-bed-early citizen knows nothing. One half the world of London is ignorant of what the other half does o' nights.

They moved on past the taxi shelter towards Knightsbridge, which was in the opposite direction to Upper Brook Street.

"I think you are certainly not fair to madame," Boyne said very quietly to the girl. "She, out of her own generous heart—for no better-hearted woman ever lived—sought you out because she felt that she had treated you unkindly. Of course, I do not know the real facts, but on the face of it I think you, mademoiselle, treated your late mistress with ingratitude. I say this," he went on, "in a perfectly friendly spirit. You may have formed some unfounded suspicion regarding poor Mr. Martin's death. Why, I don't know."

"Because I heard the truth from madame's own lips."

"Some distorted words half overheard, I suppose," he laughed. "My dear mademoiselle, it is always very dangerous to interfere with the death of anybody, because here in England there is such a thing as a law of slander, and of libel—criminal libel, which means that those who make false accusations may be committed to prison. Therefore, before you go further, I advise you to consult a solicitor. He will no doubt advise you."

"We will see the police first," declared Galtier.

"I have not the slightest objection," laughed Boyne. "If you think it will avail you, go to Scotland Yard. That is the head office of the Criminal Investigation Department, but"—and he paused—"but I tell you this, Monsieur, if either of you make any accusations against madame or myself, we shall at once prosecute you—and further, if you escape back to France, we will follow you there and prosecute you. Here, in England, we will not permit foreigners to come over and give the police a lot of trouble for nothing. So make whatever statement you like, but don't forget you will have to substantiate it with witnesses—otherwise you'll probably both find yourselves in prison. That's all I have to say. Good-night!"

And, turning abruptly upon his heel, the master-criminal walked back towards Hyde Park Corner, leaving mademoiselle and her companion utterly perplexed.

Bernard Boyne, as he hurried up Park Lane on his return to Upper Brook Street, muttered to himself:

"I've given them something to think over! They'll hesitate—and while they hesitate, we must act. It would have been fatal for them to have met Ena—and especially to-night—*of all nights*!"

Ten minutes later he was back in Ena Pollen's room, where she was sitting with Lilla.

"What's happened?" asked his wife, for the paleness of his countenance betrayed that something was amiss.

"Oh! nothing—nothing serious, I mean!" was his reply. "Get me a liqueur brandy," he stammered.

Ena went at once to the dining-room and brought a little glass of old cognac, which he swallowed at a gulp, and then sat for a few moments staring straight before him.

"Tell us, Bernie. What's happened? Where have you been?" demanded his wife.

"Been! I—well, I've been right into the camp of the enemy!" he said hoarsely.

"Enemy! What enemy?"

"Céline is here. Wants to see you. The fellow Galtier is with her. They are on the track of old Martin, and want to see you!"

The two women exchanged glances, for the light in the faces of both had died out.

"Céline here!" gasped Ena. "How much does she know?"

"How can we tell? I've simply defied her."

"But why didn't you offer to pay? They, of course, want money."

Rapidly he described to the two excited women what had occurred. Then at last Lilla said:

"Well, the only thing we can do is to sit tight. We must—if we are to get the money paid on dear Augusta's policy."

"Of course, we can't slip out, or it would be an admission, if Céline really goes to the police."

"There is nothing to prevent her," remarked Ena. "The girl is dangerous."

"So is that girl Ramsay. I've always said so," Lilla declared. "Her lover is out of the way, and the sooner she herself is silenced the better, for as long as that pair are alive they will always be a menace to us."

"I quite agree," said the red-haired widow. "You said that many weeks ago."

"Well, it is all in Bernie's hands. It's no use getting the insurance company to pay without taking due precautions to protect ourselves, is it?" asked Boyne's wife.

The death-dealers thereupon took counsel together. For an hour they sat discussing plans, each putting their idea forward. In the whole of criminal London no three persons were so callous, so ingenious, or so regardless of human life. They had discovered a means of making money with little exertion and with certain results. Boyne, expert as he was in insurance and of a scientific turn of mind, could deal death whenever and wherever he desired, and in such a manner that no coroner's jury could pronounce a verdict other than that death had supervened as a natural cause.

Not before three o'clock in the morning did Lilla and her husband leave Upper Brook Street, and when they did an elaborate and ingenious plan had been decided upon which left no loophole for discovery.

Mrs. Augusta Morrison of Carsphairn had died, and Ena would, of course, excuse herself from going to the funeral. She had mourning which, as a matter of fact, she had worn on more than one occasion when a wealthy friend of hers had died. But in this case she dared not put in an appearance.

At home in Pont Street, Boyne sat with his wife and discussed the situation at considerable length.

"You must get rid of that girl Marigold," she said very emphatically, as she lounged upon the silk-covered sofa in the elegant little room. "She suspects something at Bridge Place, just as her lover suspected. Well, we've successfully sent him off, and he can thank his lucky stars he didn't get a dose."

"I only wish now I had given him a little dose that would have caused him trouble about ten days after he sailed," Boyne said.

"Yes, Bernie. Recollect, I suggested it. They could have buried him at sea, and we should not have been troubled by him any further."

"I was a fool not to take your advice, Lilla."

"You always are. But take my advice about the girl. She's distinctly dangerous! A menace to all of us! And so is your *ménage* at Hammersmith — especially if Céline really does go to the police. You should end it all, and above everything close Marigold's mouth. That girl is the greatest peril we have before us!"

Her husband, who had lit a cigarette, and was lounging in a chair, agreed with her.

"But," he said, "how am I to do it? We are in a devilish tight corner, Lilla! The game has been a great and very easy one up to now. Nobody has ever yet tumbled to the scientific insurance stunt. And there's lots of money in it. We've found it so. We've got between us eighty thousand or so. A very decent sum. And we could make a million, given a quiet market. Look at the lots of red- or golden-haired women who are wealthy and who are not of any use on earth. Life assurance companies are always on the look-out for business, and pay commission to any and every little tin-pot agent who can put through a proposal. Remember that young fool of a solicitor in Manchester. And there are hundreds about the country everywhere."

"That's so, Bernie," replied his wife in a matter-of-fact tone, she having taken a cigarette to smoke with her husband. "But here we have a peril before us. We were never in such a tight corner before. This may finish us!"

"Oh! my dear Lilla, don't get flurried. I am not. The fellow Durrant is on the high seas as a man who has had a nervous breakdown. Oh, that description! What a godsend it is to us all, isn't it? Nervous breakdown is responsible for a thousand and one evasions of the law—theft, bigamy, assault, forgery—in fact, almost any crime in the calendar can be committed and ascribed to the 'nervous breakdown' of the defendant. We've a lot to be thankful for from the doctors, Lilla," he said, "a lot to be thankful for!"

"Well," she said, puffing thoughtfully at her cigarette, "if the secret of Bridge Place were exposed, then I fear that you couldn't ascribe it to a nervous breakdown, eh?"

Boyne laughed.

"No, Lilla. You are always alive—you are amazingly clever!" he declared. "I did my best with that French girl, Céline, but—well, I'm not quite certain whether she won't go to the police and make a statement."

"Ah! I see," Lilla said quickly. "So we ought to clear out—and quickly."

"Out of London, but not abroad. But not yet. If all of us left suddenly, the insurance company might get scent of a mystery, especially if Céline says anything about old Martin to the police."

"But what of Marigold? Has she any suspicion that Durrant is on the sea?"

"None. Durrant telegraphed to her to urge her to be patient and that he will return. So she's waiting—and she'll wait a long time!

"Ah! really, Bernie, you are wonderful. That was a glorious idea of yours—those telegrams."

"Yes. They've worked well," he said. "Both the girl and his sister, as well as the fellow's employers, have all been reassured."

"But the girl is a menace, I repeat," the woman declared, "and as such you must see that her activity comes to an end. There are a dozen ways in which you can manage it. Adopt one of them, and lose no time about it," she urged.

"Yes," he said in a hard voice, "I ought to have taken your advice long ago."

"Well, take it now," she said. "There are enemies around us—Céline, Galtier, and this girl Ramsay. So be careful. We are in very serious peril!"

"True. How serious we have yet to learn. But let's remain cool and we shall most certainly win."

Almost as he spoke, however, the electric bell at the front door rang, causing them both to start.

"Whoever can it be at this hour?" gasped Lilla, jumping to her feet.

"Wait!" said Boyne, in a changed voice. "I'll go down and see."

He did so. Lilla stood breathless, listening. She heard him unbolt the door and open it.

Then she heard him give vent to a loud cry, half of surprise, half of terror, as a man's deep voice spoke.

CHAPTER XXV
THE RECLUSE

The commotion caused in Bridge Place by the fire at Mr. Boyne's was not of long duration. Ere the fire brigade arrived, however, so swift was the fire that the two top floors were gutted, thus destroying the secret of that locked chamber.

A woman who lived a few doors off, and who knew Mrs. Felmore, gave the deaf old woman and her niece shelter, and while the police kept back the crowd at both ends of the street the four engines which had arrived were soon pumping water upon the roaring flames. The house was an old one with much woodwork, therefore it burned like tinder, and Marigold had certainly only escaped with her life. The superintendent in charge of the firemen had already ascertained that no person remained within, and the men in their shining helmets, their figures illuminated by the glare from the flames, were clambering across the neighbouring roofs with their hose-pipes.

Soon the flames were got under by the powerful rush of water, but not before the roof had fallen in, and only the ground floor remained intact, while the houses on either side were badly damaged. Every now and then, when a beam fell, or a portion of wall collapsed, showers of sparks shot upward, and there was a burst of flames through the smoke.

A fire in any crowded district of London at whatever hour always attracts a large number of onlookers. That night was no exception, for a big crowd had assembled at either end of the street, and in the centre of the crowd towards Hammersmith Bridge, wedged between several women of the lower class, stood a shabbily-dressed man in a golf cap watching intently the progress of the fire.

He watched it with satisfaction, and saw the flames as they descended and burst through the windows of the second floor. When the roof fell in he smiled, though none noticed it.

The man saw that all evidence of his diabolical work had been destroyed, for he was none other than Bernard Boyne.

What had happened to Marigold and her aunt? He asked the woman standing next to him if any people were in the house.

"Yes. They say there's two women and a man there," was the reply. "The man got out, but the two women 'ave been burnt to death, poor dears! Ain't it terrible? They were asleep when the fire broke out. The firemen 'aven't got the bodies out yet."

"Terrible!" declared the man in the golf cap; and then he elbowed his way out of the crowd filled with satisfaction.

As he did so a youth shouted:

"Lucky for 'em—eh? Both the women got out just in time."

"Is that so?" asked Boyne.

"Yes," said the youth. "One of the firemen 'as just told me."

"There was a girl there, wasn't there?" Boyne queried.

"Yes; she was got out, with an old woman!"

"Where are they?"

"They say they're in a house just along there," was the reply.

Boyne held his breath and went on. At first he had believed that his dastardly plot had been successful, and that Marigold had fallen a victim to his clever machinations. At least, the two upper floors had been destroyed and certain evidence wiped out. The clock, the pocket-lighter, and the child's rubber airball filled with petrol, which had been in the box he had so silently introduced into the house while Marigold was at the police-station, had done their work just as he had intended. But he was filled with disappointment and chagrin when, after several other inquiries of firemen and others, he became convinced that old Mrs. Felmore and her niece had escaped.

At last, after watching until the excitement of the scene had died down and the crowd was dispersing, he learnt from one of the firemen—he dared not be seen by a police constable, for most of them knew him by sight—the house in which the two half-suffocated women had taken shelter.

Then he turned and trudged all the way back to Pont Street, for, dressed as he was, he did not wish to get there until the servants had retired.

He had made another great coup, it was true, but the peril of Marigold still existed. That was the one thought that obsessed him as he strode up the long Kensington Road, past the Albert Hall, and on towards Hyde Park Corner.

The night of Augusta's death had been fraught with sufficient perils in all conscience. He recollected the unexpected appearance of Céline and her companion, of how he had defied them, and how, later that night, a caller had come to Pont Street—a caller who could not be refused admission—the man who had for so long been in hiding in that upstairs room which had now been totally wiped out by the flames. "I shall have to reappear at home to-morrow full of surprise," he muttered to himself, as at last he let himself into the house in Pont Street, the door of which Lilla had left purposely unbolted.

Next day about noon, carrying a suit-case and dressed as he usually was when going about his duties in Hammersmith, he arrived in Bridge Place utterly amazed at finding his house wrecked and ruined. A constable was on duty—a man who knew him.

"Well, sir," exclaimed the man in uniform, "this is pretty bad, ain't it? The fire broke out late last night, but it's fortunate the two women got out in time."

"What?" gasped Boyne, apparently staggered at the sight. "What's happened? I've been away in Liverpool, and have only just got back!"

"Well, that deaf old woman will be glad you're back, sir. She's been round to the police-station telling 'em that you were away."

"Where is she?"

"In the house over there," and he pointed to it.

"You said there was another woman in the house. Who was she?"

"A girl. The old woman's niece, I've heard. She's all right, and went away early this morning."

"Oh, yes, I know her. Came to keep the old woman company while I was away, I expect," he said. "But how fortunate they were saved! How did it happen? Does anyone know?"

"The superintendent of the brigade was here about two hours ago, and they examined the ruins. They think that the fire must have broken out in the top room upstairs. I went over it with them. We found a lot of fused glass, which rather puzzled them."

"Oh, yes. A lot of bottles I kept upstairs. I suppose they melted in the heat," Boyne replied. "Did they find anything else?"

"No, nothing of any importance."

"Then they don't know how it broke out?"

"No; except that there must have been something up there very inflammable, they say, for the fire spread so quickly."

"Perhaps it was a bottle of benzine I had up there for cleaning my clothes," said Boyne. "But, any case, it's rough luck on me—for I'm not insured."

"Sorry to hear that, sir," replied the constable. "They said, you being an insurance agent, you would be certain to be covered against loss."

"No. It's the old story over again," Boyne said, with a grin, "'the shoemaker's child is the worst shod.' I was a fool not to insure against fire—an infernal fool! But it can't be helped. It's ruined me!" and he turned away and crossed the road to the house which the constable had indicated as the one where old Mrs. Felmore had sought shelter.

For half an hour Boyne sat listening while the old woman shouted to him excitedly her description of the fire. He adopted that mealy-mouthed attitude which he could assume at will—that attitude he adopted so cleverly when he went to church so regularly—and condoled with her.

"Of course, Mrs. Felmore, all this horrible catastrophe shall not make any difference to you. I hear you had Miss Marigold to keep you company. Quite right! But I'm so very sorry about it all. The poor girl must have been very frightened. Where is she?"

"She went back to Wimbledon Park about an hour ago, sir. She telegraphed to the bank excusing herself for to-day, as she only had clothes that were lent her."

"Ah! I am so sorry about that. But have you any idea how it all happened?" Boyne asked the old woman.

"No, sir, I haven't. I'm always so careful about fire," she answered. "I was burnt when I was a child, and therefore I always look at the kitchen grate and rake the cinders out before I goes to bed."

"But it seems to have been upstairs where the fire originated."

"Yes, sir," replied the old woman. "I expect it was the kitchen flue. I asked old Mr. Morgan, the sweep, to do it three weeks ago, but he was very busy, and he didn't come. I've cleaned out the range all right—but that's what I think. I'm sorry, sir, but it wasn't my fault, really it wasn't."

"Of course not, Mrs. Felmore. Morgan should have come when you ordered him," Boyne said.

Afterwards he succeeded in entering the gaunt blackened wreck of his home. With satisfaction he saw the frameless windows of the two upper floors, but inside a spectacle of utter ruin met his gaze. The water had come through the ceiling of his sitting-room, half of which was down, the stairs consumed, and all the remaining furniture ruined beyond repair.

From the cupboard, however, he took his pet "Nibby," who was still alive, and probably wondering at all the commotion.

"Poor little fellow!" he exclaimed, stroking the rat's pointed pink nose, and afterwards placing him in his pocket, as he did sometimes. "I shall give you to Mrs. Felmore."

And after a final look round at the scene of the wreckage, he returned to where his deaf old housekeeper was staying, and presented her with the tame rat.

Late that same afternoon Boyne hurried along Theobald's Road, past the railings of Gray's Inn, and crossing the busy road with its procession of tramcars, turned the corner into Harpur Street, a short, dingy thoroughfare of smoke-grimed, old-fashioned houses, once the residences of well-to-do people, but now mostly let out in tenements.

Before one of the houses on the left-hand side he halted, and pulled the bell. The door was opened by a young girl wearing a dirty apron and whose hair was in curlers.

"Good-afternoon, Mr. Bennett. Yes, 'e's upstairs," she exclaimed.

So up the uncarpeted stairs Boyne went to the top of the house.

"It's only me," he said reassuringly as he turned the handle of a door and unceremoniously entered a small, barely-furnished, ill-kept room.

A cheap oil lamp, smoking badly, was burning on the table, while near it, back in the shadow, sat the figure of a man huddled up in a ragged old armchair.

"You!" he grunted. "You've been a long time!

"I couldn't get here before, Lionel. It was too dangerous. I had to see that all was clear before I to enter this street. There's always a detective or two about here, and it wouldn't do for you to be seen outside."

"No," grunted the man, who, rising slowly to his feet came within the feeble zone of light which revealed a thin, bony face, with high cheek bones, an abnormal forehead, and a pair of deep-set dark eyes. The faded grey suit he wore was several sizes too big for him, yet his arms seemed of unusual length, and his hands were narrow and long, with talon-like fingers.

His countenance was truly a strange one, being triangular, with very narrow chin and very broad brow—the face of a man who was either a genius or an idiot.

"I waited all night for you!" he said in plaintive tones. "And you never came."

"Well, I'm not going to risk anything—even for you!" replied Boyne roughly. "I've got quite enough of my own troubles just now."

"Oh! What's happened?"

"Lots. It's a good job I got you away from Hammersmith, my friend. The place has burned up!"

"Burned up?" echoed the strange-looking man. "Oh! Then you've had the beautiful fire you used to talk about, eh? And has it all gone?"

"The lot. And a darned good job for you!"

"And that beautiful microscope?" the man asked regretfully. "Has that gone, too?"

"Yes. The whole bag of tricks has been consumed. That's why I didn't come last night," Boyne said.

"Oh! the beautiful mike!" exclaimed the abnormal creature, as though to himself. "And it cost such a lot—oh, such a lot!"

"Don't trouble about the microscope, you fool!" cried Boyne roughly. "Just try and pull yourself together and save your own skin. Where are those tubes? I want them."

The lean man in the over-large suit ambled across the room, his head bent forward, for he was very round-shouldered, and going to an old leather bag in the corner, slowly unlocked it and drew out a thick cartridge envelope which contained something hard.

Boyne took it from him quickly, and tearing it open, took out two dark-blue tubes of glass, the corks of which were sealed with wax.

"Are they all right?" he asked harshly. "Can you guarantee them? Now don't tell me a lie," he added threateningly, "or it will be the worse for you. I had a good mind to give you over to the police when you came to Pont Street the other night. You deserved it—venturing out like that."

"I got to know where you were, and I had to come and see you," whirled the ugly creature as he ambled back to his chair.

"Don't do it again! Remain in hiding. Keep close here. You are in comfortable quarters. Old Mrs. Sampson below is always silent as regards her lodgers. Lots of men who have had this room have hidden from the police till they found a way out of it. Take my advice, and do the same. But don't attempt to come round to Pont Street—for we don't want you there, *understand that*?"

And he put the little glass tubes, which contained fatal bacteria, back into their envelope and placed them carefully in his pocket.

"But money! I must have money!" cried the other, a young-old man whose age it was impossible to determine though his hair was growing grey.

"Of course you must," laughed Boyne. "Here's fifty pounds to go on with. And keep a still tongue or it will be the worse for you. Recollect if you are unfortunate enough to be arrested, it will only be because of your own idiotic movements. Keep quiet here."

"Misfortune may befall any of us!" said the other in that peculiar whining voice which showed that his mental balance was not normal.

"True. But if you do happen to fall into the hands of the police, remember—breathe not a word. Trust to me to help you out of the scrape. Trust Mrs. Sampson downstairs—and trust me."

"Yes. But, oh, that beautiful mike! Burnt up. That beautiful mike!"

"Don't bother about that. I'll buy you another, and all the apparatus if you'll only keep a still tongue and remain in the house. I've told Mrs. Sampson not to let you out."

"Oh! I won't go out. I promise you I won't," he said with an idiotic stare. "I only went to Pont Street because I wanted to know if you were all right."

"And incidentally you wanted money!" laughed the other. "Well, you had it—you have it again now. Remain quiet and content. I'm busy. I've got lots of things to look after. I've probably got to go away, but I'll see you have money to go on with all right."

"Very well," said the strange man. "This place is better than Hammersmith, living in a locked room for weeks and months, nobody to see, and only breathing the fresh air on the roof when everybody had gone to bed."

"But you had your work—your scientific work in bacteriology! You can't live without your work!"

"Ah, yes. I had my work. But, oh! it was so lonely—so very lonely."

"You're not lonely here," said Boyne cheerfully. "So don't bother. Take your ease, and make the best of it. You're in a house which shelters people like yourself. Here everyone keeps a still tongue—and nobody knows about little Maggie."

The curious man with the triangular face blinked across at Boyne—and remained silent for several moments.

"Little Maggie!" he gasped at last. "Little Maggie! Ah! I remember. I——"

Again he paused. Then glaring into Boyne's face with a strange wild expression, he said:

"You! Why—why you're—you're really Willie Wisden!"

"Of course I am," laughed Boyne. "But keep cool, Lionel, old chap, or you'll have one of those nasty attacks of yours coming on again. Ta-ta! I'll come back very soon," he said, and turning he left the room and descended the stairs.

"Perhaps I'll come back," he muttered to himself. "But I do not think so! The idiot has served me well, and I've got the tubes. That is all I want—at present!"

And a moment later he was walking in the darkness through Harpur Street.

CHAPTER XXVI
"GET RID OF THE GIRL!"

Ten days more had passed. Poor Mrs. Morrison had been buried at Brookwood, her sister and several relatives being among the mourners.

Notice had been given through a solicitor to the insurance company of the assignment of the policy for ten thousand pounds to Mrs. Braybourne. The solicitor, a perfectly respectable man practising in the City, had received a call from Mrs. Braybourne of Pont Street, and she had handed him the policy and the assignment. Boyne had first made secret inquiries regarding the unsuspecting lawyer, and found him to be a man with a very high reputation in his profession.

Hence the Red Widow and her two associates, having successfully defied the French ex-maid and her lover, were now awaiting payment by the insurance company. Boyne, on his part, had cleverly destroyed all traces of the secret of that upstairs room in which had lived for some time the half-demented, eccentric Lionel Gosden, who was so blindly obedient to every order of the criminal who held him in control.

"There only remains that girl!" remarked Boyne as he sat with his wife one night.

"Yes. The sooner she's out of the way the better, my dear Bernie. She knows far too much."

"I've got the remainder of the stuff from Lionel."

"Then it will be quite easy. I needn't tell you the way."

Boyne smiled as he took another cigarette from his case.

"Yes," he said. "And then I think that Ena and I will clear off abroad and leave you as the lone widow in whose favour dear Augusta insured her life."

"True. We ought to part as soon as possible. What do they think of your absence from Hammersmith?"

"Oh, they know my home is burned up, but I put in an appearance now and then and collect up a few premiums just to show myself."

"I wonder what the girl told the police?" Lilla remarked thoughtfully.

"Some story which they, no doubt, put down to be a cock-and-bull statement—about the locked room, most probably. She might have heard Lionel moving about, or coughing, before I got him away from there. If so the noise would naturally excite her suspicion."

"What about the man Durrant?"

"Oh, we needn't trouble about him. It will be months before he can get back again, and when he does, he'll find none of us here, the girl dead—of natural causes, of course—and the house being rebuilt. We have nothing to fear from him, providing we can get rid of the girl."

"And that must be done at once," the handsome woman repeated. "While she is alive she will be a constant menace to us."

Next morning, when he left Pont Street, he went to the City, and, knowing that Marigold always went out at a quarter to one to her lunch, he waited outside the bank.

At last she came, a neatly-dressed and dainty figure of the true type of business girl, and at the corner of Fenchurch Street he met her as though by accident, and raised his hat.

"Why, Mr. Boyne!" she exclaimed in surprise.

"Yes. This is an unexpected meeting, Miss Marigold! I haven't seen you since the fire," he said. "How lucky that you and your aunt escaped! I can't think how it was caused, except that your aunt perhaps dropped a match upstairs before going to bed."

"No, Mr. Boyne," she said. "It's a mystery. I'm glad, however, that auntie is recovering from the shock."

"Have you heard anything lately of Mr.—what is his name?—Durrant, isn't it?"

"Not a word. I can't think what has become of him. They've heard nothing at his office since his last telegram."

"Oh! I shouldn't worry. He told you in his message not to worry, you know," he said cheerfully.

Marigold distrusted the man, yet she remembered how she and Gerald had resolved, at all hazards, to penetrate the mystery surrounding him. She could not deny that he had always been polite and generous towards her, and her aunt would never have a more kind and considerate master.

"Come and have some lunch with me," he suggested suddenly, as he glanced at his watch. "I'm just going to have mine. And I want to talk over your aunt's future—what she is to do while my house is being rebuilt."

Marigold hesitated a few seconds. Then she replied:

"I'm awfully sorry, Mr. Boyne, but my assistant is away ill, and we're most awfully busy in the bank to-day. I am only out for ten minutes this morning, I usually have half an hour."

"Then come somewhere and have dinner with me to-night."

"I can't to-night. I'm going to the theatre with a girl friend."

"To-morrow night, then," he said. "I'll meet you at Piccadilly tube station, say at seven, and we'll dine somewhere—eh?"

Again Marigold hesitated. She was naturally distrustful, yet she argued within herself that perhaps if she accepted his invitation she might learn from him something of interest.

"No," he laughed merrily. "I'm sure you won't refuse me, Marigold. I want to see what I can do for your aunt—because—well, perhaps I may not set up house again. And I don't want to leave her in the lurch, poor deaf old soul."

His solicitude for her aunt touched her, and so she promised to meet him as he suggested.

Then two minutes later he raised his hat and they parted.

As the girl sat with her glass of milk and sandwiches before her in the little teashop, strange thoughts crowded through her mind. The refusal of the police to assist her to find Gerald had hipped her, and ever since the night of the fire she had gone about utterly disconsolate and broken-hearted. The fire was mysterious, coming within an hour or so of her visit to the police. Yes; the more she reflected, the stranger still appeared the whole enigma.

She returned to the bank and sat hour after hour her books, but her only thought was of Gerald the reason of his disappearance.

Next day, just before noon, while she was busy at the bank, one of the male clerks came to her desk, and said:

"Miss Ramsay, you're wanted on the telephone."

"Me!" exclaimed Marigold, much surprised, for none of the staff were allowed to speak on the telephone except upon urgent family affairs. "Was this one?"

She hurried to the telephone-box and heard a female voice, which she recognised as that of Gerald's sister at Ealing.

"You there, Marigold. Listen!" she said. "I've just had a wire from Gerald. It's sent from Folkestone Harbour, and says:

"'Back again. Don't worry. With you soon, but not yet. Marigold knows why. Have wired her.—GERALD.'"

"Oh, how lovely!" cried the girl over the 'phone in wild delight. "I expect I've got a wire at Wimbledon. I'll tell you what he says. Such lots of thanks for ringing up. Good-bye. I'll come over and see you soon, dear. Righto!"

And she hung up the receiver, her cheeks flushed with the excitement of the good news.

Gerald—her Gerald—had spoken at last!

Further adding of figures that day was out of the question. She could not work, but, ever and anon, she raised her eyes to the big clock, the hands of which moved, oh! so slowly. At last five o'clock came, and she put her books away in the trolley ready to be wheeled to the strong room by the uniformed messenger, and putting on her hat and coat hurried away home in the crowded tube.

She missed her train, and things seemed to move too slow for her, but on arrival at the station she raced home. Yes, in the narrow hall of the little suburban villa lay a telegram on the hat-stand.

She tore it open with frantic haste, and read:

"Do not make inquiry about me. Am quite safe, and am in possession of some very important facts. Just returned from abroad. Be watchful, but do not feel anxious. Am quite all right. Love.—GERALD."

It reassured her. She dressed and went out to meet Mr. Boyne, carrying in her handbag the treasured message from Folkestone Pier, together with her powder-puff, her little mirror, and a few hairpins.

She had no idea, however, that at the moment when she was dressing to dine with her aunt's benefactor, a lady with red-brown hair, having taken tea at the Pavilion Hotel in Folkestone, was in a first-class carriage in a boat express for London, and that that same lady had only arrived in Folkestone a couple of hours before, and on meeting the boat had handed in the message at the office at the harbour.

She was at Piccadilly tube station quite early, and it was fully ten minutes before Boyne put in an appearance, smiling and happy.

"I'm so glad you've been able to come, Miss Marigold," he exclaimed, as he shook hands with her warmly. "Now, we'll just go and have a little dinner together, and talk about your aunt, eh?"

And he placed his hand upon her arm in a paternal manner, and started to cross the road to Coventry Street. "There's a little Italian place in Wardour Street where they do you excellently. A man I know told me of it the other day, and I dined there a couple of nights ago and found things very good. Not much of a place to look at, but good, well-cooked food. So let's go there."

She walked with him, but unable to contain her joy at receiving that reassuring wire from Gerald. She said, as they walked along Coventry Street:

"I've had a wire to-night from Mr. Durrant. He's all right."

"Have you really? How excellent!" exclaimed Boyne. "What does he say?"

"He wires from Folkestone pier. He's just arrived back in England, and he says he's all right. That's all."

"Well, what do you want more? Your boy is back, and no doubt you'll see him soon. I've always had in my mind that his absence has been due to some secret mission given to him by his employer. Those food people in Mincing Lane are profiteering out of all conscience, and Durrant's absence is only what might well be expected. He will get a big bonus for carrying out some little bit of delicate diplomacy with regard to food supplies from abroad."

They turned up Wardour Street, and presently stopped in front of one of the small, unpretentious little foreign restaurants, where one can always rely upon good cooking, even though the quality of the food sometimes leaves a little to be desired.

Not more than half a dozen people were in the white-enamelled little place, but the proprietor, a well-dressed, prosperous-looking little Italian, came forward to greet them.

"Table for two—oh! yes. You reserved it, sare—I know! This way, please." And he conducted them to a cosy spot in a corner where a table was laid à deux.

Marigold, flushed with excitement on account of the telegram in her bag, threw off her coat, settled her blouse, and sat down opposite the man, while an elderly waiter was quickly in attendance.

"I've ordered dinner," said Boyne, rather impetuously. "Antonio will know." And he dismissed him.

"I've told them to get a nice little dinner for us," he said, looking across at the girl. "Well, now, Miss Marigold," he went on. "First, I'm delighted that you could come and have dinner with me to-night. Now that my house is no longer inhabitable, I live in rooms at Notting Hill Gate. But rooms are not like one's own home, and especially with your aunt as housekeeper. A more economical woman never lived. She'd save the egg-shells and turn them into money, if she could!"

And they both laughed.

"Yes; auntie is very saving," replied the girl, whose sole purpose in accepting the unusual invitation was to try and draw her host, and so further the plans set by her lover.

"Saving! What I always say is that she's the most perfect housekeeper anyone ever had. That's why I want to do something for her."

"It's really very good of you, Mr. Boyne," said the girl, "I know now keenly she has always looked after your interests."

"And I appreciate that, Miss Marigold. Now, my idea is to allow her two pounds a week till I get settled again."

"Very generous of you, I'm sure," replied Marigold. "With her infirmity, it's most difficult. Her deafness has increased the last six months, and she could never get another situation now. I'm sure of that."

"Then you'll look after her if she has two pounds a week regularly.— eh?"

"Yes. She can come and live with me at Wimbledon," the girl said. "I'm sure auntie will be very grateful," she added. "Only a couple of days ago she told me she was wondering what she would do now that the house is burnt, and she couldn't live with a neighbour for ever."

Boyne was silent for a few seconds. The waiter had placed the little plates of sardines, olives, and sliced beet upon the table, the usual hors d'oeuvres of the foreign restaurant.

The girl's host looked her in the face suddenly, and asked:

"Tell me, Miss Marigold, what friends have you?"

"Relatives, you mean? Well, practically none who count, except auntie and my sister," she replied, little dreaming that the man had put that question with an ulterior motive—and a very sinister one, too.

"And also Mr. Durrant," he laughed.

Marigold blushed.

"Don't fear. He'll soon be back with you, and no doubt explain matters."

The girl made no reply. It was her own secret that his absence was due to the inquiries he was making concerning the past career of the plausible and hard-working man who was at that moment her host.

The soup was served, a clear *pot-au-feu*, hot, and as the waiter turned away, Boyne drew handkerchief from his trouser pocket, and next moment a number of coins fell upon the floor.

Instantly Marigold drew her chair away from the table and bent down to see where they were. At that moment Bernard Boyne executed a clever trick which he had done before. He flicked into the girl's hot soup a piece of very soft gelatine that had been extracted only half an hour before from one of those mysterious blue glass tubes he had obtained from the idiot-scientist hiding in Harpur Street.

The piece of gelatine fell into the soup unnoticed by the girl, whose eagerness was centred upon the picking up of the lost coins, and the other diners only glanced across for a second, and did not notice the dropping of that fatal dose.

"Don't bother," he said airily next moment. "The waiter will find it. They are really only coppers. I was foolish to put my handkerchief there. Please don't bother. Your soup will be cold."

And, thus reassured, the girl drank her soup with her spoon and greatly enjoyed it—for it was excellent.

Boyne watched her with complete satisfaction and confidence.

The other courses were served: fillets of sole, and a chicken *en casserole*, with mushrooms, in true Continental style. Then a cup in which were fruit, ice-cream, and champagne, and black coffee afterwards.

The dinner Marigold agreed was excellent. Boyne smoked cigarettes and chatted merrily the whole time, until at last he paid the bill and walked back with her.

They shook hands, and she thanked him heartily. Then they parted, Boyne promising to see old Mrs. Felmore and pay her the amount he suggested.

As he strode along down the Haymarket, however, on his way back to Pont Street, he laughed aloud and muttered to himself:

"I don't think we shall be troubled with you, young lady, after a few more days!"

CHAPTER XXVII
"THE DAY AFTER TOMORROW"

Three days passed. Marigold, on rising in the morning of the third day, felt hot and feverish. Her sister had suggested that she should telephone to the bank excusing herself.

"I think I've got a chill," Marigold remarked. "I felt rather queer yesterday."

"Then stay at home, dear."

"I can't," the girl declared as she put on her hat. "We're so awfully busy just now. Miss Meldrum and Miss Page are both away with influenza. I'm bound to go."

So she went, but feeling very ill. At the bank one or two of the girls remarked how unwell she looked, and as the morning wore on the pains in her head became worse. She could eat no lunch, and at two o'clock she was compelled to return home to Wimbledon.

She went straight to bed, but her friends troubled little, for it was evident that she was run down by the eternal anxiety over Gerald's absence, and that she had caught a severe cold.

Next morning she seemed worse, therefore her sister went for Doctor Thurlow, who lived in Kenilworth Avenue; but he was so busy that it was not possible for him to put in an appearance until nearly seven o'clock that evening.

He examined the girl, and though he could not diagnose the cause immediately, he at once recognised that she was decidedly ill. He prescribed a mixture, gave certain instructions, and promised to call early next morning.

This he did and found that her temperature had risen, and that she was much worse and a little delirious. In her delirium she called constantly for Gerald in a pathetic, piteous voice.

"Will my Gerald never come back to me?" she cried. "Will he never return?"

"She is ill—very ill," declared the doctor gravely to her sister. "We shall have to be extremely careful of her."

Marigold was coughing badly, for already a large area of her lungs had become involved and consolidated. Hence the doctor carried a portion of the sputum to his surgery, and that afternoon discovered the presence of the deadly streptococcus. On establishing the actual disease he at once telephoned for some anti-pneumococcic serum, and this he injected into the patient early next morning.

Having done so, he turned to her sister, and said:

"I am extremely sorry to tell you that this is our last hope. She is, I fear, collapsing fast. The organism I have found is most deadly, and I think it only right to tell you that my personal opinion is that the disease has gone too far."

"What, Doctor?" gasped the young woman, pale and anxious. "Will she die?"

"That I cannot say, but I never like to deceive my patients' friends in cases so critical as this. To me she seems to be growing weaker. I will be back at noon."

And the busy, white-headed doctor went out and drove away in his car.

Now on that same morning about eleven o'clock a tall, gaunt, hollow-eyed young man in a shabby tweed suit and golf cap walked quickly up from the Empress Dock at Southampton and across Canute Road to the railway-station, where he bought a third-class ticket for Waterloo.

"Back in England at last!" he muttered to himself as he entered an empty compartment. "I shall soon see Marigold again! Then we will get even with our enemies."

The unshaven man was Gerald Durrant, changed indeed from the spruce young secretary of Mincing Lane. He looked ten years older, for his face was pinched though bronzed, and the suit he wore was certainly never made for him.

The truth was that the steamer *Pentyrch*, of Sunderland, ran into very bad weather in the Bay of Biscay, and during a great storm off the Morocco coast Captain Bowden thought it wise to put in for shelter at the little port of Agadir. One night, just before the vessel weighed anchor to leave, Gerald dived into the sea and succeeded in swimming ashore.

His absence was not noticed until three hours later, when the vessel was well out to sea, and Captain Bowden, having lost so much time, did not deem it worth while to bother about a man who was no doubt half a lunatic.

Gerald, however, succeeded, with the aid of a friendly English trader, in getting by road from Agadir to Mogador, where he told his strange story to the British vice-consul, who in turn arranged a passage for him on a small steamer homeward bound, and gave him a little money, sufficient to pay his railway fare from Southampton to London.

Truly, his had been an astounding adventure, and now he was eagerly looking forward to the happy reunion with the girl he loved so passionately.

All his belongings were in the small brown paper parcel on the rack above him. At the station he had bought a packet of cigarettes, and as he smoked he gazed reflectively out of the carriage window. The train was an express, but in his mood it seemed to be the slowest in the world.

What would Marigold think of his long absence? He had once or twice thought of telegraphing to her from Mogador, or from Brest, where they had touched, but he had deemed it best to return to her suddenly and then wreak vengeance upon those who had so cleverly plotted to inveigle him to that flat on that never-to-be-forgotten night.

Waterloo—the new station with its bustle and hurry! He sprang from the carriage and took the next train back to Wimbledon and then on to Wimbledon Park.

At last he halted before the neat little villa with its white painted balcony, and knocked.

Marigold's sister opened the door.

"Good heavens!" she gasped. "Mr. Durrant, is it really you?"

"It is! I'm back again. Where is Marigold?"

"Come in," she said. "I-I-hardly know what to say. Marigold is—she's not very well."

And then in a few brief words as he stood in the narrow hall she told him of his beloved's sudden illness.

A second later he dashed upstairs, and then in silence, treading, noiselessly, he advanced to the bedside of the delirious girl, who with flushed face was calling for "her Gerald."

Tenderly he placed his cool hand upon her brow.

"But surely she will live!" he cried in blank despair.

"The doctor has grave doubts," her sister replied. "She had such deep and constant anxiety regarding your absence, Mr. Durrant, that her constitution has become undermined. And now she has caught this terrible chill which has developed into acute pneumonia."

"But people get over pneumonia!" he exclaimed. "Surely Marigold will recover."

"The doctor told me this morning that the malady is of the most virulent type. There are few recoveries."

"Few recoveries!" he echoed, while at the same time the poor girl was murmuring something incoherent regarding "Gerald."

"Yes. He said that if she got well again it could be only by a miracle. The serum might do its work, but—well, Mr. Durrant, I must tell you what he really said—he told me that he regarded the case as hopeless. The crisis will be the day after to-morrow."

"The day after to-morrow," he said. "And she will not recognise me till then!"

All that the poor fellow had been through—the tortures and horrors of that bondage in which everyone believed him to be mentally irresponsible— were as nothing. He loved Marigold Ramsay with the whole strength of his gallant manhood. His soul was hers. They were soul-mates, and yet she was slowly slipping away from him just at the moment of his return and his intended triumph.

Her sister led him downstairs. In the modest, well-kept little dining-room below they had a further conversation.

"She was, of course, from time to time reassured by your telegrams. By them she knew that you were alive. And they renewed her hope that you would return."

"Telegrams!" echoed the man, who looked more like an unkempt tramp than a business man. "I sent no telegrams! What do you mean, Mrs. Baynard?"

"Why, the messages you sent. She has them all in her handbag."

"But I was unable to communicate with her. I was declared to be mad, and was sent upon a sea voyage for the benefit of my health. I now know that it was for the benefit of Bernard Boyne!"

"I'll get her bag and show you. Marigold has kept them all," her sister said, and she left the room for a few moments, returning with the dying girl's black silk vanity bag, from which she drew several telegrams carefully folded.

These he opened and examined, standing aghast as he read them.

"Why! I never sent a single one of them!" he said. "They're all forgeries!"

"What?" cried Marigold's sister and Hetty in one breath—for her sister-in-law had entered the room and greeted the man who had returned.

"I tell you I never sent any message to her," he said. "Somebody has done this. Who?"

"Who can it be?" asked Hetty.

"I think I know," replied Gerald in a hard voice. "If I am not mistaken my enemies have been revenged upon me."

"Enemies! What enemies?" asked Marigold's sister. "Surely you have no enemies. I'm sure Marigold hasn't."

"Wait and we shall discover the truth," said the young man. "Marigold must get well. I have certain questions to put to her. She can tell us much that is still mysterious concerning Mr. Boyne."

Hetty looked him full in the face and said:

"Jack, my husband, was over at Hammersmith two days ago. The place is all boarded up."

"What place?"

"Mr. Boyne's house in Bridge Place. There's been a fire there, and all the upper part has been burned out. Marigold was staying with her aunt that night, and they both escaped just in the nick of time."

"Repeat that," he said, half dazed.

Hetty repeated what she had said.

"Ah! So the place has been burnt up, has it? That's more than curious, isn't it?"

"Why?"

"Because of the mystery surrounding that man Boyne," he said.

"Marigold ten days ago said that she didn't believe that Mr. Boyne was as honest and sincere as people believed, but really, I have never taken any notice of her suspicions. We all of us suspect one of our friends."

"Marigold spoke the truth! I agree entirely with her. There are certain facts—facts which I have established—which show that this man Boyne— most modest of men—is an adventurer of a new and very extraordinary type. He is engaged in some game that is very sly, and by which he somehow enriches himself by very considerable sums."

Gerald Durrant an hour later went up to Waterloo and on to Hammersmith, where in the evening he stood before the boarded-up ruins of the fire. He saw that the top floor had been destroyed.

"So the secret of that top room has been wiped out," he remarked to himself. "Why? Did Boyne suspect us of prying? If he did, then what more likely than he should put his slow, but far-reaching, fingers upon us both. That I should have been drugged and placed on board a ship bound for the other side of the world, and branded as a semi-lunatic, is only what one might expect of such a master-brain!"

At a public-house in King Street, a few doors from the end of Bridge Place, he got into conversation with the landlord, who told him of the events of that night when the house caught fire.

"It's an awful thing for poor old Boyne," he added. "Although he is an insurance agent, it seems that, though he insured other people, he never insured himself. So he's ruined—so he told Mr. Dale, the corndealer in Chiswick High Road, a week ago."

Gerald smiled but said nothing. His thoughts were upon the hooded recluse who lived on the top floor of that dingy house. What could have been the real secret of that obscure abode?

A few other inquiries led him to the sombre house with smoke-grimed curtains where deaf old Mrs. Felmore had taken refuge, a few doors from the smoke-blackened, half-destroyed house.

As he sat with the old woman he spoke to her with difficulty, moving his lips slowly.

"Yes," replied the old woman in her high-pitched voice, for all the deaf speak loudly. "It is all very curious—most curious! They've never found out how it caught fire."

From Bridge Place Gerald walked direct to the Hammersmith police-station and, demanding to see someone in authority, was ushered upstairs to that same room into which Marigold had been shown, and there sat the same detective-inspector, rosy-faced, quiet and affable.

He listened to the roughly-clad young man's story, until presently he said:

"Oh, you are Gerald Durrant, are you?"

"Yes," was his visitor's astonished reply. "Why?"

"Well, we had a young lady inquiring about you a little while ago. She said you were missing, and asked us to make inquiry. But as you had wired to her several times we considered that you had gone off on your own account."

"Was Marigold here?" he asked, surprised.

"Yes, she came one night and told us of your disappearance. Where have you been?"

"Abroad. I only returned to-day."

"That's what I told the young lady. You promised in your telegrams to come back."

"But I never sent any telegrams; they were all forged."

The detective regarded him steadily and with an air of doubt.

"Then why did you go away? What was your motive in frightening the poor girl?" he asked.

"I went involuntarily. I—well, I suppose I must have been drugged and put on board a ship at Hull."

"H'm! What ship?"

Gerald gave the name of the ship and of its captain, which the detective scribbled down.

"Yes. You'd better tell me the whole of your story. It seems rather a curious one."

"It is," declared Durrant, and he proceeded to describe what happened on that fateful night when he met the two ladies in distress outside Kensington Gardens.

The detective listened attentively, but noting Gerald's unkempt appearance and rough dress, together with his excited manner, he came to the conclusion that what he was relating was a mere exaggerated tale concocted with some ulterior motive, which to him was not apparent.

At last, when Durrant began to describe Bernard Boyne's strange doings in Bridge Place, the inspector interrupted him.

"The house has been burned, as I dare say you know."

"Yes," replied Gerald vehemently, "purposely burned for two reasons. First, to destroy evidence of whatever was contained in that upstairs room, together with its occupant— —"

"Then you think someone lived up there—eh?"

"I feel absolutely sure of it."

"You only believe it," said the officer. And after a pause he asked: "And what was the second motive?"

"To get rid of Miss Ramsay—for that night, after visiting you, she went back and slept there in order to keep her aunt company."

The detective smiled. Then, after a pause, he said:

"Mr. Boyne is very well-known and popular in Hammersmith, you know. Everyone has a good word for him. He is honest, hard-working, and often shows great kindness to poor people whose insurance policies would lapse if he did not help them over the stile. No, Mr. Durrant; Bernard Boyne is certainly not the daring and relentless criminal you are trying to make him out. Indeed, I hear that, by the fire at his house, he's lost nearly all he possessed. He wasn't insured."

"Why is it that by day he collects insurance premiums here, and yet at night puts on an evening suit and dines at the most expensive restaurants in the West End?" demanded Gerald, furious that his story was being dismissed by the police.

"Ah! He may have some motive. Many men who earn their money in a hard manner by day go into the West End at night dressed as gentlemen. He may have some motive. He may have some rich clients, for all we know."

"I see you are dubious of the whole affair!" exclaimed Gerald. "I've only come here to tell you what I know."

"And I thank you for coming," replied the detective. "But we cannot act upon your mere suspicions. You must bring us something more tangible than that before we institute inquiries. I regret it," he added; "but we cannot help you. If you had any direct evidence of incendiarism it would be different."

And, thus dismissed, Gerald Durrant descended the stairs with heavy heart and hopeless foreboding, and walking out, made his way back to Wimbledon Park, where Marigold lay dying.

CHAPTER XXVIII
AT THE WINDOW

On that same afternoon the Red Widow was seated with Boyne in Lilla's pretty drawing-room in Pont Street.

She had come there hurriedly in response to a telephone message from Boyne's wife, and they were now holding a council of war to decide upon their actions in future.

"The only danger that can possibly threaten us is that infernal French girl and her lover," Boyne assured them, as he leaned back lazily in a silken easy chair, and puffed at his cigarette. He was smartly dressed with a white slip in his waistcoat, fawn spats, and patent leather shoes. "At the present moment they hold their tongues in the hope of squeezing more money from us. Meanwhile we shall collect the sum assured upon dear Augusta, and quietly leave England for a little while. A pity the sum is not larger," he added.

"I was only thinking the same the other day," said Ena. "But how about that girl Ramsay?"

"Oh, the end ought to be to-day, or at least to-morrow. I've made secret inquiries in Wimbledon Park, and I hear that the doctor gave her up a day or so ago," he said grimly.

"That will be another distinct peril removed," remarked Lilla. "It serves the girl right for being too inquisitive."

"And the man Durrant cannot be back yet, eh?" asked Ena.

"No," was Boyne's reply. "I see by the papers that the ship has arrived at Cape Town. Even if he escaped there, and found his way back, he could not arrive in London for another three weeks or more. So when he does return—if he ever does—he will find Marigold silent in her grave, that a disaster has occurred in Bridge Place, and that we are no longer in London."

"And Lionel?" asked the Red Widow.

"Oh, we have nothing to fear from him. He's only a gibbering idiot who believes my story that he committed a crime—killed a little girl named Maggie—although he was quite innocent. I made him wear a hood whenever he saw me, and I did the same. He believed me to be a man named Wisden, the witness of his crime! And because of that he executed in blind obedience every order I gave him. The fact that for months he never saw my face impressed him, and thus the terror of the police has so got upon his unstrung nerves that he is fast going from bad to worse. As a bacteriologist he is, of course, wonderful. He was marked out as a coming man by the professors at the Laboratory at Oxford, before he took to drugs and his brain gave way."

"Where is he now?" asked Ena.

Boyne explained the man's hiding-place, adding: "I've given him money to go on with. When that is finished—well, we will consider what we shall do."

"We shall want him again, no doubt," laughed Ena.

"Probably," said Boyne. "But remember, if there are any awkward inquiries—as there may be if we can't settle completely with Céline—then we must be absent from London for a year or two."

"That's a pity," declared the Red Widow. "Recollect what I said regarding that woman Vesey, whose hair is almost similar to mine. I met her at Brighton some time ago, and we became very chummy. She has a place in Gloucestershire. And that other woman Sampson. Both affairs would be so easy—ten thousand each."

"I know, my dear Ena, but let us square up this present deal first. That solicitor in the City is horribly slow. He is out of town till to-morrow. Time is going on. Each day brings us nearer open hostilities with Céline, therefore I suggest that Lilla should remain to receive the money and settle up, while you and I get away. I propose going to Spain, and you—well, you know Sweden well. Why not slip over to Stockholm? We will all meet again, say, at Trouville in six weeks' time, and hold another consultation," suggested the man.

"Yes," Lilla said. "That's all very well. But it means that I'm to be left alone to face Céline!"

"Well, it's the only way," declared her husband. "It is not wise for all of us to await the payment. I agree that the solicitor might easily have obtained a settlement of the claim ere this—especially as it is not disputed. But the more respectable the solicitor the slower he is."

"Are you sure that the fire at Bridge Place has aroused no suspicion?" asked Ena. "After a fire there's always an inquiry as to how it originated."

"Yes, when the place is insured. But mine was not—intentionally," Boyne replied, with a grin. "We couldn't afford that upstairs laboratory to be discovered. Besides, there was enough stuff in the tubes to kill a whole town—all sorts of infectious diseases, from anthrax to bubonic plague. Lionel dabbled with them, and gleefully cultivated them with his broth and his trays and tubes of gelatine."

"Well, as long as you are quite certain we are not watched, I don't care," said the handsome woman, who was so often seen at table at the Ritz, the Carlton, and the Berkeley. "If we were, it would be most dangerous to meet, even as we are doing now."

"Bah! You are both growing very nervy!" laughed Boyne derisively. "It is so foolish. Nothing serious can happen. Even when the French girl grows greedy, we can always settle with her. Between us we have laid up a nice little nest-egg for the future. I reckoned it out yesterday. The game is one of the few which is worth the candle."

"And the people in their graves are better off!" laughed Lilla, who was utterly heartless and unscrupulous.

Boyne rose and obtained a fresh cigarette, while his wife rang the bell for tea.

The latter was brought in upon a fine old Sheffield plate tray, and Lilla poured it out.

When the man-servant had gone, the Red Widow, turning to Boyne's wife, said:

"I really think, Lilla, after what Bernie has suggested, that I shall plead illness and get away. I shall tell my friends I am going to Sicily, but instead I shall run over to Stockholm. I know lots of friends there. Indeed, we might carry on our affairs there later. The Scandinavian is a good insurance company."

"English companies are better," Boyne declared. "I have little faith in foreign insurance companies. They always want to know just a little too much to suit our purpose. I've studied them all. My first case was in Milan eight years ago, and it nearly ended in disaster. I had to clear out suddenly and leave my claim—which has never been paid. And I wasn't clumsy, I assure you. I got the stuff from old 'Grandfather' of Frankfurt."

"Oh! 'Grandfather.' I've heard his name before," said Ena. "He sells tubes, doesn't he?"

"Sells them! Of course he did—and still does. You have to be well introduced, and he charges you very high, but his stuff is first-class—quite as good as Lionel's. 'Grandfather' I met once in the Adlon, in Berlin—a funny old professor with long hair. But, by Jove! he must have made a big fortune by this time. He charged a hundred pounds for a single tube of anthrax, sleeping sickness, or virulent pneumonia—and double for a certain poison which creates all the post-mortem symptoms of heart-disease, and cannot be detected."

"Well now?" asked Lilla, sipping her tea from the pretty Crown Derby cup. "What are we to do?"

"As Bernie suggests, I think," said Ena. "I'll get away, and next day Bernie can go to Paris, and on by the Sud Express to Madrid."

"Then on to Barcelona," said Boyne. "I'm known there as Mr. Bennett. I've stayed once or twice at the Hôtel Colon."

"No. I really can't be left alone," said Lilla. "As soon as you have gone that girl Céline will call."

"Don't see her, dear," urged the Red Widow.

"Oh! That's all very well, but I can't be out each time she comes. I should be compelled to see her. And no doubt she would have the man with her. Then, when she found out that you had both gone, she would turn upon me."

"No, no," laughed Boyne. "You will have money ready to give her if she turns very hostile, so as to afford us further time. Their only game is blackmail. They suspect something concerning the old man at Chiswick—thanks to talking too loud in the presence of one's servants. It ought to be a lesson to us all."

"It is, Bernie," said the Red Widow, rising from her chair and crossing the room to get her handbag which she had left on the sofa by the window.

As she took it up, she chanced to glance out into the street.

"My God!" she gasped. And next second she sprang from the window. Her face was white as paper. "My God!" she repeated, reeling, and steadying herself by the back of a chair.

"What's happened?" asked Boyne, springing up.

"No, no! For Heaven's sake, don't go near the window. He has seen me—I'm sure he recognised me!"

"Who?"

"Emery—that solicitor in Manchester! He—he—knows me as—as Augusta Morrison—the dead woman!"

"And did he see you?" cried Boyne in a low, hoarse voice. "Are you certain?"

"Well—no—I—I'm not absolutely certain. He was looking up at the house, and he's coming here."

At that second the front door electric bell rang.

All three started.

"Why is he here?" asked Lilla. "Are inquiries already on foot?"

"If they are, then our game is up," declared Ena. "You must receive him, Lilla, but you must deny all knowledge of me. You know nothing of Augusta Morrison."

"But he may call at Upper Brook Street," said Boyne quickly. "You must not return there."

"Did he recognise me? That's the question," asked Ena, still pale to the lips.

A second later the man entered with a card upon his salver—the card of the Manchester solicitor, Mr. Emery.

"Oh!" exclaimed Lilla, taking it up. "Oh, yes—show him up."

Then as soon as the man had left, Ena slipped upstairs into one of the bedrooms to hide, in company with Bernard Boyne.

When the young Manchester solicitor was ushered in, he found the tea-things cleared—which had been effected several minutes before—and Lilla rose to greet him.

"I believe you are Mrs. Braybourne," he said, bowing. "My name is Emery. I am the solicitor who effected a policy on the life of the late Mrs. Augusta Morrison in your favour. My client, I hear, with much regret, has died, and I understand from the company that you have put in your claim."

Mrs. Braybourne admitted that it was so, and offered her visitor a seat.

"I came this morning from Manchester, in order to consult with your solicitor," he went on. "Mrs. Morrison was a personal friend of mine, and she told me that she had, since her husband's death, discovered that she was indebted to Mr. Braybourne, hence her insurance on the assignment of the policy."

"It came as a great surprise to me," said Lilla, with her innate cleverness. "I had not the pleasure of knowing Mrs. Morrison, though I met her husband several times, years ago. My late husband was a friend of his."

"So she told me when we were together at Llandudno," Emery said. "It was certainly very generous of her to try and make reparation for some wrong which her husband did to Mr. Braybourne. But I confess I am somewhat surprised."

"At what?" asked the pseudo widow.

"Well—she gave me the impression that you were a person of limited means. But that does not appear so," he said, glancing around the luxurious little apartment.

Lilla smiled quite calmly. She was uncertain whether her very unwelcome visitor had recognised Ena through the window as his client, the false Augusta Morrison.

"Of course, I have no idea what Mrs. Morrison told you concerning myself. I only know that my late husband was interested in certain business transactions with Mr. Morrison up in Scotland," she said, with an air of ignorance.

"True, Mrs. Braybourne; but how is it that you have instructed your solicitors here to press a claim of which you now declare you had no knowledge?"

For a second Lilla was cornered; but her quick woman's wit came to her aid, and smiling quite calmly, she said:

"Well, to tell you the truth, a solicitor of Mrs. Morrison in London wrote me quite recently, explaining in strict confidence the position and the efforts your client had made to make reparation for her husband's swindling. All I know is that Mr. Morrison's business morality left a great deal to be desired, and we came very near ruin. Indeed, we should have been ruined, had it not been for assistance I received from my father."

"In what way?" asked the keen young lawyer.

"Well—I think I need not go into such details," said the clever woman with whom he was confronted. "Your client, no doubt, admitted to you her husband's double-dealing and how he very nearly ruined us. It was because of that Mrs. Morrison of Carsphairn insured her life in my favour."

Young Mr. Emery nodded, but his lips curled in a smile of incredulity. He paused for several moments, his gaze fixed upon the woman.

"Well," he said at last, "I have been at the head office of the company to-day, after I found that your legal adviser was absent, and—well, to tell you the truth, they are not altogether satisfied."

"Who?" asked Lilla, in surprise.

"The insurance company."

"Why?"

Again Mr. Emery paused, again he fixed his eyes upon the woman before him. He slowly rose from his chair and walked to the fireplace, whereupon he drew himself up. Placing his hands in his trousers pockets, he said, in a changed voice:

"Mrs. Braybourne, just because I have interested myself, rather unduly perhaps, in the affairs of my late client, Mrs. Morrison, I find myself confronted by several problems. I want you to assist me to solve at least one of them."

"And what is that?" asked Lilla, quite calmly.

"Simply this," he said, fixing his dark eyes upon her. "I want you to explain the fact why, as I came along the street, I should see, standing here in your window, my late client, Mrs. Augusta Morrison?"

CHAPTER XXIX
ON THIN ICE

Lilla drew herself up, and looked her unwelcome interrogator full in the face with unwavering gaze.

"Mrs. Morrison?" she echoed. "What do you mean?"

"I mean, madam, that as I approached this house Mrs. Morrison was looking out of the window."

Lilla laughed. Though greatly perturbed, she had been forewarned, and preserved an outward calm.

"Really, Mr. Emery," she laughed, "you must be mistaken. I have not the pleasure of knowing Mrs. Morrison. I only knew her husband, who came to see us several times when we lived in Kensington. His wife lived in Scotland, but I was never acquainted with her."

"Do you mean to insist that you have never seen her?"

"Never in my life—to my knowledge," was the frank reply.

"But I insist that my eyes have not deceived me, and that she was in your window a few minutes ago."

Again Lilla laughed.

"Well, Mr. Emery, though you and I have never met before, I can't help thinking that you are—well, just a little eccentric," she said. "You come here and declare that you have seen at my window a woman who is dead."

"Ah, but is she really dead, Mrs. Braybourne?" asked the shrewd young man, who had of late been getting together an extensive legal practice in Manchester.

"My dear Mr. Emery, ask yourself," Lilla replied. "I understand that the poor lady's sister was present at the end and took a last look at her before the coffin was screwed down. Surely her sister would know her? I am, of course, in utter ignorance of the facts, But I think, before you make such foolish mistakes as you are doing, you had better inquire—don't you?"

Her argument was rather disconcerting. Charles Emery felt certain that he had seen the face of the dead woman at the window. Yet, if it were true that her sister had seen her in her coffin, then surely his eyes had deceived him.

Upstairs Boyne and Ena stood together in breathless wonder at what was in progress below. Boyne knew how clever his wife was, and how, when faced with difficulties, she always became so calm and innocent. Of that he had had proof many times. Their marital relations had been such that he had long ago felt she was a super-woman in the art of deception.

But here she was faced with a perilous problem, and both Ena and he knew it.

They stood together, conversing in whispers.

"Trust Lilla," said Boyne in a low voice. "She will wriggle out of anything. Besides, she had the tip that the fellow may have recognised you."

Below the young solicitor and Lilla were still in open hostility.

Emery had grown angry. The woman had accused him of an undue suspicion.

"Lots of people, especially those who are spooky, believe in a sixth sense," she said. "Surely you don't believe in it, do you, Mr. Emery? I do not. Do you really insist that in my window you have seen the face of a woman who is dead and buried? If so—well, you've got the sixth sense, and it would be more profitable to you to go into the Other World Combine—which, I believe, is being formed—than to practise law. Personally, I only wish I had a sixth sense. Oh, what a lot concerning other people's affairs I should know—eh?"

And she laughed lightly, as though highly amused.

Emery stood in silence. She could see that he was still unconvinced. The situation was one of the most perilous they had ever faced.

"To tell you the truth, Mrs. Braybourne, I'm not at all satisfied," said the young man frankly. "I feel confident that the woman's face I saw at your window was that of Mrs. Augusta Morrison."

"How utterly ridiculous!" declared the clever adventuress. "If Mrs. Morrison's sister and other relatives saw her at the nursing home before and after her death they must have recognised her. How therefore, can the lady possibly be alive? It's silly to imagine such a thing!"

"Well," he asked, "who first informed you that the late Mrs. Morrison had assigned her life policy to you?"

"A man I know named May, who was a friend of my husband and of the late Mr. Morrison."

"And how did he know, pray?"

"How can I tell? He knew Mrs. Morrison, I believe, and he used to stay at her house-parties at Carsphairn. Possibly she might have told him."

"When did you see him?"

"I haven't seen him lately," she replied quickly, a fiction ready to her lips. "He rang me up about three days after Mrs. Morrison's death and told me of the sad event, of which I, of course, was in complete ignorance. Then he told me that she had insured her life for my benefit. I asked him how he knew that; but he only laughed and said that he knew, and would send, me particulars of the assignment of the policy, and that I had better take steps at once to establish my claim—which naturally I did, after receiving a few notes of the assignment. I made out a full account of my late husband's dealings with Mr. Morrison—how he had very nearly brought us to ruin—and placed them with the notes of the assignment in the hands of my solicitor, who, I suppose, in due course approached the insurance company. Previously, however, I had heard of the fact from another source—a solicitor—as I have already told you."

"H'm!" Emery grunted. Then, after a pause, he asked:

"Do you happen to know a certain lady living in Upper Brook Street named Mrs. Pollen?"

"Pollen? Pollen?" repeated Lilla. "The name sounds familiar. She's a society hostess—a woman who often has her photograph in the picture papers, isn't she?" she asked, with well-affected ignorance.

"I think not. I've never seen her portrait in the papers. She was, however, a friend of Mrs. Morrison."

"I'm afraid I know nothing of Mrs. Morrison's friends. My husband knew some of them, of course. And I have to thank Morrison for bringing ruin to us. He made huge profits over these business deals and bought Carsphairn, while my husband went under and would have been down and out had it not been for my family, who assisted him on his legs again."

"Well, in any case, you seem to live in very easy circumstances to-day, Mrs. Braybourne," he remarked, glancing around the luxurious room.

"Oh, I don't know," Lilla laughed lightly. "In London we put all the goods in the window—you don't up in Lancashire."

An awkward pause ensued.

"Well, Mrs. Braybourne," he said at last, "I cannot conceal from myself that there are certain peculiar circumstances which must be cleared up."

"About what?" she asked in pretended innocence.

"About this curious claim of yours. The assignment of the policy was, of course, in my hands, and it is not at all clear how your mythical friend Mr. May gained knowledge of what the late Mrs. Morrison desired to keep secret."

"As I've told you, Mr. May gave me particulars regarding it, which I duly handed to my solicitors. If Mrs. Morrison, in a fit of remorse for her husband's sharp practice, as it seems, chose to insure her life for my benefit, I don't see, Mr. Emery, why you should raise any objection," she protested. "She was your client, I presume?"

"She was," he replied. "And because I also acted as agent of the insurance company, I now consider it my duty to put all the facts before them, together with my allegation that the dead woman is actually in this house, or was when I entered here."

"Really, you are most insulting!" declared Lilla with well-feigned indignation. "I think it gross impertinence and a breach of professional etiquette that you should come here to see me and accuse me of lying when the matter is in the hands of my solicitor."

"Ah, Mrs. Braybourne. Pardon me, please; I only wish to straighten things out," he said blandly. "At present they are a little too tangled to suit me," he went on. "When I have given over the facts to the company my responsibility is at an end. Your solicitor returns to London to-morrow, and I will have a consultation, with a view to a settlement—in some way or other," he added in a meaning tone.

Then he bowed coldly and took his departure.

The instant he had left, the trio of dealers in secret death held a hurried and excited council.

"The game is up!" declared Ena, her countenance blanched to the lips. "The Fates are against us. How dare we press our claim further, and if we do not, then our failure to do so is self-condemnation."

"He's a shrewd young chap. He certainly recognised you—curse it!" cried Boyne.

"We must get away," said Lilla. "We all of us have old Jackie James's passports. And it only remains for us to clear out at once."

"Old Jackie's passports" to which she had referred were those cleverly fabricated since the war by an old man named James who lived at Notting Hill Gate, and who had at one time been a notorious forger. He now made a very excellent living by supplying crooks and criminals of all classes with false passports in neat little blue books, on which then photograph was fixed, and he himself embossed it with the stamp bearing the British royal arms and the words "Foreign Office," as well as the rubber date stamp, at an inclusive cost of fifteen pounds each.

These passports were beautifully printed in Bilbao, in Spain, together with the British red sixpenny stamp, but completed ready for the purchaser at Notting Hill Gate.

"Though I never like leaving good money behind," said Boyne, "I must admit that our luck is quite out this time, and we must all lie doggo for a bit."

"Ena must not return to Upper Brook Street, for Emery is certain to go there," Lilla said.

"Curse the fellow!" cried the Red Widow. "It's all my fault! I ought to have exercised more care, but Bernie has always been so cocksure that everything was plain sailing."

"No," he protested. "Surely I can't be accused of your indiscretions, Ena. I've done my best—just as we all have done—but we've fortunately received warning in time that the game is at an end—at least, for a little while. We can resume it in France, or probably in America later on. All that remains now is for us to swiftly and quietly fade out and leave them all guessing."

"One good feature is that the girl Ramsay will not be able to tell them anything," said Lilla. "I've always doubted her from the first. She's a cunning little cat."

"Yes. The end ought to be to-day—or to-morrow at latest," Boyne said.

"And by that time we shall all three be well on our way abroad."

Then they began to discuss ways and means, the destination of each of them, and the matter of money, there being three deposits in different London banks in different names.

The Red Widow and her companions had long ago taken every ingenious precaution in case of enforced flight at a moment's notice. There were, indeed, three separate sets of baggage lying at the waiting-room of Victoria Station. But the banks were closed and no money could be obtained.

In the meantime the young Manchester solicitor, much puzzled, of course, had taken a taxi and alighted in Upper Brook Street.

Of the hall-porter he made inquiry regarding Mrs. Pollen, and was taken up in the lift.

At the door of the flat he rang, and a smart maid answered.

"I want to see Mrs. Pollen," he said with his best smile.

"Mrs. Pollen isn't at home, sir," the girl replied.

"Dear me!" he said, deeply disappointed. "I've come up from the country specially to see her. When will she be back?"

"I don't know. Perhaps not till the evening, sir."

Emery paused. He was arriving at an estimate of the maid's loyalty to her mistress.

"Well," he said, "my business is most important—upon money matters. May I come in and write her a note?"

"Madam has forbidden me to allow anyone inside during her absence," replied the good-looking, dark-eyed girl.

"Of course, she fears thieves. But I'm a solicitor," and he showed her his card. "Please don't think I'm a thief—eh?" and he laughed merrily.

The girl looked at the card and then allowed him in, showing him into the dining-room, upon the table of which was a great bowl of La France roses—the room in which his client, Mrs. Augusta Morrison, had been entrapped and done to death so insidiously.

"There's paper there, I think, sir," she said, indicating a small writing-table set near the window.

He seated himself, though his quick eyes took in all the surroundings.

Before he began to write, he saw in a broad silver frame before him a large photograph of his client, Mrs. Morrison.

"That's a beautiful portrait," he remarked to the girl.

"Yes, sir. Mistress had it done about three months ago. It's very good of her."

Charles Emery bit his lip and managed to stifle the ejaculation which rose to his lips.

The truth was out! It was Ena Pollen whom he had seen at Mrs. Braybourne's window, and Ena Pollen had, he saw, posed for insurance purposes as Mrs. Augusta Morrison—the rich widow of Carsphairn.

For a moment the discovery dumbfounded him. He scribbled a few lines. Then he tore them up, and, making excuse for troubling the maid, he rose and said he would call next day. Then he pressed into her hand a ten-shilling note.

But just before he took his leave, he turned to her in the hall, and asked suddenly:

"Oh, by the way, has Mrs. Morrison been here to visit your mistress lately?"

"Not lately, sir," she answered. "Poor lady, she's dead, so I hear."

"Did she often visit your mistress?"

"Yes, sir. The last time she was here was at a dinner party with Mr. and Mrs. Braybourne."

"Oh! Then Mrs. Braybourne is a friend of your mistress, is she? I know her quite well. She lives in Pont Street, eh?"

"Yes, sir; she's a very great friend," was the girl's reply. "So is Mr. Braybourne."

"And who is Mr. Braybourne?"

"Why, Mrs. Braybourne's husband, of course."

As Emery descended the stairs to the street he wondered who could be "Mr. Braybourne"—if Mrs. Braybourne was a widow, as alleged.

At the end of the street he hailed a taxi and returned at once to the head office of the insurance company, where he revealed certain other suspicions which had arisen in his mind after his interview with Mrs. Braybourne.

CHAPTER XXX
THROUGH THE DARKNESS

Events happened apace.

The criminal dovecot in Pont Street was now seriously disturbed.

Even Boyne, usually so calm and unruffled in face of any peril or difficulty, saw that matters had grown very serious. He was in complete ignorance of the return of Gerald Durrant. Nor did he know that at Wimbledon Park the doctor, on calling again late that afternoon, had pronounced that the serum was doing its work, and that Marigold was decidedly better.

It had been just a toss-up. According to his judgment, the serum injected to fight the germs of disease had been administered a few hours too late. The human machine is, however, a curious thing, and the throw of the dice with Death is always weighted upon the side of the living.

Gerald, pale, anxious, and emaciated after all the hardships he had gone through, sat by the bedside of his well-beloved, watching her eagerly.

To his delight, she was slowly recovering. It is one of the features of the malady from which Marigold was suffering—thanks to the brutal plot to kill her—that after a certain fixed period, death supervenes or recovery comes very quickly.

In her case the doctor himself was agreeably surprised. She was recovering, he had said! She would yet live to cheat her enemies!

Gerald, realising this, was in the seventh heaven of delight. He was, of course, in ignorance of what had transpired at Pont Street, or of the suspicion of Charles Emery, the man who had made the actual assignment of Mrs. Morrison's insurance.

On the following morning, after hearing the doctor's good news, he sat beside Marigold's bed, and by slow degrees the girl recognised her lover as he bent over her and tenderly kissed her upon the brow.

The light of recognition suddenly shone in her eyes, and smiling, she gripped his hand.

"Yes, darling, I am home again!" he said in a soft voice. "Home—to find that you are getting better. You've been very ill. But you'll soon be well again, thank God!"

For some moments the girl was too overcome by emotion to speak, but at last her lips moved, and in a voice scarcely audible she pronounced his name.

"Gerald!" she articulated with difficulty, raising her hand until it rested against his cheek. "Gerald! *My Gerald*!"

"Yes, darling! I am here with you!" he assured her soothingly, for they were alone together, the doctor having just left. "You have been very, very ill."

"Yes," she whispered, "very ill."

Then she closed her eyes for fully five minutes, as though the strain of speaking had been too much for her, while he sat at her bedside watching breathlessly the white countenance of the girl who was all in all to him.

At last she again opened her eyes, and in a voice scarce above a whisper, asked:

"Where have you been all this long, long time?"

"Abroad, dear. But don't worry about that! I'm back," he said cheerfully. "Back with you. Rest, and you will soon be quite well again."

Again she closed her eyes and turned her head slightly upon the pillow. And as she did this, Gerald again kissed her upon the brow.

About two hours later her condition showed a marked improvement, but Gerald had not left her side for a moment.

At noon she seemed so much better that he decided to go over to Ealing and obtain a suit of his own clothes, so as to make himself more presentable. This he did.

His sister was naturally delighted to see him, but save for a brief explanation of his absence he did not enter into any details concerning it. His anxiety was to return to Wimbledon Park. He had at first contemplated going to Mincing Lane to explain his absence, but had now decided to postpone that until the morrow.

So about three o'clock he was back again at Marigold's bedside, delighted to find the great improvement which had taken place during the past few hours. The serum was doing its work, and slowly she was returning to her old self again.

When they were alone, and Gerald was once more seated beside her, she turned to him, and in a low, intense voice asked if her sister had told him of the fire in Bridge Place.

"Yes, dearest," he answered. "I know all about it. I've seen the ruin, and I've talked to your aunt. You both had narrow escapes!"

"Mr. Boyne—set—it—on—fire—Gerald," she said weakly, "so as to get rid of what was in that upstairs room!"

"Without a doubt."

"I—I tried to learn more about it. That's—well, that's why I dined with Mr. Boyne."

"You dined with him?" echoed her lover.

"Yes—in order to try and learn something more. Did we not agree to keep a watchful eye upon him?"

"We did. But I fell into a cunningly devised trap on the night I disappeared," he said. "I will describe it to you later. Well, when you dined with the fellow, did you discover why he spends his evenings among those smart people in the West End?"

"No, Gerald; but I came to the conclusion that he is a very remarkable crook."

"Of that I'm certain, dear. We've both had proof of it. He knew we were watching him, and his intention, no doubt, was to get rid of both of us."

"Yes, I quite agree," replied the girl faintly, yet smiling into his face. Then she added: "Do you know, Gerald, that—that ever since I dined with Mr. Boyne I haven't been the same. I felt ill next morning, and gradually the illness increased, until I had to go to bed and the doctor came to see me."

Gerald Durrant knit his brows.

"By Gad!" he gasped. "I—I never thought of that! He invited you to dinner—eh?"

In reply to his question, Marigold described the chance meeting near the bank and the invitation that followed.

"Ah!" he exclaimed, after a pause. "He had got rid of me, and intended that you should die—truly a most diabolical plot! I see it all! But we will be even with him yet, darling—never fear!"

Assuring the girl that he would return very soon, Gerald Durrant left the house determined to take direct action. His failure to convince the police at Hammersmith that "Busy" Boyne, the pious insurance agent, was a master-criminal, had irritated and angered him. Probably if he went direct to Scotland Yard and re-told the story, laying stress upon the plots against Marigold and himself, they would hear him and make some investigation.

The mystery of that upstairs room and its weird occupant was ever uppermost in his mind. And now that it was destroyed, it made it plainer than ever that there had been some guilty secret hidden there.

He went to Charing Cross, and presently entered the headquarters of the Criminal Investigation Department at Scotland Yard, where he was courteously received by Detective-Inspector Shaw in one of the cold, bare, official waiting-rooms.

The inspector, a short, stout, brusque man, listened very patiently to the strange story related to him, and once or twice jotted down notes. But his countenance was imperturbable, and Gerald's heart had already sunk within him, for he saw that he was quite unimpressed.

At last Shaw stirred himself, and said:

"Well, Mr. Durrant, all that you've just told me is extremely interesting. Will you wait a few moments?" and rising, he left the room. On his return five minutes later, he asked Gerald to accompany him. They went together down a long corridor, where the young man was ushered into a comfortable office. A well-dressed man of rather dapper appearance was seated at a table, and Gerald was invited to a chair, when he was closely questioned, more especially regarding his observations and those of Marigold upon the houses in Pont Street and Upper Brook Street, and also concerning the trap into which he himself had fallen, and Marigold's inexplicable illness.

"Is the young lady yet fit to see anyone, do you think?" asked the superintendent. "Is she well enough to make a statement?"

"Not to-day, I fear. Perhaps she will be to-morrow."

His interrogator reflected for a few moments.

"When is that appointment due with Mr. Macdonald and the Frenchman—Galtier is his name, isn't it?" he asked his secretary, who was seated at a table on the opposite side of the room.

"They are due here now," was the latter's reply as he glanced at the clock.

"Mr. Emery is also to be here, is he not, Mr. Francis?"

"Yes, sir," replied the secretary.

Five minutes later there assembled in that room five other persons. Charles Emery was shown in with the inquisitive little man, Alexander Macdonald, who had arrived in Ardlui, and, giving his name as John Greig, had watched the Red Widow by orders from the detective office in Glasgow, and had gone back down Loch Lomond only half convinced that he was on the wrong track, and that she was not the notorious woman, Sarah Slade, for whom he was in search.

Alexander Macdonald was, however, a very shrewd person, and when the first suspicion of a new case was aroused against Ena Pollen, as she now called herself, he saw that he had been sadly misled. Therefore, unknown to Scotland Yard, the Glasgow police had been doing underground work in order to fix the identity of the lady of Upper Brook Street.

Almost simultaneously with the arrival of the two men there came Céline and Galtier, together with a well-dressed elderly man, the manager of the insurance company in which the false Mrs. Morrison had taken out a policy.

For a full hour they sat with the superintendent of the Criminal Investigation Department, who, with a shorthand writer at his elbow, heard the further statement of each in turn. At last, turning to Inspector Shaw, he said:

"There is certainly sufficient evidence to justify the immediate arrest of the two women and the man Boyne. We must get the statements of Miss Ramsay and her aunt later."

Then, taking a sheet of pale-yellow official paper, he scribbled one or two lines, signed them, and handed it to Shaw.

"I think that is all we can do at the moment," he said, addressing the party. "It is quite evident that a great insurance conspiracy has been attempted, and not for the first time. Apparently the late Mr. Martin was a victim, together with other persons, whose names and circumstances we shall later on discover. To me it seems that great credit is due to the intelligence of Miss Ramsay and of Mr. Durrant, who watched the man Boyne so ingeniously until they must have somehow betrayed themselves, and thus have placed their lives in jeopardy."

"I think," said the Manchester solicitor, "that if Mrs. Braybourne had pretended to remain in ignorance for a month or so, and not sought to establish her claim, the company would have, no doubt, paid the sum without question."

"Yes," laughed the superintendent. "But criminals always betray themselves by overdue anxiety. But we have here to deal with a very dangerous gang. and it only shows to the insurance world how easily they may be defrauded by a well-established organisation."

Shaw had left the room, and already the telephone was at work to ensure the arrest of the criminals.

"It will certainly be highly interesting to discover how many innocent people have actually been the victims of this desperate and relentless trio who dealt secret death in order to enrich themselves," remarked the superintendent.

"There was a grave suspicion of the woman Pollen in another case about two years ago," said Macdonald. "Therefore, on a report from Ardlui, I ran up from Glasgow, but I failed to identify her as the woman who had called herself Slade, though I had very strong suspicions. Her social standing deceived me, I admit. Poor Mrs. Morrison of Carsphairn!" exclaimed Macdonald in his strong Glasgow accent. "She was a good lady—a very good lady!"

"Well," said the superintendent, rising from his chair. "We have to thank you all for your combined efforts, and especially Mademoiselle and Mr. Durrant. Let's hope we shall get the guilty ones, and then we shall all meet again as witnesses at the Old Bailey."

And thus, just after five o'clock, he dismissed them, Gerald, excitedly and with all haste, making his way back to the bedside of his loved one in order to tell her the intentions of the police.

At last the devilish crimes of the Red Widow and her accomplices were to be exposed, and the trio of death-dealers punished.

CONCLUSION

Scotland Yard is difficult to arouse, but when once actual evidence of crime is forthcoming it is quick of action.

At half-past five that afternoon a small, under-sized man, who wore the uniform of the Metropolitan Water Board, rang at the basement entrance of the house in Pont Street, and the cook opened the door. "Well, missus?" he exclaimed merrily. "What's the trouble with the water here—eh?"

"Trouble? There's no trouble," replied the cook, who never suspected that four other men were in close vicinity awaiting their leader's call.

"Oh! but we've had a report that you've got a bad leak in one of your pipes. So I'll just have to look at it," and he carried in what looked like a walking-stick in wood with a wide trumpet end.

The cook took him into the scullery, and he placed the end of his stick upon the pipe. He listened intently, using it like a huge stethoscope. Then he went from pipe to pipe, chatting merrily with the cook and the man-servant all the time.

"Are your people at home?" he asked the cook.

"No. They went away an hour ago in a car down to Brighton for three weeks. So we're all off for a bit of a holiday, so hurry up! Do you find anything wrong, mister?"

"No," replied the shrewd little man. "There must be some mistake, I suppose. There's no leak here, as far as I can detect. But what a time you will have—eh? Did they take much luggage?"

"No, not very much. Madam said she would come up and get some more on Tuesday."

"Went sudden-like—eh?"

"Yes. All of a hurry. Their friend, Mrs. Pollen, slept here last night—which is a bit unusual. But my mistress had a 'phone message. Then they rang up for a car and all three went off. They left their address—the Metropole."

"Do you know where they got the car from?"

"No. That I don't! Why? I heard Mrs. Pollen ordering it on the 'phone. But where it came from, I don't know."

"You think that they're at the Metropole, at Brighton?"

"Of course they are. But are you going down there to report a leak of water, mister? If so, yours must be a nice comfortable job."

The little man laughed mysteriously, and leaving, walked to the corner of Pont Street, where he reported to his colleagues that the birds had flown.

Inquiry at Upper Brook Street brought no better result. Mrs. Pollen had not been seen there since the previous day.

Already news of the flight had been telephoned to Scotland Yard, who, in turn, telephoned to the Brighton police, and within ten minutes the telegraph wires were at work to the various ports of embarkation, circulating descriptions of the trio—Boyne's description being furnished by the police at Hammersmith, where he was so well known.

That night Gerald sat with Marigold, and both were filled with wonder at what was happening.

Expert criminals of the type of the death-dealers never fail to arrange for a safe bolt-hole in case sudden escape becomes necessary. The police knew this well, and had already taken certain precautions for their arrest.

The story, of what followed is a brief, but dramatic one.

The car hired to take them to Brighton conveyed them only as far as Redhill, where they dismissed it. The Red Widow, having already alighted at Sutton, in Surrey, and returning to Victoria by train, claimed her two trunks. Then, by the aid of her false passport, and adding age and shabbiness to her appearance, she managed to travel third-class from Folkestone to Boulogne and, passed by the police and passport officer there, went on to Paris, where already she had a safe asylum awaiting her.

At Redhill Boyne and his wife halted at an hotel, and after being inside for ten minutes the fugitives came out, paid the man, gave him a handsome douceur and said that they had changed their minds. Thus dismissed the man returned to London well satisfied.

The pair separated half an hour later, Boyne returning as far as Clapham Junction, where he changed and went on to Waterloo. His idea was to get away by Southampton that evening to the Channel Islands, and thence, after a few days, across to Havre. He knew too well that the game was up and that his only chance was to get abroad.

On arrival he went into the refreshment room at Waterloo, for he had a full hour to wait for the next train to Southampton. Having leisurely drunk a cup of tea, he was just about to emerge when three men near the door dashed out and pounced upon him.

In an instant he fought like a tiger, but just as quickly the men gripped him, though not a word was spoken, except that a terrible imprecation escaped the assassin's lips.

He was a master-criminal, and the detectives had not gauged the extent of his wily cleverness.

"Very well," he laughed grimly at last. "You needn't hurt my arm. Really, this is all extremely annoying."

A crowd had at once assembled at the first sign of a struggle, but the detectives hurried him unceremoniously to a taxi, into which they bundled him. Of that very act Bernard Boyne was swift to take advantage, for ere they could prevent him he had managed to slip his hand to his mouth and swallowed something—so quickly, indeed, that the detectives who sat with him could scarcely realise his action.

Then, as the taxi sped across Waterloo Bridge on its way to Bow Street, Boyne, turning to his captors with a gay laugh of defiance, said:

"Gentlemen, you have done your duty, but you've bruised my arm very badly. Yet I forgive you. Bernard Boyne has had a long life and a merry one. But"—he gasped, his face suddenly changed—"but he cheats—he cheats you—after—after all!"

Next second their prisoner collapsed, and his captors saw to their horror that he was dead.

Lilla, in ignorance of what had happened, spent the night with a friend at Reigate, and went next day to Victoria, where she presented the voucher and obtained her luggage, which she took with her to Liverpool, having succeeded in purchasing a second-class passage to Canada in the name of Anna Mansfield, the name upon her forged passport.

When, however, two days later she had boarded the big liner and was sitting comfortably at tea within an hour of sailing, she was politely invited by the steward to step ashore again as a friend was awaiting her. She at once realised that she had been followed. Two minutes later she was under arrest. In the night she was brought to London, and before the magistrate at Bow Street next morning.

The suicide of Bernard Boyne prevented the whole details of the amazing conspiracy from being explained at Lilla's trial, which later on took place at the Old Bailey. She was, however, sent to penal servitude for life as the accomplice of her husband—a just sentence she is still serving.

Not until nearly three months afterwards was anything heard of the Red Widow, until one night she was arrested in Lyons, and on being brought to Paris it was found by the Sûreté Générale that she was wanted by them for a similar offence in Biarritz—the mysterious death of a red-haired Englishman named Pearson about three years previously—and that she had, even then, been in active association with Boyne and his wife.

She was brought before the Examining Magistrate, M. Decoud, and her guilt proved. Just before the date of her trial at the Assize Court of the Seine she followed the master-criminal's example by poisoning herself with one of the same tiny pilules which the insane toxicologist of Harpur Street had prepared for emergency. This little white pilule she had succeeded in secreting in the hem of her skirt for nearly four months, hoping to escape justice. But at last, being convinced of the terrible sentence which awaited her, she ended her notorious career.

The demented scientist in Harpur Street, whom Boyne had held so completely in his power, came to the end of his resources in a month, and was certified as insane and sent to an asylum. He made wild allegations against a person named Wisden, but they were always unintelligible to the attendants.

The insurance company which had issued the policy on the life of the unfortunate Mrs. Morrison, combined with three other companies which had also been defrauded, awarded to Gerald Durrant and Marigold Ramsay the very substantial sum of one thousand pounds each for their services in breaking up the dangerous and unscrupulous gang, for had the truth not been discovered they would in all probability be carrying on their murderous work at the present moment.

The reward which the young people received went a long way towards buying the pretty little home they occupy at Hampstead, for they are now united as man and wife.

Gerald is back again at Mincing Lane, where he has been promoted to a responsible and lucrative position as assistant manager, but Marigold, of course, no longer goes daily to the City.

They are never tired of talking of those dark days of their danger and distress, but there is one person to whom they have agreed never to refer—that handsome woman of many crimes both known and unknown—the Red Widow.